The Loner:
HARD LUCK MONEY

The Loner:
HARD LUCK MONEY

J. A. Johnstone

PINNACLE BOOKS
Kensington Publishing Corp.

www.kensingtonbooks.com

PINNACLE BOOKS are published by

Kensington Publishing Corp.
119 West 40th Street
New York, NY 10018

All Kensington titles, imprints, and distributed lines are available at special quantity discounts for bulk purchases for sales promotions, premiums, fund-raising, educational, or institutional use. Special book excerpts or customized printings can also be created to fit specific needs. For details, write or phone the office of the Kensington special sales manager: Kensington Publishing Corp., 119 West 40th Street, New York, NY 10018, attn: Special Sales Department; phone 1-800-221-2647.

ISBN-13: 978-0-7860-2852-8
ISBN-10: 0-7860-2852-1

First printing: July 2012

10 9 8 7 6 5 4 3 2 1

Printed in the United States of America

Chapter 1

Texas State Penitentiary, Huntsville, Texas

Quint Lupo knew something was wrong. Five years spent behind the thick walls, barbed wire, and iron bars of the prison had honed his instincts to a keen edge.

He figured somebody was going to kill him.

He had plenty of enemies in there, that was for sure. A man couldn't stay locked up for very long without getting on somebody's bad side. Look at a man wrong in the yard, bump into some fella in the mess hall by accident, and the strain of being in prison made everything seem worse than it really was. When that happened, pride often turned it into a killing matter.

When you got right down to it, pride was just about all a locked-up man had left.

As Lupo walked across the yard, his eyes moved constantly, searching for the first sign of trouble.

It was a hot day, and being outside for a few minutes caused him to sweat through his gray convict's uniform. Squinting against the sun's glare, he glanced up at the brassy Texas sky. He looked at the guard towers in two corners of the yard, where guards with Winchesters were posted, ready to open fire instantly if they needed to.

It was Sunday afternoon and convicts were scattered around the yard. Any other day, most of them would have been out working in the fields. The penitentiary raised an assortment of crops, some to feed the prisoners, others to sell. The convicts had to work hard, but truthfully, it wasn't much harder than it would have been if they'd been trying to eke out a living for their families from their own hardscrabble farms.

It wasn't the work, it was the lack of freedom and the memories of being able to come and go as he pleased that got to a man. Lupo remembered vividly how it felt to race across the plains on a good horse. He'd loved it . . . even when there was a posse on his trail.

"Hey, Lupo," someone called behind him.

Lupo stopped and turned.

A convict named Leroy Boozer was coming toward him, followed by several of Boozer's friends. The man was tall and burly, with massive arms and a black beard. He looked even bigger and more threatening compared to Lupo's lean build and gray hair.

"What do you want, Boozer?" Lupo asked, thinking once again his instincts had proven accurate. Boozer was a troublemaker, plain and simple. He spent a week or two every month in solitary as a result of the problems he caused.

With a murderous glare, Boozer said, "I hear you been sayin' things about me. Bad things."

Even though he knew it probably wouldn't do any good, Lupo shook his head. "I haven't said anything about you. We have never had anything to do with each other."

"Yeah, because some fancy bank robber like you thinks he's too good to associate with the likes of me!"

Lupo wasn't going to admit that and make the situation worse, but Boozer was right. The man had been sent to Huntsville because he had beaten his own wife and his brother to death with his bare hands. He'd thought they'd been fooling around with each other.

There was no truth to that suspicion, the way Lupo understood it. He figured the real reason Boozer had killed those two people was because he was blind, crazy drunk at the time. He'd been lucky to escape hanging and sentenced to life in prison instead.

Quint Lupo, on the other hand, might have robbed banks and held up trains from one end of Texas to the other, but he had never killed anyone in his life and prided himself on that fact. It was one reason he was determined to serve the remaining ten years of his sentence and then walk the straight and narrow once he was released.

The other reason was his daughter Kate.

"Boozer, I don't want any trouble with you," Lupo said. "I give you my word I haven't been talking about you, and I don't intend to. Whoever told you that was just trying to stir up a fight."

Boozer's glare darkened even more. "Are you callin' my friends liars?" he demanded as he stepped closer. His big hands balled into knobby-knuckled fists. "Are you callin' *me* a liar?"

It was looking more and more like there was no way out, but Lupo shook his head and tried one more time to ward off violence. "I'm not calling anybody a liar. I'm just saying that someone is mistaken."

"That's the same thing!" Boozer bellowed.

Lupo glanced around. Several guards were in the yard, and they usually kept their eyes on prisoners like Boozer who were known to start trouble.

On that hot afternoon, however, they all seemed to be looking elsewhere.

Lupo wondered suddenly if that was a coincidence. "Listen—"

"I'm tired of listenin' to you!" Boozer yelled. He lunged forward, swinging a big fist at Lupo's head.

The punch would have taken his head off if it connected, so Lupo made sure it didn't. He ducked and let Boozer's fist whip harmlessly over his head.

Boozer wavered, a little off balance.

Stepping in close, Lupo hammered a left and a

right into Boozer's midsection. It was almost like hitting the wall of a log cabin. He was quick, and straightened up, driving the top of his head into Boozer's face.

Blood spurted hotly as Boozer's nose flattened under the impact. He roared in mixed pain and anger as he bulled forward, flailing punches that would have done a lot of damage if they'd landed.

Lupo darted this way and that and avoided the big fists. He couldn't match Boozer's strength or reach, but he had superior speed on his side. He landed a couple jabs on Boozer's nose and sprayed more blood into the air. Boozer tried to catch him in a bear hug, but Lupo stepped quickly to the side, thrust his foot between Boozer's ankles, and with a hard jerk of his leg upended the bigger man.

Dust flew in the air as Boozer crashed to the ground.

Before Lupo could take any satisfaction from that, Boozer's cronies were on him, punching and snarling. Lupo blocked as many blows as he could, but some got through and slammed into him. The impact rocked him back. He fought to keep his balance. He knew if he fell, they might kick and stomp the life out of him.

Where were the guards? Why hadn't the men in the towers fired any warning shots? Usually a fight was broken up almost as soon as it started, as long as so many men didn't join in that the fracas turned into a riot.

Lupo got his feet set and drove punches back at

the men attacking him. He was badly outnumbered and couldn't hope to win, but his goal was to stay on his feet and fend them off until the guards arrived. His fists cracked against jaws, knocking Boozer's friends away from him, and giving him a momentary respite.

It ended as someone tackled him from behind and knocked him to the ground. A heavy weight pinned him down. Foul breath gusted in his face as Boozer panted, "Now we'll teach you a lesson, bank robber!"

Boozer heaved to his feet and brought Lupo up with him. Lupo's arms were pinned to his sides, so he couldn't defend himself as Boozer's friends closed in and slammed punches to his head. He tried to kick at them, but he couldn't keep them all away.

"Get back! Get back, damn it!" roared a harsh, commanding voice.

Finally, the guards were going to step in. It was about time, Lupo thought. The convicts fell away to the sides, clearing a path for a brawny man in a blue uniform who was carrying a club. Lupo recognized him as one of the guards named Hagen.

He expected Boozer to let go of him, but that didn't happen. Instead the big prisoner's grip on Lupo tightened. Hagen stepped closer, raising the club.

"What are you . . ." Lupo managed to gasp out.

"Start a fight in my yard, will you, Lupo?" Hagen yelled. "I'll put a stop to that!"

The club rose and fell. Lupo saw it coming, but there was nothing he could do, nowhere to go. The club smashed against his head with stunning force. Red light exploded through his brain.

"But I didn't—" That was all he got out before the red light turned to the black of oblivion and claimed him.

Chapter 2

The Menger Hotel, San Antonio, Texas,
several months later

The man called Kid Morgan woke up and stretched his right arm. The redheaded woman cradled in the crook of his left arm stirred as well.

"Is it morning?" Lace McCall murmured in a sleepy voice as she snuggled against him.

The Kid squinted at the bright yellow light coming in around the edges of the curtain over the hotel room window. "Actually, I'd say it's closer to noon."

A smile tugged at the corners of his mouth. He asked himself how long it had been since he'd slept this late, this well, and woke up with a beautiful woman in bed beside him.

Actually, not that long, he thought wryly. The previous morning, to be precise. And that's what he'd done every morning for the past two weeks.

But it still seemed like a novelty. After all the danger that had dogged his trail over the past few years, all the grief and tragedy that had haunted him, to spend even a little time in pleasant surroundings was unusual. To spend a month that way was unheard of.

And yet that was exactly what he'd been doing. Ever since he and Lace had arrived in San Antonio and had their final showdown with the outlaw they'd been trailing, they had taken life easy and enjoyed being with each other.

The Menger was San Antonio's finest hotel, and staying there for such a long time certainly wasn't cheap. Financier and industrialist Conrad Browning could afford it, though. Since Kid Morgan, the young gunfighter with a growing reputation as a fighting man, and Conrad Browning were actually the same person, The Kid didn't worry too much about the expense. The hotel had orders to send the bill to Conrad's lawyers in San Francisco, and they would take care of it.

That allowed him to enjoy himself . . . although he did have one worry nagging at his mind.

Lace turned in his arms and raised her head so she could kiss him. The Kid responded eagerly.

Before things could progress any farther, she pulled back slightly. "We can't just go on being this decadent forever."

The Kid grinned. "I don't see why not."

"Well, for one thing, I'm not rich like you are. I have people depending on me."

The Kid frowned, and Lace instantly looked like she regretted the words. They were a reminder that

Conrad Browning's wife was dead, and the only family he had left was his father, the notorious gunfighter Frank Morgan.

The Kid pushed that thought away, unwilling to let it intrude on his good mood. It had been a long time since he'd been happy for more than a moment here and there, so he was going to hang on to the pleasant interlude as long as possible.

"Any time you need to send money to your mother and your little girl—" He stopped abruptly, knowing right away *he* had said the wrong thing. Lace McCall was a prideful woman, something The Kid considered a good quality for the most part, but it sure made her stiff-necked sometimes. It certainly did on the subject of her career as a bounty hunter.

"You can forget that, Kid," she said in a flat, hard voice. "I don't mind letting you pay for hotel rooms and dinners at fancy restaurants, even though some folks would say that makes me a whore. But I draw the line at you taking care of my mama and my daughter. That's my job."

"Of course it is," The Kid said, but knew it was too late. The mood between them had evaporated.

Just as well, he tried to tell himself. The morning was nearly over. It would be time for dinner soon, and he was hungry.

Lace sat up, swung her legs out of bed, and stood. The Kid didn't look at her. She might not be what people would consider classically beautiful, but she had an impact on him like the smash of a bullet.

While they were getting dressed, she said, "Asa's liable to be downstairs waiting for you."

The Kid sighed. "I know. I owe him an answer. I promised I'd think about his proposition and let him know my decision."

"Have you made up your mind?" Lace asked. "Are you going to take him up on the job offer?"

"I don't know," The Kid replied honestly.

Three weeks earlier, in the aftermath of the deadly quest that had brought them all together, Texas Ranger Asa Culhane had come to see The Kid and Lace at the Menger. He'd had a proposition for The Kid. In his mind's eye, The Kid could still see the badge in the shape of a silver star in a silver circle Culhane had held out to him on an open palm.

"This is yours if you want it, Kid," Culhane had told him that day.

It wasn't everybody who was asked to join the Texas Rangers. The Kid had done a lot of things in his life, before he gave up his identity as Conrad Browning and after, but becoming a Ranger wasn't one of them. He'd never even considered anything like that.

He didn't think it was a good idea. He had gotten in the habit of drifting and being his own boss. If he was a Ranger, he'd be tied down and would have to follow orders. So he was leaning toward rejecting Culhane's offer.

On the other hand, he had a great deal of admiration for the crusty old lawman, and if Culhane thought he'd make a good Ranger, maybe he would. Culhane had talked his superiors into offering the job to The Kid, so in a way his own reputation was riding on The Kid's answer.

"I don't want to think about it right now," The Kid said as he reached for his black Stetson with the concho-studded band.

Lace shrugged as she finished buttoning the high neck on her dress. Whenever she was on the trail of a wanted outlaw, she wore boots, buckskins, and range clothes, but in town, when she wasn't working, she seemed to enjoy dressing like a lady.

"That's up to you." She turned to face him. "But if it makes any difference, I think you should know I'm going to be leaving pretty soon."

The Kid frowned. "What are you talking about?"

"I told you, I have to take care of my family. I've heard a rumor that Jake Cisneros has been spotted down around Del Rio. There's a fifteen hundred dollar bounty on his head, and I could sure use it."

The Kid had to bite his tongue to keep from saying he could send a wire to Claudius Turnbuckle in San Francisco and have the lawyer send fifteen hundred dollars to Lace before the day was over. He could have ten times that much sent to her, and the accounts Turnbuckle managed for him would never miss that drop in the bucket.

But if he said anything like that, Lace would have her horse saddled and ride out of San Antonio so quick it would make a person's head spin. The Kid knew it, so he said, "I haven't heard of Cisneros."

"He's one of those border bandits who raid back and forth across the Rio Grande. The U.S. and Mexico both have rewards out for him."

"Sounds like a mighty dangerous man," The Kid commented.

"He is." Lace gave him a meaningful look. "But I'm dangerous, too."

The Kid couldn't argue with that.

Before leaving the room, he buckled a gunbelt around his hips. Most men didn't carry guns in a big city like San Antonio, but The Kid had gotten into a habit of it and found that habit hard to break.

The gun on his hip as he and Lace started downstairs wasn't the Colt .45 he had carried for the past few years. It was a Mauser C96 semi-automatic pistol made in Germany that fired 7.63mm rounds. The Kid thought he might have trouble coming up with ammunition of that caliber while he was on the drift, so he'd stocked up on it while he was in San Antonio.

Lace had one of those Mausers, too. They had taken the pair off Warren Latch, the outlaw they had tracked to San Antonio. Being dead and all, he didn't need them anymore.

The foreign-made pistol held rounds in the clip that extended below its breech and could spew them out in a hurry. The Kid had ridden out of town several times to practice with the weapon and had taken quite a liking to it. If he needed to shoot a bunch of hombres in a short period of time, it would come in handy.

He had asked around and found a Mexican artisan who crafted custom leather goods. The old man had fashioned a special holster for the Mauser and equipped it with a spring that made The Kid's already fast draw even faster. In his hands the pistol was a supremely efficient killing machine.

Of course, some people said the same thing about Kid Morgan himself.

When they reached the lobby of the hotel, The Kid saw that Lace's prediction was correct. Asa Culhane was sitting next to a potted palm reading a copy of the San Antonio newspaper. The Ranger was actually watching for them, which he proved by folding the newspaper and setting it aside as soon as he spotted them at the bottom of the stairs.

Culhane stood up and crossed the lobby. The Menger played host to travelers of all types, from eastern businessmen to Texas cattle barons to dandies who hailed from San Francisco. Culhane stood out as impressive even in that crowd, with his broad, barrel chest, his rugged, weathered face, and the Texas Ranger star pinned to his coat. He was the sort most men stood aside from, and that was as true in the lobby of the Menger Hotel as it was anywhere else.

"Howdy, Kid," he said in his deep, rough voice. He lifted a hand to the brim of his cuffed-back black Stetson and added, "Miss Lace."

"How are you this morning, Asa?" Lace asked.

"Well, it ain't quite mornin' no more," Culhane replied, casting a glance at the big clock on the wall behind the registration desk. The hands stood at three minutes past noon. "But I'm fine. Ain't even usin' my cane no more."

"I noticed that," Lace told him with a smile. "I'm glad to see you're doing better."

"Yes'm, so's my cap'n. He says I been lollygaggin' around long enough and it's time for me to get back to my Rangerin' chores."

Considering that Culhane had gotten shot up in the line of duty, The Kid figured he had the right to take off and recuperate for as long as necessary, but he also understood the Ranger was eager to get back in harness.

"We were just on our way to eat dinner," he said. "You're welcome to join us, Asa."

Culhane frowned. "Actually, I've been sent to fetch you, Kid. The cap'n wants to have a word with you."

"If this is about that badge you offered me—"

"It ain't. This is somethin' else. If you're interested, though, you'd be helpin' out the Rangers, even if you don't join up with us regular-like."

The Kid was puzzled, even intrigued. He looked over at Lace, who said, "Go ahead if you want to, Kid. I'm going to be busy this afternoon anyway."

"Oh?"

"That's right." Her voice took on a tone of determination. "I need to start rounding up some supplies for that trip down south."

To Del Rio, The Kid thought. Where Jake Cisneros had been spotted.

So that was how it was going to be, he told himself. Well, he had known it couldn't last forever, no matter how much a part of him wanted it to.

Nothing lasted forever, did it?

He nodded to Culhane. "All right, Asa. I'll go listen to whatever it is your captain has to say."

Chapter 3

Huntsville

When Quint Lupo regained consciousness, his head hurt like blazes. He had already absorbed quite a bit of punishment before Hagen came up and clouted him with that club. Getting knocked out cold made the pain of regaining consciousness worse.

But at least the guard hadn't beaten him to death, so Lupo supposed that was something to be thankful for.

When he opened his eyes and looked around he saw whitewashed stone walls that were otherwise bare. The rough sheet he felt underneath him, rasping against his skin, told him he was in a bed.

It was the prison infirmary, he thought. He had been there before, getting patched up after various scrapes in the yard. Never for anything quite as serious, though.

He tried to turn his head, but it made more pain explode inside his skull. He groaned.

That brought footsteps toward the bed.

"You awake, Lupo?" a man asked. He leaned over so Lupo could see him. "I'll go get the doc."

Lupo recognized the weaselly little convict as Ike Calvert, a trusty who worked in the infirmary. Calvert scuttled off, and a moment later a man in a white coat came over to the bed, the prison doctor, Simon Kendrick.

Lupo had heard rumors that Kendrick was an opium addict, and the man's hollow eyes and sallow countenance seemed to confirm it. But he was a fairly competent doctor despite his personal failings. He touched Lupo's bandaged head gingerly, checking the dressing.

"It took half a dozen stitches to close the wound Corporal Hagen's bludgeon left in your scalp, Lupo," Kendrick said. "You should be careful and not move around too much. Brain injuries can be tricky matters."

"I have . . . a brain injury?" Lupo husked through dry, cracked lips.

"Possibly. It's hard to say. That's why we have to proceed carefully. You'll be here for several days before you go back to your regular cell." Kendrick smiled. "I don't suppose being out of your cell will bother you much."

It wouldn't bother him at all, Lupo thought. His cellmate, a rustler named Jack Stallings, was a surly hombre, and they had little to do with each other. Lupo was fine with staying in the infirmary, although he wished his head didn't hurt quite so much.

"You should be feeling better by tomorrow," Kendrick went on. "There's nothing for you to do now except rest, so you might as well enjoy it."

"That's fine, Doc. Thanks." Something occurred to Lupo. "What happened to Boozer?"

"The man you assaulted?" Kendrick shrugged. "Nothing, as far as I know."

"I didn't—" Lupo stopped. He'd been about to say he hadn't assaulted Boozer. It had been the other way around. Boozer had started that fight.

But he recalled how Hagen had rushed up after the fight had gone on for several minutes. Boozer and the other prisoners had already dealt out quite a bit of punishment, making him groggy and easy to handle. Hagen hadn't asked any questions, hadn't hesitated to lift his club and bring it crashing down on Lupo's head.

As if he had known all along which one of the fighters he was going to hit.

Lupo sighed and closed his eyes like he wanted to rest, just as Kendrick had told him. He heard the doctor and Calvert move away from the bed.

But Lupo wasn't sleeping. He was thinking. His ability to figure things out had made him a successful outlaw for a number of years, before the odds finally caught up to him. He went back over everything that had happened in the yard and could see how it really laid out.

The fight hadn't happened because of a misunderstanding. Boozer had jumped him because somebody had told him to. Maybe even slipped him a little payoff of some sort.

That somebody had to be Hagen. He might be only a corporal, but it was well known among the prisoners that he had a lot of power inside the prison walls. He was the man to go to if a convict wanted a special favor, and it worked the other way, too.

So Hagen had set him up, Lupo concluded. Nothing else really made sense.

But why? He'd never clashed with Hagen. He'd had very little to do with the guard and certainly had never defied him. Lupo just wanted to serve his sentence and get out of there. He didn't go looking for trouble.

He'd figured out what had happened, but had no idea of the motive and was more tired than he'd thought. Sleep dragged at his brain.

He surrendered to it. There would be time enough later to ponder on the mystery, he told himself.

By the next day, the intense pain in Lupo's head had receded to a continuous dull throb, and he was able to keep down some beans, a chunk of bread, and a cup of coffee.

Surprised he hadn't been moved to the infirmary's regular ward, he could hear other prisoners as they cursed, groaned, and complained of various ailments and injuries. He was alone in a separate room, with its single high, barred window.

Lupo didn't mind the solitude, although after a while he got bored just lying in bed.

By evening, the pain in his head had slacked off to the point that when Kendrick came around to check on him, he asked, "How much longer do I have to stay here, Doc?"

Kendrick smiled thinly. "You want to go back to work in the fields, is that it?"

"Well, I didn't say that—"

"You're in no shape to return to your normal routine yet, Lupo. If I were you, I'd just count my blessings and stop questioning things."

Lupo shrugged. "Fine."

But things weren't fine. He couldn't shake the feeling that something was wrong, that something not readily apparent was going on.

Sometime in the middle of the night, light suddenly washed over his bunk and woke him. Blinking against the harsh glare, he tried to push himself to a sitting position.

Before he could make it, strong hands grabbed his arms and hauled him off the thin, hard mattress, standing him up so his bare feet were on the cold floor. A voice growled, "Get those clothes on him."

Lupo squinted as his eyes adjusted to the light. He made out several hulking forms filling the room and casting grotesque shadows on the whitewashed walls. The light came from a lantern held high over the head of the man who had given the order. Lupo thought the voice belonged to Hagen.

Were they going to take him out and kill him, for some reason he couldn't begin to fathom? Some of the prisoners talked about things like that happening. From time to time a convict disappeared mysteriously, never to be seen or heard from again.

That thought put fear in him, and Lupo struggled as his captors yanked his prison uniform off him and began pulling civilian clothes onto his body. None of it made sense, but every instinct he possessed told him those men weren't trying to help him.

"Hurry up, damn it."

That was definitely Hagen behind the glare of the lantern, Lupo decided.

"We don't have a lot of time to waste."

Time for what? Lupo asked himself wildly.

But no answer was forthcoming.

There were too many men. Lupo couldn't stop them from dressing him in the new clothes and boots and dragging him out of the room.

When they did, he saw that screens had been set up to block off the view of the corridor from the regular ward. If any of the convicts in there had been disturbed by the commotion, they gave no sign of it.

Inside the walls, men learned quickly if the trouble didn't have anything to do with them, it was best to pretend they didn't see or hear it.

Lupo got a better look at his captors and was

surprised to see they were a mixture of guards and convicts, including Leroy Boozer, working together to hustle him along the corridor. He couldn't imagine what had prompted these natural enemies to cooperate, but it couldn't be anything that boded well for him.

The infirmary was located inside one of the prison's administrative buildings. The offices they passed were closed and dark. Only one sally port stood between that part of the penitentiary and the outside world.

The crazy idea that they were taking him out of the prison entered Lupo's head. But if he was caught out there, he would be considered an escapee. Nobody would believe the story that some guards and prisoners, working together, had forced him out of the prison. He would be brought back, and more years would be added to his sentence. He wasn't a young man, by any means, and if he had to spend an extra ten or fifteen years in there, he would probably never leave, at least not alive.

"No!" Lupo yelled. "Stop it! I don't want to go!"

Hagen paused and looked back over his shoulder with a snarl. "Shut him up!" he ordered. "We can't risk anybody who's not in on the plan hearing him!"

So there *was* a plan. The whole thing really had been a setup all along. But why?

The next instant one of the men grabbed Lupo's jaws, forced his mouth open, and shoved a rag into it. Lupo couldn't do anything but make some frantic, muffled noises.

They reached the front door of the building and his captors forced him out into the night air. They went down the steps and across the narrow gravel yard to the sally port. Two guards armed with rifles waited there.

The gates were open.

The guard towers didn't command a very good view of that location. Even if they had, Lupo wouldn't have been surprised to find the guards manning those towers were part of Hagen's scheme.

After the past few minutes, not much of anything would have surprised Lupo.

But one thing did. A sharp voice demanded, "Wait a minute! Where are you taking that man, Hagen?"

Chapter 4

The group had just started through the sally port. Hagen came to an abrupt stop and turned. "Sergeant Flynn. You're supposed to be off duty tonight."

A big man wearing only the trousers from a guard's uniform and the upper half of a pair of long underwear strode toward them. His rusty hair was tangled and his sweeping handlebar mustache was rust-colored as well.

"Does it look like I'm on duty?" he snapped. "I couldn't sleep, so I came over from the guard barracks to work on next month's duty rosters. Heard somebody go past in the hall and figured I'd better see what in blazes was going on."

Hagen handed the lantern to one of the other men and walked past the others to confront Flynn. "It's nothing for you to concern yourself with, Sergeant. I have this under control."

Flynn glared darkly at him. "I see four of my

guards and three prisoners giving a civilian the bum's rush out of here, and I'm not supposed to be concerned?" Flynn peered at Lupo, his eyes narrowing with suspicion. "My God, that's no civilian! That's Quint Lupo! What deviltry are you up to, Hagen? I've had my eye on you. I know you can't be trusted—"

"Then you should've thrown me out of here a long time before now, Sergeant," Hagen said.

Lupo saw the sudden glint of lantern light on steel, but with that rag in his mouth he couldn't call a warning to Flynn. It probably wouldn't have done any good even if he'd been able to. Hagen brought a knife up and around with blinding speed and plunged it into Flynn's chest.

Flynn took a half step back, obviously shocked by the unexpected attack. He reached for the knife with one hand, but his other hand shot out and grabbed Hagen by the neck. Flynn was big and strong and wasn't going to go down without a fight.

Unfortunately, the knife must have pierced his heart because his strength deserted him almost immediately. He let go of Hagen and pawed at the knife with both hands. His knees unhinged, and he fell. A brief drumming of Flynn's feet on the gravel signaled his death.

Hagen reached down and pulled the knife free. "Too bad," he said coldly. "Flynn was in the wrong place at the wrong time and Lupo killed him during the escape."

Lupo's eyes widened, and he made noises again

as he tried to push the rag out of his mouth using his tongue. It was bad enough they were making it look like he'd escaped. If he was blamed for Flynn's murder, every lawman in the state would be looking for him, including the Texas Rangers. He'd be caught, brought back, and hanged.

But it would never come to that, he realized as his captors once again hurried him through the night, past the sally port, out of the walls, and toward a distant stand of trees. He was convinced they were taking him out to kill him, for some reason he couldn't begin to understand.

Behind them, the prison remained quiet and sleeping.

The group plunged into the thick shadows under the trees. The growth cut off any moonlight or starlight, and when the man carrying the lantern blew it out, the darkness was almost complete. They came to a stop.

"Now we wait," Hagen said in a half whisper.

Despair made Lupo sag in the grip of the men holding him. He had never been the sort to give up, but he didn't see how he could get away.

But maybe if he could make them think he wasn't going to fight anymore, they would get careless. If one of the guards got close enough to tackle, and Lupo could tear loose just for a moment, he might be able to get his hands on a gun. . . .

He didn't harbor any foolish notion of being able to shoot his way out, but if they were going to kill him anyway, he might as well go down fighting and take some of the bastards with him, he thought.

Especially Hagen.

But he never got the chance. The men who were holding him, one of whom was Boozer, never let up. They kept him pinioned firmly between them. None of the guards came close enough for him to make a grab for a gun, either, even if he could have gotten loose.

"How long do we have to wait?" one of the men asked.

"Until the fellas I'm working with get here," Hagen snapped.

So someone else was involved, Lupo mused. That put a new angle on the situation, but didn't clear anything up. He was as much in the dark as ever, figuratively as well as literally.

Time didn't have much meaning in such circumstances. Lupo didn't know how much of it had passed when he heard hoofbeats approaching. What sounded like five or six riders were making their way slowly through the trees.

The hoofbeats stopped, and someone made a noise like a night bird.

Hagen said, "That's the signal," and scratched a match into life to light the lantern again. The men holding Lupo had to squint against the glare.

So did Lupo. The thought that it might be his last chance flashed through his mind. He tensed his muscles, about to make one more attempt to break free, but Boozer's hands tightened on his arm and the big convict growled, "Don't even think about it, Lupo."

Muttering a curse under his breath, Lupo waited to see what was going to happen.

The riders started moving again, tall, looming shapes making their way through the trees. They reined to a stop about twenty feet away from the group of guards and convicts.

One of the newcomers edged his horse forward. He was a big, barrel-chested man with an ugly face adorned by a ragged gray mustache that didn't help its appearance. "Is that him?" he asked in a gravelly voice.

"That's him," Hagen confirmed. "Quint Lupo. One of the most successful bank robbers in Texas for a long time. Held up quite a few trains, too. But the law finally caught up to him."

"And now the law's about to lose him again," the stranger said.

That brought a laugh from Hagen. "We're not losing him. We're giving him back."

"All right." The man on horseback made a curt gesture. "Bring him on over."

"There's one thing you ought to know," Hagen said.

The man stiffened, and Lupo saw his hand move slightly closer to the butt of the gun holstered on his hip.

"What's that?" the man demanded. "You'd better not have changed your mind about the price you agreed to."

"That's not it," Hagen said with a quick shake of his head. "There's a dead guard back at the prison. A couple of my men are sitting on the body right now, but they'll pretend to discover it as soon as I give the world."

"And Lupo will get the blame for the killing?"

"I don't see any other way to work it," Hagen said.

The stranger thought things over for a moment, then nodded.

"I think there's a good chance the boss can turn that to our advantage."

"If he does—"

"I know, you'll want a cut of whatever extra we make. You'll have to take that up with the boss. All I'm doing is picking up Lupo and taking him back."

"All right." The tone of Hagen's voice made it clear he would have preferred to come to some sort of arrangement right then.

The stranger motioned to one of the men with him. He led a saddled but riderless horse forward. As Lupo's captors muscled him forward, he knew he was going up on that horse. Again the thought of making a break for freedom crossed his mind. Once he was in the saddle, there weren't many men who could keep up with him.

As if reading Lupo's mind, the stranger drew his gun. So did the men with him.

"Here's the deal, mister," he said, addressing Lupo directly for the first time. "We've got a use for you . . . but you ain't the only huckleberry in the world who fits the bill. You understand me? You try to get away or give us too much trouble, and we'll just kill you and leave you layin' where you fall. Simple as that."

They had a use for him, the man said. That meant they would keep him alive, at least for a while. Lupo didn't see anything he could do except cooperate. He lifted his head and made noises through the gag.

The stranger jerked a hand toward it. "Take that out of his mouth. We don't want him to choke before we get him back to the boss's place."

Lupo wanted to meet the mysterious boss. Anybody who could set up something like what was happening had to be a pretty smart man, as well as a powerful one.

Boozer pulled the rag out of Lupo's mouth. Lupo spat and worked his jaw back and forth for a moment before he looked up at the stranger. "I'll cooperate with you, mister. Don't worry about that."

"Good. I was hopin' you'd be smart."

Hagen said, "Let him go."

Lupo took a deep breath. He put his foot in the stirrup, grasped the horn, and swung up onto the riderless horse's back.

"That just leaves one thing," Hagen said.

The stranger shook his head. "That's your lookout, not mine," he said flatly.

"You could give me a hand with the chore."

"Sorry," the stranger said, but he didn't sound sorry at all.

Hagen grunted. He put his hand in his jacket pocket and brought it out holding a revolver. With no more warning than that, he turned, pointed the gun at Boozer's head, and pulled the trigger.

The shot was sharp and vicious in the night. Boozer's eyes widened in shock as the bullet bored into his brain, leaving a small, red-rimmed hole in his temple. He went down like a dropped sack of grain.

The other guards were ready for the moment. They pulled guns, too, and emptied several rounds apiece into the other two convicts who had helped with the escape. They never had a chance.

Lupo sat on his horse, his eyes wide with shock and horror, as he watched the two men jitter around in a grotesque dance for a couple seconds before death dumped them in gory heaps on the ground.

The big, ugly man who was in charge of the riders grinned at Hagen. "Looks like Lupo's the only one who got away."

"Yeah," Hagen agreed. "Lucky son of a bitch, ain't he?"

With that, the riders closed in around Lupo and forced him to turn with them. They set a fast pace as they rode off through the trees, fast enough that Lupo worried he would run into something and bash his brains out.

The men seemed to know where they were going, and surrounded as he was, he didn't run into anything. They came out on one of the roads near the prison and paused momentarily.

Lupo was still stunned by what had happened, but he understood the reasoning behind it. Hagen would claim Boozer and the other two convicts had been part of the escape, too. He and the guards with him would be hailed as heroes for stopping three of the four fugitives. Hagen would probably even claim Lupo must have been the mastermind behind the prison break.

Back inside the walls, bells began to clang as the alarm was sounded. Soon bloodhounds would be baying through the East Texas woods, but Lupo was willing to bet Hagen would mislead the dogs somehow and put them on the wrong scent. Hagen's part in everything would be covered up completely.

"Let's go," the man in charge said. "Hagen won't be able to keep them off our trail forever."

The riders pounded along the road, with Lupo still caught in the middle of the group and unable to do anything except go along with them.

Lucky, Hagen had called him, Lupo thought. Lucky because he was out of prison and not dead like Boozer and the others.

But somehow, as he was forced to flee into the night, Lupo had a bad feeling he wasn't lucky at all.

Chapter 5

They rode for miles, following roads and trails that twisted through the thick forest. Lupo had always had a pretty good sense of direction—it came in handy in his line of work—but he knew he would never be able to retrace their path.

Finally the leader called a halt. "Put the sack on him."

One of the men crowded his horse close to the one Lupo rode and pulled a canvas sack over Lupo's head. A few stray grains of something landed on Lupo's lips. He licked them off and found that they were sweet. It had been a sugar sack.

Now it was an effective blindfold. He couldn't see a blasted thing.

"Try to sling that off and you'll be sorry," warned the man.

"Don't worry," Lupo replied. "I don't want to see where we're going."

"That's bein' smart," the leader said. "Come on."

Once more they rode through the night, one of the men leading Lupo's horse. Lupo rocked along in the saddle, waiting to see what was going to happen.

The waiting gnawed at his nerves. In the past, he'd always been the one to make plans and take action. As the captive, he was just reacting to what his captors did.

Five years in prison must have softened him up, he thought.

On the other hand, he was smart enough to know when the odds were overwhelmingly against him. Being cautious wasn't the same as being soft.

After what seemed like several more miles, the leader called another halt. "Take it off of him now," he ordered.

The sugar sack was jerked from Lupo's head. Enough moonlight shone down for him to see his surroundings. They had stopped in a straight, tree-lined lane running about a quarter mile to a large building gleaming white in the silvery illumination.

It was an old plantation house, Lupo realized. East Texas had more in common with the Old South than it did with the frontier. Cotton plantations were plentiful although many of them had been broken up after the Civil War when Reconstruction stripped the owners of their riches.

The riders moved at an easy trot toward the mansion, which had massive columns flanking its entrance. When they got closer, Lupo could see the place wasn't in as good repair as it had seemed from a distance.

The white paint was flaking and peeling in places, and the stucco on the walls had started to crumble. The flowerbeds along the front of the house were overgrown with weeds. It had been a fancy, elegant home at one time, but no longer.

The leader reined to a stop in front of the portico. "You been pretty well-behaved so far, Lupo. If you know what's good for you, you'll keep on actin' like that. The boss is a fair man, but he won't put up with any trouble."

Lupo put a hint of the old steel in his voice as he said sharply, "Can't you get it through your head that I don't want to cause trouble? Hell, you fellas busted me out of prison. I'm grateful to you."

"You looked like you wanted to put up a fight back there, where we met up with Hagen."

"That's because I thought Hagen was going to kill me! I didn't trust him. Boozer and those other two convicts shouldn't have trusted him, that's for sure."

The big, ugly hombre chuckled. "You're right about that," he admitted. "Do we need to tie your hands before we take you to see the boss?"

"Nope. All I want to do is thank the man."

That was true as far as it went. Lupo didn't trust his captors.

But maybe he was being too suspicious. Maybe the mysterious boss didn't mean him any harm.

Maybe the man had some reason of his own for wanting Quint Lupo out of jail.

The easiest way to find out, and to figure out what he needed to do next, was to play along.

The leader dismounted and drew his gun. "Don't take offense, Lupo," he said as he motioned for the prisoner to dismount. "No new man gets to see the boss without being covered."

Lupo swung down from the saddle. "None taken. Can't blame a man for being careful."

The other men dismounted as well. Some of them tended to the horses while two men drew their guns and followed the leader and Lupo into the house.

A lamp in a wall sconce burned in the foyer. Its glow revealed the shabby former elegance of the house's exterior continued inside.

The once-thick rug on the floor was threadbare, and the wallpaper was stained in places. The furnishings, which in the plantation's heyday would have been kept shined and polished to a high gleam by house slaves, were dull and tarnished.

With some work, the place could have been restored to its former glory, Lupo thought. Obviously, the current owner didn't care that much about it.

Big Ugly led the way along a corridor to a pair of double doors. He knocked on one of them. "It's Brattle, Mr. Grey."

Lupo heard a reply from the other side of the doors, but couldn't make out the words. Brattle grasped one of the once-bright knobs and turned it, so Lupo knew they'd been told to come in.

Brattle went first. Lupo followed with the guns of the other two men covering him. He stepped into a room that appeared to be a combination library and office.

Bookshelves covered three walls. They were lined with dark, leatherbound volumes, but the layer of dust on the books told Lupo no one had disturbed them in quite a while. The sour smell of mold and mildew hung in the air.

Lupo's nerves crawled. Everything about the place reminded him of death and decay . . . including the man standing in front of the old desk that dominated the room.

He was tall and thin, probably in his thirties, dressed in a dark suit. He might have been handsome if his face hadn't been gaunt to the point that he resembled a cadaver. His skin, which seemed more pale when contrasted with his shock of coal-black hair, added to his corpse-like appearance.

When he smiled, he was somehow transformed and didn't seem nearly as grotesque. He stepped forward and extended a hand with long, slender fingers.

"Quint Lupo!" he said in a deep, commanding voice. "I've heard a great deal about you. It's an honor to meet you."

Lupo took the man's hand, which was smooth and

cool, and shook it. "Most folks wouldn't consider it an honor to meet a bank robber."

That brought a laugh from his host. "I'm always glad to meet any man who's good at what he does, and you were one of the best, Mr. Lupo. Or should I call you Quint?"

Lupo shrugged. "Whatever you'd like. And I wasn't good enough to stay out of prison."

"Yes, but you've left those iron bars and gray walls behind now, haven't you?" The man let go of Lupo's hand and gestured toward a red leather chair in front of the desk. The chair had a couple small rips in the upholstery, but appeared to be in better shape than many of the furnishings. "Please, have a seat. Brattle, fetch us some brandy."

"Sure, boss." Brattle slid his gun into its holster. The other two men stayed in the background, alert and clearly ready for trouble.

"Cigar?" the pale, gaunt man asked as he reached for a humidor on the desk.

"Sure," Lupo said. The sheer bizarreness made him nervous, but he kept the feeling under control. He didn't seem to be in any immediate danger. He took the thick cylinder of tightly rolled tobacco the man held out to him.

Brattle brought over a silver tray with a couple snifters of brandy on it.

Mr. Grey smiled. "You wouldn't think someone as large and formidable-looking as Brattle here would be an excellent butler, but he is."

"I've told you, boss, I ain't a butler," Brattle objected. "You can call me your segundo if you want."

"I'll call you whatever I please," Grey said with an undertone of irritation coming into his voice.

"Well, yeah, sure, I reckon," Brattle agreed quickly as he set the tray on the desk.

"Help yourself," Grey told Lupo with a nod toward the brandy. He went behind the desk and sat down in a large, brown leather chair.

Lupo picked up one of the snifters and took a sip. It seemed all right, not drugged or anything. Grey had given him his pick of the glasses, which supported that idea.

The fiery liquor was good, although Lupo was far from an expert on such things. When he was on the owlhoot trail he'd drunk beer and whiskey.

Grey took a cigar from the humidor for himself and fired up both smokes. He leaned back in his chair. "You're bound to be wondering why I've gone to so much trouble to have you brought here, Quint."

"The thought's crossed my mind," Lupo admitted dryly.

"I'm sorry it had to be such an unpleasant experience for you." Grey touched his head, obviously making reference to the wallop Lupo had gotten from Hagen. "My influence inside the walls goes only so far. We needed you in the infirmary in order to be able to secure your freedom."

"Well, I reckon Boozer had it a lot worse in the end," Lupo said.

Grey frowned and glanced sharply at Brattle. "What's he talking about?"

Brattle's thick shoulders rose and fell. "Hagen brought some of the convicts in on the deal. Of course, we knew he'd do that to put Lupo in the infirmary, but he used 'em in the actual escape, too."

"That was running quite a risk."

"Not really," Brattle said. "As soon as he'd turned Lupo over to us, Hagen and the guards with him killed the three cons."

Grey's dark, deep-set eyes widened slightly. "Really."

"He had to kill a guard who wasn't in on the plan, too," Brattle added. "He figures he'll put the blame for that killin' on Lupo."

Grey thought about that for a moment and then nodded as if satisfied. "That's interesting." He looked across the desk at Lupo again. "It seems there's going to be quite a high price on your head after this, eh, Quint?"

"For breaking jail and killing a guard? I'd say so, yeah." Lupo couldn't keep the bitterness out of his voice as he added, "Even though I didn't do either of those things."

"Ah, but the authorities don't know that. I was going to offer you a very attractive proposition anyway, but it seems now you have even more reason to accept my offer, since we can help you stay out of the hands of the law."

Lupo downed a healthy slug of the brandy to fortify himself and asked, "Just what the hell is it you want from me, anyway?"

Grey smiled. "I want you to do what you do best, Quint. I want you to rob banks."

Chapter 6

The group of horsemen came to a stop on top of a high hill overlooking the thickly wooded valley where the Colorado River wound its way toward the Gulf of Mexico. On the other side of the river lay the town of La Grange, dominated by the big stone Fayette County Courthouse with its clock tower.

"The bank's right there on the square, so the streets will be busy around it," Brattle said. "Nobody'll be expectin' trouble, so we ought to be able to get in and out without too many problems."

Lupo shifted in his saddle and felt the weight of the revolver on his hip. "I'd feel better about things if you'd give me some bullets for this gun."

Brattle chuckled. "You know that ain't the way Mr. Grey does things. You can swear you're with us up one way and down the other, Lupo, but until you've proven it, none of us are gonna trust you. You got to earn it."

A wave of irritation went through Lupo. "What

am I going to do, start yelling for the law as soon as we ride in? If I did that I'd be sticking my head right in a hangman's noose."

"I'm not the one who makes the rules," Brattle said. "That'd be Mr. Grey."

Yes, Alexander Grey was in charge, even though he wasn't there, Lupo thought.

Grey was still in that crumbling old plantation house eighty miles away, waiting for his handpicked crew of bank robbers to return with the loot.

Before Lupo had set out with Brattle and the others for La Grange, Grey had shown Lupo the freshly printed wanted poster. Lupo's photograph was on it, an improvement over the days when wanted posters had relied on drawings, along with the information that he was wanted for the murder of a guard at the Texas State Penitentiary, as well as for escaping from that prison.

A reward of $2,500 for his arrest, or for his body, was offered, since the bounty would be paid whether he was dead or alive. The wanted poster made that clear in big, black letters.

"You'll appear to be in charge, Quint," Grey had explained, "although Brattle will really be calling the shots. But your leadership will be important. If you perform well, things will get better for you. You have my word on that."

"It still seems loco to me. I don't wear a mask, I don't get a gun with bullets in it . . . I'll be the only one running any risk on this job!"

"I've explained this to you," Grey had said with

the patient air of someone talking to a child, which also irritated Lupo. "You're already a wanted man, but none of the others are. It doesn't matter if you're recognized. As for the gun, that's simply a precaution."

"I don't stand to gain a damned thing by double-crossing you."

"And I don't stand to gain anything by giving you the opportunity to double-cross me." Grey had smiled. "Just be patient, Quint."

It wasn't like he had much choice in the matter, Lupo thought as he looked down across the river at La Grange. Grey had him over a barrel. The man could turn him in to the law at any time.

"All right," Lupo said. "Let's get this done."

They followed the road zigzagging down the side of the steep hill and clattered across the wooden bridge spanning the Colorado.

It was the middle of a warm June afternoon. The square was busy, with a number of wagons parked in front of businesses and horses tied to hitch racks. Not as busy as a Saturday, the day when farmers and ranchers in the area came into town, but still, too many people for Lupo to feel comfortable about what they were doing.

Well, it wasn't the first time he had ridden into a town in broad daylight to rob a bank, he told himself.

He and his companions moved along the street at an easy pace, not doing anything to draw attention to themselves as they approached the bank.

It sat on a corner of the square in a redbrick building with various offices on its second floor. Next to it was Al's Grocery Store, where Lupo, Brattle, and the other men reined in and dismounted.

After tying up their horses, Lupo and Brattle moved along the boardwalk and went into the bank while the other men drifted into the grocery store.

Lupo wanted to take a look around first, and of course Brattle wasn't going to let him out of his sight. The other outlaws would make their way into the bank, one by one, after approximately ten minutes had passed.

Right away, Lupo saw the place had a typical setup: a row of tellers' cages to one side, several desks behind a railing where the bank executives did their business, the massive vault in the middle and to the back.

All the tellers were occupied with customers, and several more customers stood at a marble counter filling out slips to make deposits or withdrawals.

The key to a successful bank robbery, Lupo knew, wasn't the physical layout of the place. It was the people involved.

Without being obvious about what he was doing, he studied the two men sitting at the desks. The middle-aged one, well padded with fat, would be the bank president. He had a broad, friendly face, and the reddish tinge of his nose revealed he liked to drink a little too much. He wouldn't be a danger.

Lupo would stake his life on it . . . which might well be what he was doing.

Ah, but the other man, the younger, slimmer one with the eager expression on his face as if he actually enjoyed the paperwork he was doing . . . he might present a problem. He was the bank vice-president, more than likely, and he'd have his eye on the president's job, which meant he would be quicker to defend the customers' money. Ambition nearly always equaled foolhardiness.

In one of the drawers of the young man's desk would be a gun, and when the holdup started he'd be tempted to make a grab for it.

Lupo caught Brattle's eye and gave a tiny nod toward the bank vice-president. Brattle nodded back to show he understood Lupo was telling him where the greatest danger lay. He would be ready if the vice-president tried anything.

The three tellers were men approaching middle age, all with the resigned look of hombres who knew they would never do anything else with their lives. It was possible one might put up a fight, but it was just as possible they would be more concerned with their own hides and would cooperate with the robbers. Lupo would keep an eye on them, of course, but he really didn't expect any trouble from that direction.

That left the customers. They were a mix of housewives depositing butter-and-egg money, local businessmen, and a couple rangy men in cowboy hats and boots who probably owned spreads in the area.

Those cattlemen weren't carrying guns, which was good, because they looked like the sort of hombres who would use them, if they had them. Lupo preferred they not be there, even unarmed. Maybe the ranchers would finish up their business and leave before the other members of the gang were in position, he thought.

One of the cattlemen did indeed stroll out a few minutes later, but the other lingered to jaw with the bank president.

Lupo stood at the marble counter, holding a pencil and pretending to do some figuring on a piece of paper, as he watched the other members of the gang drift in casually. Nobody in the bank did more than glance idly at them, but if they stood around doing nothing for very long, people would start to get suspicious.

It was time to move.

Lupo looked over at Brattle and nodded.

Brattle reached for the bandanna tied around his neck and pulled it up over the lower half of his face. The other robbers did the same.

Lupo was the only one with his face still uncovered as he pulled his gun, stepped back so he could cover the whole room, and shouted, "Everybody put your hands up and stand still! This is a holdup!"

Telling people to stand still worked better than ordering them not to move, Lupo had discovered through experience. People were more likely to obey if they were told to *do* something rather than to *not* do something, even if the end result was exactly the same.

But there was always somebody who wouldn't follow orders. The trick was to get on top of them right away and stop them from making trouble.

The rancher who'd been talking to the bank president whirled around and took a step toward the gate in the railing.

Lupo pointed his gun at the man and eared back the hammer. The sound of a gun being cocked when it was aimed right at him tended to freeze the blood of any man.

It worked with the rancher. He stopped in his tracks and glared at Lupo, but didn't move anymore except to raise his hands slowly.

He had no way of knowing Lupo's gun was empty . . . unless he looked closely enough to see that no bullets were visible in the Colt's cylinder. Lupo hoped the man wouldn't be that observant.

Brattle had his gun pointed at the vice-president, who had bolted up out of his chair at the sound of Lupo's shouted command. The young man froze just like the rancher as Brattle was quick to cover him.

Maybe they could get this job done without any gunplay, Lupo thought.

One robber kept his gun on the customers while the other three moved in on the tellers' cages. They pulled out canvas sacks from under their shirts and tossed them to the frightened tellers.

"Fill 'em up," one of the outlaws growled.

Lupo moved closer to the railing and told the bank president, "You're going back there to open the vault now, friend. Do it and no one gets hurt."

The man's face had turned pale and looked like lumpy bread dough. "I . . . I can't open it. I don't know the combination—"

"The hell you don't," Lupo interrupted. "Get back there and do it now."

The rancher said, "You'd better do what he says, Carl. I recognize this fella. He's that mad dog son of a bi . . . gun Lupo who broke out of Huntsville a week ago. Killed a guard on his way out, the newspaper said."

Lupo let a menacing smile curve his mouth. "That's right, Carl. So move or I'll kill you, too, and get somebody else to open the vault."

Holding his hands up in plain sight, the bank president struggled to his feet. "I'm going. I . . . I . . ."

His eyes widened and he looked like he was about to choke. Instead of moving to follow Lupo's order, he suddenly clasped both hands to his chest. With a strangled groan, he pitched forward across his desk.

That was so unexpected Brattle turned to look, giving the vice-president the chance he had been waiting for. Reaching down, he jerked open a drawer in his desk, and plucked out a gun.

He never had a chance. Brattle's Colt boomed twice and sent a pair of slugs ripping into the young man's chest. The bullets drove him off his feet and dropped him in a bloody heap.

The gunshots ended the possibility of emptying the vault—not enough time for that now.

But the canvas bags were already bulging with loot scooped from the tellers' drawers.

"Move!" Lupo shouted through the echoes of Brattle's shots. "Get to the horses!"

He swung his gun back and forth, keeping the rancher and the other customers covered as the masked men ran for the door and burst through it. Lupo was the last one out and the last one to hit the saddle.

As Lupo wheeled his horse, the rancher ran out of the bank with the gun the vice-president had dropped, and started shooting at the robbers.

Brattle returned the fire, his slugs striking the rancher and twisting the man off his feet.

The six outlaws galloped past the courthouse and headed for the river. People shouted curses and questions and scurried to get out of the way before they were trampled.

As he rode hard, leaning forward over his horse's neck to make himself a smaller target, Lupo reached into the saddlebags for the items he had told Grey he would need after he'd scouted the job. He pulled out a bundle of three sticks of dynamite tied together with twine. Their fuses were twisted together.

As the horses pounded onto the bridge over the river, Lupo guided his mount with his knees and used his other hand to snap a match into life with his thumbnail.

Sparks flew in the air as he lit the fuses, hanging back to let the others get well ahead of him.

A glance over his shoulder told him several men had mounted up and were galloping in pursuit. When he reached the far end of the bridge, Lupo wheeled his horse and gave the dynamite an underhanded toss, sending it bouncing and rolling about forty feet away onto the span.

A bullet whined over his head at the same time a rifle cracked in the distance. Somebody was shooting at him from the town. He turned his horse and galloped for the hill.

Behind him, the pursuers had raced onto the bridge when the dynamite blew. The bridge was long enough that they weren't caught in the explosion, but the blast made the horses rear up in panic. Several men were thrown from their saddles. Debris from the explosion rained down around them.

Another bridge was located two miles upstream. The closest bridge downstream was five miles away. By the time a posse could get across the Colorado and give chase, the bank robbers would have an insurmountable lead.

That was just the way Lupo had planned it.

The job would have to be considered a success, even though the take might not be as big as Grey expected. Lupo had passed his first test. He had been recognized, sure, and that would get him in deeper trouble with the law, but the undeniable truth to that old saying was they could only hang him once. The murder of that prison guard was enough to doom him to spending the rest of his life as a fugitive.

His plans to go straight were ruined. He would never be able to give Katie any sort of a normal life. She would always be the daughter of an outlaw and a killer.

He'd wait for his chance to turn the tables on Alexander Grey.

If he had to be an outlaw again, then by God he would be the boss outlaw!

Chapter 7

Three men died in the La Grange bank robbery: the bank vice-president, the rancher who'd been shot, and the heavyset bank president whose heart gave out from the fear and strain of the holdup.

The robbery itself netted a little under nine thousand dollars. Alexander Grey took about a third of that, leaving a thousand apiece for the men who had done the actual work.

That difference in the payoff might make a nice wedge to drive between Grey and the other men sometime in the future, Lupo thought.

A few days after the La Grange job, the bounty on Quint Lupo rose to four thousand dollars.

Two weeks later, Lupo, Brattle, and the rest of the gang held up the bank in Hallettsville, down on the Lavaca River. Nobody was killed, although a townsmen caught a slug through the thigh during a brief flurry of shots as the outlaws were riding out of town.

A month later, they ventured farther west to San Marcos and hit the bank there. One of the tellers made a grab for the gun in his cash drawer and got a bullet through the brain from Brattle's gun.

Three weeks after that, they stopped a train near Seguin and emptied the safe in the express car. The express messenger and the conductor both died in that holdup when they tried to put up a fight.

Three things remained constant during that stretch. Lupo was the only one of the gang who wasn't masked during the jobs, so he was recognized each time. With each new crime, the bounty on him was raised, especially after they hit the train. With the money the railroad kicked in, the reward on Lupo's head rose all the way to twelve thousand dollars.

The third thing was that Alexander Grey took approximately a third of the loot as his share, even though he didn't run any of the risks.

It was time to make his move, Lupo sensed.

No one had ever tracked them back to the old plantation. He knew all the tricks of throwing a posse off his trail, so the place was their sanctuary, where they could take it easy between jobs.

The men grew more and more restless, though. Each had a pretty good poke of stolen loot built up, with nothing to spend it on. Whiskey, women, cards . . . all those things called to the outlaws, but Grey insisted they had to lie low.

Lupo planned to use that dissatisfaction to his advantage.

He wasn't guarded all the time, as he had been at first, although Grey still didn't trust him enough to allow him to carry a gun while he was there.

At least when he went on a job, his gun had bullets in it. So far he hadn't had to fire it. Brattle and the other men had taken care of all the gunplay.

He was in his second floor room one evening when a knock sounded on the door. He'd been sitting in a chair, smoking one of Grey's cigars, and reading a book he'd taken from the library downstairs, some far-fetched adventure yarn by an Englishman named Stevenson. Some of the pages were crinkled from water damage, but he could still read them.

When the knock came, he set the book and the cigar aside and called, "What is it?"

"Boss wants to see you downstairs," Brattle replied through the door.

Lupo stood up. It had been a week since the last job, so he figured Grey probably wanted to start talking about the next one. Lupo opened the door and grinned at Brattle standing there wearing his six-gun and Stetson, as usual.

"What's so funny?" Brattle demanded.

"I was just remembering how Grey called you his butler, the night you first brought me here."

Brattle snorted. "The boss gets some funny notions in his head. Do I look like a butler to you?"

"No, you look like a bank-robbing outlaw."

"Damn right. Come on."

As they went down the stairs covered by a frayed runner, Lupo asked, "Do you know what this is about?"

"Nope. The boss don't let me in on his plans unless he figures I've got a good reason for knowin' about 'em. He just said to fetch you."

"Well, I suppose I'll know soon enough."

"I expect so." Brattle escorted Lupo to the library.

Lupo didn't say anything else as they walked through the plantation house.

A few times lately, he had made some idle comments to the other men about how they were running all the risks while Grey claimed the lion's share of the loot. The men seemed to resent that arrangement, which was encouraging for Lupo's long-term plans.

So far, he hadn't approached Brattle in the same way. Since Brattle was closer to Grey than the other men it seemed a bigger risk.

The last thing Lupo needed was somebody telling Grey that he was trying to stir up a mutiny.

Brattle didn't pause to knock on the library door, just opened it and motioned for Lupo to go on in. He did so and was surprised to see Alexander Grey sitting at the desk with a stranger in the red leather chair in front of him.

Grey looked up with a smile of greeting on his lean face and got to his feet. "Come in, Quint. We have a visitor I want you to meet."

The stranger stood, too, and turned around. He was a dour, medium-sized man with slightly graying dark hair above a tanned face. He was dressed all in black, including his gunbelt and the grips of the Colt he carried. A black Stetson sat on the corner of Grey's desk.

"This is Angus Murrell," Grey introduced him. "Angus, you know all about Quint Lupo."

"Yeah, I should." Murrell held out a hand. "Howdy, Lupo."

Lupo shook hands with the man, then asked, "How do you know about me?"

That brought a laugh from Grey. "You may have wondered how I got those wanted posters on you, Quint. Angus takes care of things like that for me. In fact, he's brought a new one tonight." Grey picked up a sheet of paper from his desk and extended it toward Lupo. "Here, take a good look at it."

Lupo took the paper. He recognized the familiar photograph of himself printed on it, but the amount of the reward listed below his face was new. He let out a low whistle to show that he was impressed. "Fifteen grand. I'm worth a lot of money."

"You certainly are," Grey agreed, and something about his voice made Lupo glance up sharply.

Boot leather scraped on the floor behind him. Brattle was still back there.

Lupo had forgotten all about him, but his instincts shrieked a warning.

That warning came too late. With stunning force, something crashed against the back of Lupo's head as he started to turn. He felt himself falling.

He didn't feel himself hit the floor in front of Grey's desk.

He was already out cold by then.

Awareness seeped back into Lupo's brain and brought with it pain and fear. He knew he had been the worst kind of fool. He had been making his plans, scheming to double-cross Grey and take over the gang, when all along Grey had been using him, setting up a double cross of his own.

He lay sprawled uncomfortably on a hard-packed dirt surface, his arms tied behind his back. He opened his eyes, and realized he was in one of the plantation's old barns. The big, drafty building was slowly rotting away, but it was still intact for the moment.

They had taken him out there because Grey didn't want to get blood on the floor of his study, Lupo thought grimly.

A lantern hung from a nail in one of the beams holding up the hayloft. Its harsh light spread over a circle that held Grey, Brattle, and Murrell. Lupo saw a couple of saddled horses waiting patiently behind them.

"I'm sorry, Quint," Grey said when he saw that Lupo had regained consciousness. "That head of yours has taken quite a pounding in the past few months, hasn't it?"

"You . . . son of a bitch," Lupo panted. He strained at his bonds, but the ropes were too tight.

"There's no need to take that attitude, simply because you were outsmarted," Grey said. "These things happen. A man figures the odds as best he can and then makes his play. It just so happens I figured them a bit better than you."

"You . . . set me up. You planned all along . . . to double-cross me."

"Of course. And as a matter of fact, we made an excellent team while it lasted. You're a very good bank robber, Quint. But the reward for you is high enough now that you're more valuable to me in other ways."

"How do you plan on collecting?" Lupo asked. He didn't really care all that much how Grey was going to work the scheme, but the longer he kept the man talking, were a few more minutes of life he could cling to. Maybe a miracle would happen. "You can't turn me in. I'd tell the law all about you."

Grey smiled and spread his hands. "Well, of course you would," he agreed. "That goes without saying."

"So you have to kill me."

"I'm afraid so."

"How will you collect the reward? You're an outlaw, too."

"Ah, but no one knows that," Grey said smugly. "I could ride into the nearest town with your body and claim the reward myself, and no one would ever be the wiser. But that might make the authorities curious about me, and I'd prefer they remain completely unaware of my existence. The same goes for Brattle here."

Lupo's gaze darted toward Murrell. "But this man—"

"He's a bounty hunter," Grey finished for him. "The law is already quite familiar with him, and no one will think twice when he brings in the body of a fugitive wanted for murder, bank robbery, and breaking out of prison."

Lupo felt like crying. But he hadn't shed tears in more than forty years and he was damned if he was going to start.

But he was damned no matter what he did, he thought. He sighed. "Get it over with."

"What? You're not going to beg for your life?"

Lupo lunged up off the floor as best he could with his hands tied behind him. It wasn't much.

"Damn you to hell, Grey! Don't taunt me! If you're going to kill me, go ahead and kill me!"

Grey took out a cigar and put it in his mouth without lighting it. He said around the cigar, "You might as well oblige him, Angus."

Murrell drew the black Colt on his hip and pulled

back the hammer. Lupo wanted to glare furiously at the killer, but he couldn't do it. He closed his eyes instead and whispered, "I'm sorry, Katie."

Grey said, "Wait, what did he—"

Murrell's finger had already tightened on the trigger. The gun roared like thunder, echoing in the old barn. Even with his eyes squeezed shut, Lupo saw an explosion of red, then . . . nothing.

No miracles tonight.

Chapter 8

San Antonio

"Let me make sure I've got this straight," Kid Morgan said. "You want to send me to prison."

Captain John R. Hughes looked solemnly across the desk at him and nodded. "That's right, Mr. Morgan."

"No offense, Captain, but you've gone loco!"

Culhane shifted uncomfortably in his chair. He and The Kid were sitting in front of Hughes's desk.

"No, sir, I'm completely serious." The grave look on Hughes's rugged, mustachioed face confirmed his statement.

Culhane had explained to The Kid that Captain Hughes was the commander of Company D, Texas Rangers, part of the famous Frontier Battalion that had brought law and order to so much of the far-flung state. They were sitting in Hughes's office in the adobe building that housed the Battalion's headquarters.

"Maybe you don't understand, Kid," Culhane said.

"Oh, I understand, all right," The Kid said. "It's pretty plain. You want to send me to prison so I can get shot in the head."

"That's what happened to Quint Lupo," Hughes said. "The idea is to keep it from happening to anybody else, and to round up the outlaws behind the scheme."

"You don't know there actually is a scheme. You said the reason that fella Lupo was behind bars to start with was because he was a bank robber."

"And a good one," Hughes said with a nod. "Or maybe I should say a talented one. I'm not sure there is such a thing as a good bank robber."

The Kid wanted to get up and walk out of the captain's office. He wished he hadn't let Culhane talk him into going there in the first place.

But now that he was, he didn't want to get Culhane in trouble with the boss Ranger, so he said, "All right. I'll hear you out, Captain. But I've got a special dislike for the idea of going to prison . . . especially when I haven't done anything to deserve it!"

"Yes, I understand. I did some checking into your background after Sergeant Culhane came up with this idea." Hughes shook his head. "But we'll get to that. Let me finish filling you in on the facts as we know them."

Hughes had already gone over some of it, but The Kid could tell the captain was the sort who liked to be thorough. He nodded. "Go ahead."

Hughes glanced down at the documents on his desk. "Five years ago, Quint Lupo was arrested, tried, convicted, and sentenced to a term of fifteen years in the state penitentiary on numerous charges of bank and train robbery. The record shows that prior to his arrest, no one was ever killed during the commission of one of his crimes."

"We don't have any evidence to show he ever took a shot at anybody," Culhane put in.

The Kid shrugged. "All that tells me is he planned his robberies well enough he didn't have to shoot anybody."

"That's how it appears," Hughes agreed. "And except for a few minor scrapes of the sort that occur all the time in prison, he stayed out of trouble while he was at Huntsville . . . until he provoked a fight with another convict and wound up in the infirmary."

"Which you think was deliberate."

"It looks like it," Culhane said. "That ain't necessarily the same thing."

"While Lupo was in the infirmary, he and three other convicts made an escape attempt," Hughes went on. "They murdered a guard, a Sergeant Alonzo Flynn, and slightly injured two others. They made it outside the walls of the prison, but were pursued by a guard detail led by Corporal Bert Hagen. The other three convicts were shot down by Hagen and his men, but Lupo gave them the slip and got away in the woods."

"Men have broken out of prison before," The

Kid pointed out. As a matter of fact, he was one of them.

"Yeah, but that ain't all of it," Culhane said.

Hughes shifted around some of the papers on his desk and picked up another document.

"Lupo dropped out of sight and wasn't spotted until a couple weeks later, when half a dozen outlaws held up the bank in La Grange. They were all masked except for Lupo, who was recognized by one of the victims. That man wound up being killed when he pursued the robbers outside the bank, but he identified Lupo in the hearing of several other witnesses before the shooting started."

The Kid frowned slightly. "Wait a minute. Lupo was the only one who wasn't wearing a mask?"

"That's right. Two men were gunned down during that robbery, and another, the bank president, died of a heart seizure."

"That doesn't sound much like the jobs Lupo pulled before."

"No, it doesn't," Hughes said.

Culhane put in, "When Rangers questioned some of the folks who were in the bank the day of the holdup, they said Lupo wasn't the one who killed those fellas. He waved a gun around, but he didn't shoot."

The Kid had to admit this was getting more interesting, even though he was still reluctant to get involved. He scratched his jaw. "All right, go on."

"Over the next couple months, Lupo turned up at several more robberies, including stopping a train and looting the express car over by Seguin," Hughes said. "Three more men were killed in those crimes, and one was wounded."

"Did Lupo do any of the shooting?"

"Not as far as we've been able to determine."

The Kid leaned back in his chair. "So probably what you've got is a fella who didn't like killing when he started out, but hardened up while he was in prison and threw in with some trigger-happy hombres after he escaped. You could explain it that way."

"And no one would doubt it for a second," Hughes said. "Just like no one lost any sleep over it when a bounty hunter named Angus Murrell brought in Lupo's body a couple weeks ago. He claimed he'd been trailing the gang and caught up to them while Lupo was away from the other out-laws. Murrell shot and killed him . . . and collected the fifteen thousand dollar reward on his head."

The Kid grunted. Fifteen thousand dollars wasn't much money to Conrad Browning, as he had thought earlier when he was talking to Lace, but it was a mighty big price for an outlaw. "Bounty hunters bring in fugitives all the time," he said, thinking about her again. "There's nothing un-usual about that."

"No, and this man Murrell is well-known to the authorities. Lupo wasn't the first wanted man he'd brought in, not by a long shot."

"So what makes Lupo's case different?" The Kid wanted to know.

Hughes smiled slightly. "It's not the differences but the similarities. Six months ago, Angus Murrell brought in the body of an outlaw named Henry Bedford. A few months before that, Bedford escaped from the penitentiary where he was serving a term for several bank holdups."

The Kid sat forward, intrigued despite himself. "Let me guess. After breaking out, Bedford turned up leading a gang of robbers, only they were all masked and he wasn't."

Culhane slapped a hand against his thigh. "Dadgummit, Cap'n, I told you this young fella was smart!"

Hughes nodded. "You're right, Mr. Morgan. That's exactly what happened. Then Murrell tracked Bedford down and killed him, earning himself ten thousand dollars bounty in the process."

"Is there more?" The Kid asked.

"One more case. Last year another bank robber named Lew Tolbert escaped from prison and took part in another series of holdups in which he was positively identified. Eventually Murrell brought *his* body in and claimed an eight thousand dollar reward for him."

"The payoff's going up every time," The Kid murmured.

"That's right. So you can see where all this is leading us, Mr. Morgan."

"It's not leading to me volunteering to go to prison, that's for sure," The Kid said. "I had enough of that over in New Mexico Territory."

Hughes tapped a finger against another document on his desk. "Yes, I've got a report here about how you were locked up in Hellgate Prison because of a case of mistaken identity. You were identified as an outlaw named . . . Bledsoe, was it?"

"Ben Bledsoe," The Kid said. "Bloody Ben, they called him, and he deserved the name."

"That matter was cleared up. There are no charges against you in New Mexico Territory or anywhere else."

"Maybe not, but I spent more than enough time behind bars in that hellhole. I'm not anxious to go back."

"Huntsville ain't like that Hellgate place," Culhane said.

"But it's still a prison."

Neither of the Rangers could argue with that statement.

After a moment, Hughes cleared his throat and went on. "It's our belief there's an organized gang breaking these men out of prison, forcing them to take part in bank robberies, and then killing them for the bounty once the price on their heads has gone up enough to make it profitable. In order to do that they'd have to be working with someone inside the prison. We want to put our hands on whoever that is, as well as the mastermind who's orchestrating the whole thing."

"You don't have any proof that theory's even right," The Kid said.

"No, we don't," Hughes admitted. "But that's where you come in."

The Kid started to get up. "No, that's where I go out. I think you may be on to something, Captain, I have to admit that, but the plan's still loco."

"It could work," Hughes said quickly, trying to keep The Kid from leaving. "We can't put a Ranger in there, because there's too much of a chance one of the convicts would recognize him. But you're not a lawman, Mr. Morgan, and you haven't spent that much time in Texas. You could get away with it."

"I'm not an outlaw, either," The Kid said.

"No, but Waco Keene is."

Taken by surprise, The Kid eased back down into his chair. "Who in blazes is Waco Keene?"

"You are, if you agree to help us," Hughes said.

"He ain't real," Culhane added. "Or rather, he was, but he's dead now. Deputy sheriff up in Comanche County killed him the other day when he tried to rob a store in Gustine. Thing is, not many folks know about it yet."

"So he was a bank robber," The Kid said.

Hughes said, "Not exactly. He and three other men stopped and held up half a dozen trains in various places around Central Texas. The other members of the gang were killed last week when a posse caught up to them. Keene got away, but he had been dodging the law on his own ever since and was pretty desperate. He tried to shoot it out with that deputy sheriff and lost."

"I suppose I happen to look like him?" The Kid asked.

"No, not at all," the captain said. "He was a scrawny little fella with dark hair, not a big strapping hombre like you. But that doesn't matter. As far as anybody inside the walls at Huntsville would know, you'd be him. Nobody he ever rode with is locked up there."

"As far as you know."

Hughes shrugged and nodded.

"As far as we know. The plan certainly wouldn't be without its risks."

"And I'd be the one running them. No thanks."

The Kid put his hands on the arms of the chair and pushed himself to his feet.

"Mr. Morgan, I can't order you to do this—"

"You certainly can't."

"But from what I know of you, you're the best man for the job. You stand a better chance than anyone else of getting on the inside of this gang and helping us bring them to justice."

"I'm sorry, Captain," The Kid said. "I mean that. But I have no interest in going back to prison, for any reason."

Culhane started to say something, but Hughes lifted a hand to stop him. "It's all right, Sergeant. Mr. Morgan certainly has every right to refuse." Hughes stood and extended his hand across the desk. "Thank you for coming in and hearing me out."

The Kid shook hands with him. "I hope you find somebody who works out better than I did."

Culhane followed The Kid out of the office, and as soon as the door was closed behind them, he said, "Dang it, Kid—"

"There's no point in arguing with me, Asa. My mind's made up." The Kid paused. "You can satisfy my curiosity about something, though."

"I ain't sure I want to," Culhane said with a frown. "But what is it?"

"If you and the captain are right about there being some sort of mastermind behind this, it's a pretty complicated scheme. A lot of things would have to go just right to make it work. But if they did, it would be really hard to detect. What made you suspicious about it in the first place? It's not the sort of thing that would jump out at anybody."

"Are you sayin' we're too dumb to have figured it out our own selves?"

"No, I'm saying you wouldn't have had any reason to think about it if somebody hadn't tipped you off."

"Well, that's true, I reckon. Somebody did just about talk my ear off, and then the cap'n's ear, too, tryin' to convince us she was right about it."

"She?" The Kid repeated.

"That's right. You see, Quint Lupo had a daughter. Katherine's her name, and she's plumb convinced her old bank-robbin' pa was murdered."

Chapter 9

By the time he got back to the Menger Hotel, The Kid hadn't changed his mind about accepting Captain Hughes's proposition, despite what Culhane had told him about Quint Lupo's daughter being convinced her father had reformed while he was in prison. What daughter wouldn't want to believe that about her father?

The idea of voluntarily going back to prison just wasn't acceptable to him. As he walked up the stairs to his room, The Kid recalled how a few years earlier his own father, Frank Morgan, had wound up pretending to be a prisoner in Yuma Territorial Prison, out in Arizona, in a deadly charade designed to find out the location of a cache of stolen bank money.

That memory made The Kid feel a twinge of guilt. Frank had taken on that dangerous job as a favor to him. Conrad Browning owned a substantial stake in that looted bank.

It didn't matter, he told himself. He hadn't known Quint Lupo, and he didn't know anybody in La Grange or any of the other places where Lupo's alleged gang had robbed a bank. He certainly didn't know Lupo's daughter Katherine.

He unlocked the door of the room and went in, calling to Lace, "I'm back."

Then he stopped short just inside the door. Lace was gone and so were her things.

The Kid bit back a curse as he whirled around. He should have been expecting it, he told himself bitterly. He should have known better than to think once her mind was made up she would stay around any longer than she had to. She wouldn't want to give him a chance to talk her out of lighting a shuck for Del Rio and that fugitive she was after.

He hurried down the stairs and crossed the lobby with long strides. "Have you seen Miss McCall?" he demanded of the clerk at the desk.

The vehement question made the slick-haired gent look nervous, but he took a small envelope from under the counter and held it out toward The Kid. "She departed a while ago, Mr. Morgan. She asked me if I would give you this note."

The Kid snatched the envelope out of the clerk's hand, causing him to flinch a little. As The Kid stalked over to one of the windows where the light was better, he ripped the envelope open, in his anger not being too careful about it.

Lace's handwriting was bold but feminine. On the card inside the envelope she had written:

Sorry to end things like this for now, Kid. I thought it might be easier this way. I know you're already thinking about charging after me and giving me a hand tracking down Jake Cisneros, but I'd take it as a personal favor if you didn't. This is my job, not yours. We'll run into each other again one of these days. Until then . . .

Lace.

His first impulse was to clench his hand on the card and crumple it, but he knew he might regret it, later. He slid it back into the envelope and tucked it away inside his coat.

She was right about him coming after her, though. If she was bound and determined to be a bounty hunter, she'd just have to put up with a partner. He wouldn't take any cut of the rewards, of course, since he didn't need the money and she did.

And she'd probably wind up hating him for horning in, he realized with a sharply indrawn breath. It would be a blow to her pride, and that was one thing Lace couldn't stand.

On the other hand, he already missed her. The pang of it was like a knife in him.

As he turned away from the window, he saw the clerk pointing across the lobby at him. The man was talking to a tall, slender young woman in a gray traveling outfit and hat. Her blond hair was pinned up in an elaborate arrangement of curls under the hat. Clearly, the clerk had just pointed him out to her.

The Kid tensed. He already had enough on his mind without more trouble, and he could tell by looking at the woman that was exactly what she was. He even had a pretty good hunch *who* she was.

She nodded her thanks to the clerk and started across the lobby toward The Kid. He glanced at the doors of the hotel. The only way he could reach them before she cut him off was by making a dash for them. He wasn't going to make a run for it across the Menger's lobby just to get away from a young woman.

She was a very attractive young woman, too, not that that changed anything. Her face was lovely, and even at a distance The Kid could tell her eyes were a brilliant blue. He still didn't want to talk to her.

But it looked like he wasn't going to have any choice in the matter. She planted herself in front of him and said, "Mr. Morgan?"

"You know I am. The fella at the desk just told you I was. And you'd be Miss Lupo."

If she was surprised by his knowledge of her identity, she didn't show it. "That's right. I imagine Captain Hughes told you about me."

"Actually it was Sergeant Culhane."

Culhane's name brought a smile to her lips. "The sergeant told me the two of you are friends."

"Not good enough friends that I'm willing to go to prison just because he asks me to," The Kid said.

Katherine Lupo's smile disappeared. She looked worried. "We shouldn't be talking about that here. There are too many people around."

"Doesn't matter," The Kid told her with a shake of his head. "I'm sorry, Miss Lupo, but I can't help you."

"You mean you won't help me," she shot right back at him.

He shrugged. "Call it whatever you want."

"It's not so much about helping me. It's about restoring the reputation of . . . well, I suppose you really can't call my father an innocent man."

"Since he was behind bars for bank robbery and holding up trains, I reckon not."

Anger flared in those compelling blue eyes of hers. "My father never denied what he'd done. Once he was caught, he was willing to serve his time. But he'd been in prison for five years, Mr. Morgan, and every time I visited him during those years, and in every letter he wrote to me, he made the same promise—that once he had served his sentence and been released, he would never break the law again. I believed him then, and I still do."

"Of course you do," The Kid said. "He was your father. And for your sake I'm sorry about what happened to him, by the way."

"But you don't think I'm right about him." The words came out of her mouth in a flat, hard voice.

The Kid sighed. "Look, maybe we shouldn't stand here in the middle of the lobby talking about this.

Why don't we go in the dining room, maybe get some tea?"

And maybe that would help get his mind off Lace leaving the way she had, he thought.

Katherine hesitated for a moment, then nodded. "All right. I'd like to explain."

"It won't do you any good," The Kid told her, "but I'll listen."

They went into the Menger's well-appointed dining room and sat at a table in the corner. A waitress came over and The Kid ordered tea. He hadn't managed to get any dinner before he went with Culhane to the headquarters of the Frontier Battalion, but with Lace gone, he wasn't particularly hungry.

While they were waiting for the tea, Katherine Lupo said, "Captain Hughes told you about what happened to my father, I suppose."

"That's right."

"You probably don't believe that he wouldn't have broken out of prison unless he was forced to."

"Being forced is not something that happens very often," The Kid said. "Or ever."

Again her eyes sparked with anger. "You don't know that," she insisted. "But even if you don't believe that, you can believe this. My father would never, ever kill anyone. He just didn't have it in him. Why do you think he was able to carry out all those other robberies without anyone ever getting hurt?"

"Some of that could've been luck."

Katherine shook her head. "No. It was because he never wanted anyone to get hurt. He was a good man."

"Except for stealing other people's money."

For a second The Kid thought Katherine was going to stand up and slap him. He probably had it coming, he mused. He wasn't being very nice to her.

But he didn't feel very nice.

Finally she said, "I'll admit that he had a few . . . moral shortcomings, I guess you could call them. But he wouldn't have killed that prison guard."

"Maybe one of the men who broke out with him was responsible for that," The Kid suggested. "They may not know exactly what happened during the escape."

"One of the guards, Corporal Hagen, swore that he saw my father stab Sergeant Flynn. He's lying, Mr. Morgan."

"Why would he do that?" The Kid asked.

The question was barely out of his mouth when a possible answer suggested itself to him.

Hughes had said the Rangers suspected the gang was working with at least one person inside the prison, probably more. The guard Hagen could be part of the scheme, he thought. In that case, if the Rangers—and Katherine Lupo—were right about her father being forced to escape against his will, it made sense Hagen would lie about Lupo killing the other guard. That would give the gang even more of a hold over him.

In spite of himself, The Kid found himself thinking again about everything he had heard . . . and realizing there was a good chance Hughes, Culhane, and Katherine were right.

Katherine watched The Kid's thought play across his face and smiled. "Now you're beginning to understand, Mr. Morgan."

The Kid frowned. He understood, all right, but that didn't change the facts of what they wanted him to do.

The waitress arrived with their tea. They sat quietly for a few moments, sipping from the delicate china cups.

Katherine placed her cup on the accompanying saucer and said, "I know it's not fair. The Rangers are asking you—*I'm* asking you—to risk your life. You didn't know my father and you don't know me. You have absolutely no reason to be willing to run that sort of risk."

"I don't like outlaws," The Kid said. "If what Hughes told me is true, this is a pretty vicious bunch. They're responsible for the deaths of quite a few people."

"Yes, including my father. I'd track them down myself if I could, Mr. Morgan, but that's just not possible."

He smiled faintly. "You'd stand out pretty good in the penitentiary, all right."

"When Sergeant Culhane first came up with this

idea, I told him and Captain Hughes I didn't want them to do it. I wasn't going to ask a perfect stranger to put his life on the line simply to get justice for my father."

"That's not the only reason to do it."

"Perhaps not, but it's the reason that matters the most to me. Sergeant Culhane assured me things would be arranged so that whoever went into the prison would have help. They would have ways of communicating with you and stepping in if the situation became too dangerous."

That sounded good and might be reassuring to Katherine, The Kid thought, but he knew how quickly things could change once a fella was in the middle of a fight. All the plans in the world might not be enough to save him if his luck deserted him at the wrong moment.

But that was true of just about everything in life, he reminded himself. Anything could happen, at any time. The tragedies that had dogged his own life the past few years were proof enough.

A man would go loco if he thought about it too much.

So the choices facing him were simple ones, at least on the surface. He could ride after Lace and risk making her so angry at him she'd never have anything to do with him again. He could sit in San Antonio and drink and brood, maybe gamble a little like the bored rich man he used to be. He could go back to Boston or San Francisco and actually resume the identity of Conrad Browning again, something he had sworn he would never do.

Or he could go along with the Rangers' plan and maybe wind up dead.

But if he *didn't* wind up dead, he might be able to get to the bottom of the mystery and put a gang of brutal killers out of business. That would be a good thing.

And so would taking some of the pain out of this young woman's eyes.

Those thoughts flashed through his mind in a matter of seconds. He looked across the table at Katherine Lupo and said, "Tell you what I'll do. I'll talk to Culhane again."

Chapter 10

"Didn't expect to see you again so soon, Kid," Asa Culhane said.

"Someone came to see me at my hotel," The Kid said.

"The girl?"

"You didn't put her up to it, did you?" The Kid watched Culhane's rough-hewn face intently as he asked the question.

"No, sir, I did not," the Ranger replied, sounding a little offended by the idea. "I knew she'd been here and talked to the cap'n, and I figured he told her you said no to the idea, but that's all I know about it. Cap'n Hughes wouldn't have sent her to beg you to help, neither. He ain't got an underhanded bone in his body."

The Kid smiled. "That's the impression I got, too. Miss Lupo's really determined to clear her father's name, at least as much as that's possible considering his history."

Culhane nodded. "Can't blame her for feelin' that way about her pa."

"The same thought occurred to me," The Kid agreed. He'd caught up to Culhane at the headquarters of the Frontier Battlion. Even though the grizzled old Ranger claimed to be surprised to see him again, The Kid thought Culhane didn't really look all that surprised, as if he'd suspected all along The Kid wouldn't be able to resist the challenge.

"Let's go in the office and talk," Culhane suggested. The Kid nodded.

They went into the adobe building. Culhane rapped his knuckles on the open door of Captain Hughes's office and was told to come in.

Hughes raised his eyebrows when he saw The Kid. He looked genuinely surprised.

"The Kid's had second thoughts about our plan," Culhane said.

"I wouldn't go quite that far," The Kid corrected him. "But I'm willing to discuss it some more. Miss Lupo said you had some ideas about how to cut down on the danger for the man who goes into the prison."

"Miss Lupo came to see you?" Hughes asked.

"She found me at the Menger Hotel."

"I didn't send her there, Mr. Morgan."

"That's what Sergeant Culhane told me. I believe you, Captain."

"Well, in that case," Hughes said, "sit down and we'll talk about this."

"We'd have to keep who you really are mighty

quiet," Culhane said after he and The Kid took seats in front of Hughes's desk, "since we figure somebody inside the prison is workin' with the gang and we don't know who."

Hughes said, "Just about the only person who's above suspicion is the warden."

"You're sure of him?" The Kid asked.

"I've known Preston Jennings for more than twenty years," Hughes said. "He's incorruptible."

The Kid wasn't sure anybody fell into that category, but since he was going to have to trust *somebody* if he became a part of this, he supposed he might as well trust the captain's judgment. Nodding, he said, "Go on."

"We'd let Jennings know who you really are and that you're working with us. We'll leave it up to him to tell one subordinate he trusts."

"Just in case somethin' happened to the warden," Culhane added. "We wouldn't want you to wind up gettin' stuck behind bars for any longer than you had to be there."

"I wouldn't want that, either," The Kid commented with a smile.

"Other than that, though," Hughes continued, "everybody inside the prison would believe you're actually Waco Keene, the train robber."

"None of the convicts in there know Keene well enough to recognize him?"

Hughes shook his head. "We can't rule that out entirely, of course, without checking the background of every single prisoner, but the chances of it are slim. Keene's never been in prison. He was locked up a few times in local jails, but those are the only times he's been behind bars. And all the men who rode with him on his holdups are dead. All the paperwork will say you're Waco Keene, and I don't think anyone will challenge it."

"Sounds like this Keene was pretty small-time, and he wasn't even a bank robber," The Kid said. "Not like Lupo. What makes you think the gang will find him an attractive enough target to go after?"

"Keene was beginning to develop a reputation as a desperado. We can make it even stronger by spreading the word he was responsible for a number of robberies he really didn't have anything to do with and inflating the amount of the rewards that were offered for him. A prison is like any other community, Mr. Morgan. To a certain extent it lives on gossip and speculation. Also, we know Lupo took part in at least one train robbery after he was broken out of prison. The gang doesn't limit themselves to bank robberies." Hughes shrugged. "Anyway, Waco Keene is the one who's conveniently dead right now."

"It sounds like you might be able to pull off that part of it," The Kid said. "But if I found myself in trouble, the guards wouldn't help me. They'd believe I was Waco Keene, too."

"Well . . ." Hughes smiled thinly. "You'd have to be able to take care of yourself, that's certainly true. But if you found yourself in such danger the plan had to be abandoned, you could ask to see the warden. He'll know who you are."

"The guards might not let me see him."

Hughes shrugged. "The plan has risks. I won't deny that."

"So what you're saying is it would be up to me to stay alive in there until the gang comes to bust me out," The Kid said. "Or until you give up on the idea. How long's that going to be? Lupo was in there for five years before they recruited him, remember?"

"They've been making a move about every six months," Hughes said. "It hasn't been that long since Lupo escaped, but we're hoping they're starting to get greedy and will make their next move sooner."

"Owlhoots usually do get greedy," Culhane put in.

The Kid leaned back in his chair and cocked his right ankle on his left knee. "Let's say it works and they break me out of there. What happens then?"

"We'll be keeping an eye on the prison, and with any luck we'll be able to follow them," Hughes said. "We wouldn't want to close in on them just yet, though. We wouldn't be able to charge them with anything except the breakout. To get proof of everything they've done, you'd have to be part of their organization for a while. Once you've found out as much as you can, you get word to your contact, and the Rangers will move in and grab them."

"What contact?"

"We'll have a man stationed somewhere close to the gang. He'll signal you, so you'll know where to look for him. After that, he'll wait for your signal, and when he sees it, he'll alert the other Rangers."

The Kid thought it all over and then slowly shook his head.

"Sounds like there's an awful lot that could go wrong."

"Of course there is," Hughes agreed without hesitation. "And if it does, you could easily wind up dead. I won't try to deny that. But it's the only way we can think of to find the people who are really behind this."

"If you're even right about it being some sort of gang," The Kid said. "Maybe you're wrong about Lupo, and his daughter is, too."

"In that case, nothing will happen, and in a few months we'll pull you out of the prison."

"A few months," The Kid repeated wryly.

"I don't think that's how it's going to turn out. I think we're right about the gang."

The Kid thought there was a good chance the Rangers were right, too. And from the sound of it, they had devoted quite a bit of planning to the idea and would try to protect their inside man as much as they could.

In the end, as Captain Hughes had said, it would be up to the man masquerading as Waco Keene to stay alive while he was behind bars.

"What do you think, Kid?" Culhane asked.

The Kid smiled. "I think I'm a damned fool to even be here."

"Does that mean you're going to do it?" Hughes said.

Surviving inside the prison would take razor-sharp instincts and complete concentration, The Kid thought, and so would capturing the gang after they broke him out.

If something like that didn't take his mind off Lace leaving him like she had, then nothing would.

He looked at Culhane and Hughes. "Say howdy to Waco Keene."

The Kid spent the rest of the afternoon in Hughes's office going over the plan with the two Rangers. It would take several days to get everything ready. Hughes asked The Kid to stay in San Antonio during that time and not draw attention to himself.

"That won't be hard," The Kid assured him. "I'll lie low at the hotel."

"When we're ready, Sergeant Culhane will come and get you. There's nothing unusual about the Rangers delivering prisoners to the penitentiary, so he'll take you there with several men as an escort."

"You want whoever's keeping an eye out for new targets to believe that Waco Keene is a dangerous man, is that it?"

"Exactly," Hughes said with a nod. "You'll have a reputation to live up to, Mr. Morgan."

That wouldn't be anything new, The Kid reflected. For years he had walked in the shadow of Frank Morgan, the famous gunfighter known as The Drifter, and he had his own reputation as a fast gun, a reputation he had largely invented in the beginning to help him track down his wife's murderers. As it turned out, real life had more than lived up to those dime novel exploits.

By the time he left Ranger headquarters and returned to the Menger Hotel, his stomach was reminding him he had skipped the midday meal. He stopped at the desk and asked the clerk to have some supper sent up to him.

"Of course, Mr. Morgan," the man said.

"Any messages?" The Kid asked. "Anybody been around looking for me?" It was too much to hope Lace might have changed her mind and come back, but that didn't stop the thought from crossing his mind.

The clerk shook his head. "No, sir."

The Kid nodded and went up the stairs. Just as well, he told himself. If Lace had returned, it would have ruined the plan hatched by the Rangers. He wouldn't have been willing to go through with it then.

He needed to focus all his attention on the dangerous job facing him.

When he reached the room, he turned on the gas lights, since dusk was stealing over the city. The Menger was known for its luxuries, which were the equal of some of the fancier hotels back east, including hot and cold running water. The Kid started the hot water in the claw-footed bath-tub, intending to soak in it after he ate supper.

He hung his hat and his gunbelt on the chair next to the bed, took off his coat and hung it in the wardrobe, then stripped off his shirt and string tie, leaving him bare to the waist. When a knock sounded on the door, he left the water running in the tub and went to answer the summons, assuming he'd find a waiter with his supper standing in the corridor.

When he swung the door open he found himself looking into the beautiful, but rather startled face of Katherine Lupo.

Chapter 11

"Mr. Morgan. I'm sorry. I didn't mean to intrude on you."

"It's all right. What can I do for you, Miss Lupo?"

"I can come back later," she offered.

The Kid shook his head. "That's not necessary."

He supposed she had talked to Hughes and knew he was going to help the Rangers with their plan after all. She had probably come to thank him, but he wasn't really in the mood for it. He wasn't doing it to help her, but rather to distract himself.

He decided it was best to get the conversation out of the way. "Go ahead and say whatever it is you came here to say."

She drew in a deep breath and her chin came up a little. "All right. But may I come in first?"

The water, fed by a tank on the roof of the building, didn't run very fast, so he knew it would still be a few minutes before the tub was full. He stepped back, holding onto the edge of the door. "Sure. Come on in."

Katherine stepped past him, and he closed the door behind her. If she wasn't worried about being alone in a hotel room with a man who was stripped to the waist, he wasn't going to worry about protecting her maidenly sensibilities. He turned to face her and found that she was regarding him with a frank stare.

"I've thought about it a great deal," she said, "and I'm convinced you're the only man who can prove my father wasn't a killer. Accomplishing that means a great deal to me. So I'm prepared to do whatever it takes to persuade you to go along with Captain Hughes's plan." With that, she reached up and started to unbutton the top button of her blouse.

"Wait just a minute," The Kid said sharply. "You're saying that you're willing to go to bed with me to get me to do what you want?"

For a second she looked like she wanted to bolt, but he could almost see her spine stiffening with resolve as she said, "That's right." The top button was undone, and her fingers were headed for the second one.

"Miss Lupo." The Kid reached out and took hold of her wrists. "You don't have to do that."

"I don't mind. Really."

He could tell she was trying to make her eyes bold as she looked at him. He didn't let go of her wrists as he said, "You haven't been to Ranger headquarters since earlier in the day, have you?"

"No, I . . . I've been thinking about what I need to do."

"It's not this," The Kid said. "Don't think I wasn't tempted for a second. I'm as human as the next man. But I have to tell you the truth. I've already told Captain Hughes and Sergeant Culhane that I'll go along with their plan."

Katherine's bright blue eyes widened. "Oh. Oh!" She pulled back, and The Kid released her wrists. "Then you must think I'm some sort of . . . of loose woman—"

"I think you're a woman who loves her father and wants to clear his name," The Kid interrupted her. "That's all. At this point, it's the only thing you can still do for him, so it's very important to you. There's no shame in that."

Unable to meet his eyes, she looked down and hurriedly fastened the button she had undone. "I'm not ashamed," she said with a trace of defiance in her voice. "I probably should be. But I was desperate."

"I understand," The Kid said.

"When you opened the door and I saw you standing there . . . like that . . . I took it as an omen . . ."

"I thought you were the waiter bringing my supper," The Kid explained. "I'm not in the habit of parading around shirtless in front of women I don't really know. I'm sorry for the misunderstanding."

"That's all right. I should go." A tiny smile tugged at the corners of her mouth. "Although you really, ah, don't owe me an apology."

It had taken him a long time to get over his wife's

death and reach a point where he was willing to admit to the human needs he still felt. Lace was the only woman who'd been able to get beyond the wall of grief and resolve he had built. At least, she was the only woman so far . . .

If things had been different, he might have been intrigued enough by Katherine Lupo to consider getting to know her better. Under the circumstances, with him still smarting from Lace leaving earlier, he knew it wouldn't be smart.

Also, as soon as Hughes and Culhane had everything set up, he would be leaving for Huntsville with a Ranger escort, for all intents and purposes a prisoner. So it was a terrible time all around to be getting romantically involved with anyone.

"Maybe we'll see each other again before things get started," he said.

"Maybe. If not . . . I can't thank you enough for what you're doing, Mr. Morgan. I know you're risking your life, and I have no right to ask you to do something like that."

"I wouldn't be doing it if I didn't want to."

"I know. Still, I appreciate it so much."

For a second he wondered if she was about to offer to go to bed with him to thank him for what he was doing, but then another knock sounded on the door. He thought he was a little relieved by that. "That's bound to be my supper this time."

"I'll leave you to it, then." She turned toward the door.

"Hold on a minute. You're not worried about your reputation?"

He knew if the waiter saw her leaving the room, with him stripped to the waist, there was liable to be gossip about her.

She shook her head. "The only reputation I'm worried about is my father's, and you're going to help repair that. I've made my peace knowing he was a bank robber. I can live with that. But I don't want people thinking he was a murderer, too."

The Kid hoped for her sake that was how the whole thing was going to turn out.

He went to the door and opened it. A waiter in a red jacket stood there, all right, with a tray containing several covered dishes in his hands.

"The lady was just leaving," The Kid said as Katherine stepped past him. The waiter moved aside to give her some room. The Kid saw the man's eyes widen slightly at the sight of her, but a quick glare from him made the waiter's expression turn neutral again.

Katherine turned back long enough to say, "Thank you, Mr. Morgan. Good night."

"Good night," he told her with a nod. Then he jerked a thumb to indicate the waiter should bring in the food.

The man stepped inside and placed the tray on a table. He straightened to find The Kid had drawn the Mauser from its holster. The sight of the odd looking but definitely menacing pistol made the man's face turn pale. He swallowed hard as he stared at it.

The Kid held the gun down at his side. In his other hand he had a twenty dollar gold piece he had taken from the pocket of his trousers. He held the coin up so the waiter could see it.

"Your choice is pretty simple," The Kid said. "You can keep your mouth shut about what you just saw and earn yourself this double eagle. Or you can spread rumors. If you do and they get back to me, I'll know who started them. You understand me, amigo?"

The waiter licked dry lips. "Yes, sir, I sure do. And that gold piece looks mighty nice to me."

"I thought maybe it would." The Kid flipped the double eagle toward the waiter, who plucked it deftly from the air. "I'll put the dishes in the hall when I'm through with them."

"Yes, sir!" The waiter couldn't leave fast enough.

The Kid smiled, shook his head, and slid the Mauser back into its holster. He went into the bathroom and turned off the water in the tub, which was about to overflow. Then he sat down to eat his supper before he started his soak in the steaming water.

He tried not to think about Katherine Lupo, but that proved to be quite a challenge.

Chapter 12

The Texas State Penitentiary at Huntsville was ugly as hell, The Kid thought, but at least it wasn't a hole in the ground like Hellgate Prison over in New Mexico Territory. In Hellgate, the prisoners' cells had been blasted out of the rock itself. The Kid had never seen a place any more bleak and depressing.

The prison at Huntsville might wind up running it a close second.

He rode in an enclosed wagon with small, barred windows in front and back. He could see the prison when he looked through the window in front, past Asa Culhane's shoulder.

Culhane rode on the seat next to the driver, a shotgun cradled across his lap. Four more Rangers, each of them heavily armed, flanked the wagon on horseback.

The Kid sat on a hard wooden bench, wearing leg irons and manacles connected by a length of chain. He knew he would barely shuffle along when he got out of the wagon.

He'd been wearing the restraints only for the past twenty miles or so. No reason for him to be uncomfortable all the way from San Antonio, Culhane had said, although The Kid had traveled the whole journey inside the wagon.

Just in case the gang they were after had anybody watching the approaches to the prison, Culhane had called a halt a couple hours earlier and told The Kid through the window to go ahead and snap the irons into place. The metal had already started to chafe his skin, even though he hadn't worn the irons for very long.

"There it is, Keene," Culhane called in a booming voice through the window as he turned his head to look toward The Kid. "Your home for the next twenty years."

"That's good," The Kid said. "You ever think about going on the stage, Asa? Becoming an actor?"

Culhane chuckled. "Reckon you and me ought to team up and go on the stage. I can sing and dance a mite, tell a few jokes."

"No thanks," The Kid said. "Making everybody in there think I'm Waco Keene is all the playacting I'm interested in doing."

The other five Rangers with Culhane were in on the plan, of course, and Warden Jennings was expecting them. Other than Captain Hughes and Katherine Lupo back in San Antonio, no one else knew Kid Morgan had taken the place of the late Waco Keene, and that was the way it had to remain.

The wagon drew to a halt in front of the prison's main gate. A couple blue-uniformed guards carrying shotguns came out of a guardhouse to greet Culhane.

"Six Rangers?" one of them said with a grin. "Whoever you've got locked up in that wagon, he must be a ring-tailed terror!"

"He's a bad hombre, all right," Culhane said as he handed down some papers to the guard. "Train robber and shootist named Keene."

"Yeah, I heard he was comin' in," the other guard said. "Papers look all right, Casey?"

The first guard grunted and handed the papers back to Culhane. "Yeah, signal the fellas inside to open the gate."

The second man went back into the guardhouse, and a moment later the big metal gate began rolling back. The Ranger handling the team of horses drove through and had to stop again at a wooden gate topped with barbed wire. The guards manning it didn't unlock it and swing it open until the outer gate had closed behind the wagon and its escort.

The gates were well guarded, The Kid thought, and yet Quint Lupo and the other prisoners had been able to get out through a single sally port leading from the administrative area where the infirmary was located to the outside.

During the past week, The Kid had gone over

every known detail about Lupo's escape with Hughes and Culhane. He wondered if that weakness in the prison's security had been addressed since Lupo's escape.

Once through the second gate, the Rangers were directed to the part of the sprawling prison compound where the offices were. The Kid supposed the routine varied from prison to prison, but he knew from his time at Hellgate that new prisoners would be processed in, examined by a doctor, issued a convict's uniform, and might even be spoken to by the warden. He figured in his case, that was a pretty safe bet. Warden Jennings would want to have a word with a notorious new convict like Waco Keene.

As the wagon came to a halt in front of one of the stone buildings, The Kid heard an unfamiliar voice say, "We can take him from here, Ranger. Just unlock the back of that wagon."

"No, sir." That was Culhane. "I ain't turnin' this one over to anybody except the warden his own self. He ain't your run-of-the-mill owlhoot."

The other man snickered. "Who have you got in there, the second comin' of Jesse James?"

"Reckon he might've turned out to be as bad as ol' Jesse if the law hadn't got lucky enough to nab him now. Name of Waco Keene."

"Yeah, I think I've heard some talk about him. You say you want to hand him over to the warden?"

"That's right."

"Well, I guess it's all right if you stay with him

while we're gettin' him checked in. I'll go let Mr. Jennings know you're here."

"Much obliged, son," Culhane said.

The Kid felt the wagon shift as Culhane and the driver climbed down from the seat. A moment later, a key rattled in the heavy padlock holding the thick wooden door at the back of the vehicle closed.

The door swung open, letting more sunlight into the enclosed wagon. The Kid had to squint a little against the glare.

"Climb out of there, Keene," Culhane ordered sternly. "And don't try anything or you'll be sorry. So says me and this scattergun."

The Kid grinned to himself. Culhane was putting on a pretty good performance, but he needed somebody to write better dialogue for him.

The wagon was parked in front of a squat stone building as unappealing as all the other buildings inside the prison. The area housed the offices, the infirmary, the guards' barracks for those who didn't live nearby in the town of Huntsville, storage buildings, and everything else that made the prison a nearly self-sufficient operation.

Beyond the area were more fences and walls cutting it off from the prison's main buildings, large, hulking gray structures where the prisoners were housed. The kitchen and the laundry, which were manned by convicts, were there, too, and in the center of those buildings was the exercise yard.

The layout wasn't that different from Hellgate,

The Kid saw as he climbed awkwardly out of the wagon and looked around. He supposed most prisons were similar. There was no point in getting fancy to keep men locked up.

The Rangers surrounded him, along with three blue-uniformed prison guards wearing stiff-billed black caps. Trying not to overdo it, The Kid put a sneer on his face as he looked at them. He hadn't shaved for several days, so brown stubble covered his cheeks.

"Follow me, Keene," one of the guards said.

The Kid didn't move for a second, just long enough to make it clear he wasn't going to jump to obey, then reluctantly shuffled along behind the guard. Having his ankles shackled made him feel like he was about to pitch forward onto his face, and he didn't like it at all. The sensation stirred up bitter memories of the time he'd spent in Hellgate.

They went into one of the ugly buildings and along a corridor to a room empty except for a bench along one wall.

"You'll take your clothes off here," the guard said.

As much as the chain connecting his wrists to his ankles would allow him, The Kid lifted his hands to display the iron fetters. "That's gonna be kind of hard."

The guard gave him an unpleasant smile. "Don't worry. We'll get 'em off you."

The guards closed in and cut The Kid's clothes

off. Of course, the garments weren't actually his. They were rough work clothes the Rangers had provided for the masquerade.

The Kid protested anyway, thinking that was something Waco Keene would do, but it didn't do any good. He was left standing naked except for the chains, and despite the warmth of the day outside, something dank about the stone-walled room made him shiver.

One of the guards knocked on a door on the other side of the room, and a moment later it opened to admit a slender man in a white coat.

As soon as The Kid saw the man's hollow eyes and pale skin, he knew something was wrong with him. He had seen opium addicts before, and had a hunch he was looking at one now.

The man stopped in front of The Kid. "I'm Dr. Simon Kendrick. I'm going to examine you now, Mr. Keene."

"You don't have to do that," The Kid said. "Ain't nothin' wrong with me."

Kendrick smiled. "I'm afraid it's standard procedure. This won't take long."

The doctor was right about that. The examination was cursory at best. But it was still humiliating, and The Kid was glad when it was over.

He recalled that Quint Lupo had been taken to the infirmary after a fight in the yard. Someone in the pay of the gang could have started that fight in order to get Lupo removed from the other convicts.

Did that mean Kendrick was part of the gang, or at least being paid off by them?

A man addicted to opium would certainly be vulnerable to something like that, The Kid thought. He would have to keep an eye on the doctor.

The only other name he knew was Bert Hagen, who had testified that Lupo murdered a guard during the prison break. For all The Kid knew, Hagen could have been one of the blue-uniformed men who had brought him into the building.

After the doctor was gone, one of the guards said to Culhane, "All right, take the chains off him."

Culhane handed his shotgun to one of the other Rangers. He wasn't wearing a handgun. He went over to The Kid, took a key from his vest pocket, and unlocked the leg irons and manacles.

When that was done, Culhane backed off, letting the restraints dangle from his hand. The other Rangers and the three guards had kept The Kid covered the whole time Culhane was turning him loose.

"You fellas must think I'm loco," The Kid muttered. "An hombre would have to be crazy to try anything with that many guns pointin' at him."

"You just keep reminding yourself of that, Keene," said the guard who had done the talking so far. "You do that and you'll be all right."

A small, ferret-faced convict in a gray uniform brought in a bundle of clothes, including a pair of boots and some socks. The man was one of the trusties. He set the clothes on the bench and left.

"That's what I'm supposed to wear?" The Kid asked as he gestured toward the bench.

"That's right," the guard said. "They suit you?"

"I reckon they'll do." The Kid got dressed. The gray uniform was rough and ill-fitting—a far cry from the luxurious clothing Conrad Browning had purchased from the finest tailors in Boston and New York. If some of the men who had sat in board-rooms with him could see him now . . . of course, some of those men were probably as crooked as many of the prisoners already locked up, he reminded himself.

"All right, the warden ought to be ready for you now," the guard said. "Let's go."

They weaved through corridors until The Kid figured he would have a hard time retracing their steps if he'd needed to. They went outside, crossed a short area covered with gravel, and entered another building. It was a little nicer, and The Kid wasn't surprised to see that it housed the prison offices.

The guard stopped and knocked on a polished wooden door. Gilt letters reading PRESTON JENNINGS were painted on it, with the title WARDEN underneath the name.

"Come in," a man said from inside.

The guard opened the door and went in first, turning so he could cover The Kid. Culhane and the other two prison guards followed, leaving the other Rangers in the hall.

The warden's office was simply but comfortably

furnished with a rug on the floor, several leather chairs, and a large desk. The window behind the desk didn't command much of a view. A high stone wall rose only a few feet from it.

The man standing behind the desk wore a brown tweed suit. He had thinning gray hair and a salt-and-pepper beard. Spectacles had slid down his nose and were perched on the end.

"This is the new man?" he asked, and The Kid was a little surprised to hear his voice contained a hint of an English accent.

"That's right, sir," the guard said. "Waco Keene."

"Waco, eh?" Warden Jennings smiled at The Kid. "Is that what your mother named you, Mr. Keene?"

"It'll do as good as any," The Kid replied in a surly voice.

"Suit yourself. My name is Preston Jennings. I'm the warden here. I want you to know we allow no troublemaking, but if you comply with our rules, you'll be treated fairly."

The Kid didn't say anything, but he thought, *You don't allow any troublemaking . . . just breakouts.*

He hoped Captain Hughes was right about Jennings being trustworthy. If he wasn't, The Kid's life wasn't going to be worth a plugged nickel.

"Do you understand what I just told you, Mr. Keene?" Jennings asked with a trace of impatience.

"Yeah, sure," The Kid said, keeping his voice and expression surly.

"Very well." Jennings looked over at Culhane. "I

understand you wanted to turn this prisoner over to me personally, Sergeant Culhane."

"That's right," the Ranger said. "My cap'n told me not to take my eyes off him until I was sure he wouldn't be able to get away. Keene's a tricky one. If he hadn't had some bad luck, I ain't sure we ever would've caught him."

Don't lay it on too thick, Asa, The Kid thought.

"Well, you can see for yourself he's not going anywhere, Sergeant," Jennings said. "You can tell your captain we'll take good care of him."

"Yes, sir, I'll do that." Culhane turned to The Kid. "So long, Waco. Don't reckon I'll be seein' you again. But if I do, you can bet I'll be shootin' to kill."

"Maybe," The Kid said. "Unless I see you first, Ranger."

"That's quite enough of that," Jennings snapped. "Lawrence, take the prisoner to his cell."

"Yes, sir," the guard said.

The Kid and Culhane traded hard looks for a second, then the guards closed in around The Kid and marched him out of the warden's office. He was taken out through a side door and escorted to a heavy wooden gate in the wall. Again, there was a fence beyond the wall, and the gate in it wasn't opened until the other one was closed.

A couple guards were waiting inside the fence. They were armed with clubs instead of guns. Lawrence handed his shotgun to one of the men who'd come with him before he went through the gate in the fence with The Kid. That gate was closed and locked behind them. No guns were allowed beyond that point, The Kid guessed.

But guard towers with sharpshooters posted in them loomed above the walls. The Kid could feel the eyes of those marksmen on him as he walked across the yard with the guards. He might as well have had a bull's-eye painted on his back.

He ought to get used to the feeling, he told himself. It was probably going to be there for a while.

Chapter 13

The guards escorted The Kid into one of the big buildings. There was an open area in the middle with three levels of cells on either side. He was surprised to see most of the cells were empty until he realized that because it was the middle of the day, most of the prisoners were out working, either in the fields or in one of the shops located at the prison. Probably the few men who were in their cells were either sick or had been excused from work for some other reason.

A few of them called out jeers at the guards, who ignored them for the most part. One convict hung on the bars of his cell and spewed filthy comments.

In the lead, Lawrence didn't look over, but slammed his club against the bars only a couple inches below where the prisoner gripped them, causing the man to jump back in alarm. If the club had hit his fingers, it probably would have broken them.

Other than that quick strike, Lawrence gave no sign he had even heard the invective.

About two-thirds of the way along the block, on the first level, Lawrence came to a stop in front of an open cell. He motioned with the club for The Kid to go in. "You'll be issued an extra uniform later. One of the trusties will bring it by later, along with a blanket for your bunk. Since it's past the middle of the day, you're excused from work, but only for today."

"What job are you going to have me doing?" The Kid asked.

"New men work the laundry. That's where they can do the least damage if they decide to act up. Once you've shown you're not going to make any trouble, maybe you can move on to something else."

The Kid nodded. He didn't really care what task he was assigned. Hughes had told him it was all right for him to act surly and not eager to cooperate, but to not cause any real trouble. That might delay the gang making their move.

"Who's my cellmate?"

Lawrence smiled. "I'll let the two of you introduce yourselves when he gets back."

The Kid had a feeling the guard's comment might not bode well. If he didn't get along with his cellmate, the time he spent in there would get even more challenging.

He sat down on the bare mattress. There was nothing else to do.

Lawrence slammed the cell door. The crash of

metal against metal had a terrible finality to it, and for a second The Kid was tempted to call the whole thing off. Then he steeled his resolve. He had agreed to help, and he wanted to keep his word.

But if the gang he was after was going to strike again, with him as the target, he hoped they didn't take too long to get around to it.

The same ferret-like trusty showed up a while later with The Kid's extra uniform and blanket.

As he handed the items through the small opening in the cell door designed for such things, he introduced himself. "I'm Ike Calvert, Keene. You need anything around here, you let me know. If I can't put my hands on it, chances are I'll know somebody who can."

"It's like that, is it?" The Kid said.

Calvert snickered. "Well, yeah. Within reason, I mean. Don't go askin' me for no Gatlin' gun or anything like that!" He laughed again.

The Kid smiled. "All right, no Gatling gun." He asked the expected question, the one convicts always asked of each other. "What are you in for, Calvert?"

The trusty's grin disappeared. He looked down at the floor and shuffled his feet uneasily. "I don't like to talk about that. I done some bad things, really bad things. Just as soon forget about 'em."

Calvert looked relatively harmless, but The Kid

knew how looks could be deceptive, especially in a place such as this. "That's fine with me."

"I know why you're here, though." Calvert glanced up again. "I heard you robbed trains all the way from one end of Texas to the other!"

The Kid shrugged. It was possible Calvert had some connection to the gang, but even if he didn't, The Kid wanted to play up the reputation the Rangers had manufactured for him.

One way to do that was to not boast about it. Patently false modesty would reinforce the image he wanted to create. "I held up a few trains in my time, yeah."

"More than a few, I heard. And you blowed up more than one express car, too."

"Well, you have to get the door off the safe somehow, don't you?" The Kid asked with a grin.

Calvert snickered again. "You're gonna do just fine in here, Keene. Better keep your eyes open, though. Not everybody in here is like me. Some of 'em you can't trust."

"I'll remember that." The Kid tossed the extra clothes and the blanket on the bunk. "Thanks for bringing those things."

"Just doin' my job." Calvert lifted a hand in farewell and scuttled away, reminding The Kid more of a rat than a ferret.

The Kid returned to the bunk to sit and wait some more. He thought about the likelihood Calvert was working with the gang on the outside and had to admit it was possible. Even if Calvert had no connection with the outlaws, he struck The Kid as the sort who would gossip and help spread the word about the notorious new convict, Waco Keene. The more of that that went on, the better.

Time dragged by, but eventually the afternoon waned and the guards began bringing the prisoners back in from their day's labors. The Kid stayed where he was on the bunk when a guard paused outside the door of his cell and unlocked it. The guard stepped aside to let a middle-aged convict walk past him into the cell.

The door clanged shut as the prisoner stopped just inside the cell and looked at The Kid.

He was at least fifty, probably older. His gray hair had quite a bit of white in it, as did his mustache. His face was weathered to a permanent tan, which told The Kid that he worked outside quite a bit. The man didn't have the pallor people usually associated with convicts. He reminded The Kid of old cowboys he had seen, men who had punched cows their entire life until they were too stove up to do it anymore.

After a few seconds, the man said, "Nobody told me I was getting a new cellmate today, but I'm glad to meet you anyway, son." He held out his hand. "I'm John Schofield."

The Kid stood up and gripped Schofield's hand. "Waco Keene," he introduced himself.

Schofield's rather bushy gray eyebrows rose. "The train robber I've been hearing all the talk about?"

The Kid put a cocky grin on his face. "Word got around the place that I was coming, eh?"

"You could say that," Schofield replied with a nod.

His voice held a note of education and culture The Kid hadn't expected. He revised his opinion of Schofield. Instead of a cowpuncher, he wondered if the convict had been a businessman or a professor of some sort.

The Kid also wondered if Jennings had assigned him to that cell so he wouldn't be in with someone who might prove to be a threat. The whole plan hatched by the Rangers would fall apart if The Kid was killed or even badly injured by a brutal cellmate.

"I've heard that you're quite a train robber," Schofield went on.

The Kid took the same tack he had earlier. He shrugged. "The railroads and the express companies have plenty of good reasons not to like me."

Schofield chuckled. "I can imagine. I also imagine you're curious about me."

"I don't believe in pryin' into a man's personal business," The Kid said.

"Oh, it's perfectly all right, and understandable as well. We're going to be spending a lot of time together. Of course you'd like to know what sort of man I am. I used to be a Baptist minister."

The Kid was a little surprised by that information. "Is that so?"

"Yes, but I had a crisis of faith. I suppose you could say the Lord and I had a falling-out." Schofield cleared his throat. "It was prompted by a woman, of course, as such things all too often are. The spirit may be willing, but the flesh is weak, so weak."

"I didn't know they put preachers in jail for back-sliding," The Kid said.

"They don't. They do, however, put preachers in jail who burn down their own churches . . . with the congregation still inside."

"Good Lord!" The Kid couldn't stop the startled exclamation that came from him. He caught himself and went on. "Sorry, Reverend, I didn't mean—" He stopped short when he realized he was apologizing for maybe offending a man who'd just admitted to carrying out mass murder.

"It's all right, Waco," Schofield said. "Can I call you Waco? I understand how people feel about what I did. It's shocking, especially when you consider I never committed any other act of violence before or since that day. But I was tormented, you see, absolutely tormented, and I thought I might be able to cleanse my soul with fire. I fully intended to die right along with the others. I locked all the doors, set the fire in a back room, and climbed to the pulpit to confess my sins before the end."

Schofield shook his head sadly as he paused.

"When the congregation smelled the smoke and realized what I had done," he resumed a moment later, "some sidewinder in the choir shot me. I didn't know he was carrying a gun under that robe. The men were able to break out some windows and most of the congregation escaped. Only ten people died. I'm sorry to say they dragged me outside instead of leaving me there to die, as I would have preferred. But I suppose the Lord still has plans for me . . . or at least I would assume He did, if I still believed in Him."

Schofield talked like a preacher, all right, the words just flowing out of him like a river. He wore a serene expression the whole time he was talking about the horrible thing he'd done, and The Kid could come to only one conclusion.

His cellmate was loco. Pure loco.

But that didn't really matter as long as Schofield didn't interfere with the plan. The Kid nodded. "Thank you for tellin' me about that, John. Must have been rough on you, all right."

"I've made my peace with it," Schofield said. "I may not have burned in the church that day, but I know I'll burn in hell when my time comes."

"Wait a minute," The Kid said with a slight frown. "I thought you said you didn't believe in God."

"I don't."

"Then how can you believe in hell? You can't have one without the other, can you?"

"I believe that you can."

"I don't see how." The Kid wasn't sure why he was debating theology with this lunatic, but if he was going to be sharing a cell with Schofield it was probably a good idea to learn as much about him as he could.

"Look around you," Schofield said.

"At this prison?"

"At this world. If this isn't the anteroom of hell, what else can it possibly be? Think of all the sin and suffering that goes on constantly, the human misery and degradation that's all around us. When people tell me to go to hell, Waco, I tell them there's no need. I'm already there."

With that he started to laugh softly, and The Kid felt an unaccustomed chill go through him.

Loco or not, John Schofield was friendly and unassuming. Knowing what he did, The Kid didn't think he would ever actually like the man, but figured they could get along all right. And since Schofield had been locked up at Huntsville for seventeen years, he certainly knew how things worked in the prison.

For instance, as they were walking toward the mess hall that evening, The Kid mentioned Ike Calvert, the trusty who had brought him his blanket and extra uniform, and Schofield frowned. "Never trust that little weasel."

"He told me he can get just about anything a fella might want."

"He probably can, but the price might wind up being more than you'd want to pay. He's an evil man, Waco. I know that after the things I've done, I'm not one to be talking, but Calvert is truly an agent of the Devil."

"I'll keep that in mind." The Kid didn't expect to have any dealings with Calvert, but it was good to know if he did, he should tread carefully.

The tables and benches in the mess hall were bolted to the floor. Guards prowled constantly between them, keeping an eye on the prisoners to make sure nobody tried to swipe a spoon that could be used to make a weapon.

"They keep a close count on utensils, bowls, and anything else that might prove to be dangerous," Schofield explained. "If even a single spoon turns up missing, we're all searched and so are our cells until it's found."

"I'll bet fellas manage to steal one every now and then anyway," The Kid said.

"Of course. Every man harbors the desire to commit murder inside him. Some are unable to control it."

The Kid might have argued with that . . . but he remembered how he had once pulled the trigger of a rifle he was holding to a man's head. Did the fact that the man was one of those responsible for his wife's death make a difference? Was that cold-blooded killing any less murder?

The Kid had long since stopped worrying about it except on the occasional dark night of the soul.

"Who are some of the troublemakers in here?" he asked quietly as he and Schofield ate.

"Well, there was a man named Boozer . . . but he was killed in an escape attempt several months ago. He may have been the worst. But nature abhors a vacuum, you know. Do you understand what I mean?"

"Whenever something happens to one SOB, another SOB comes along to take his place," The Kid said.

"Exactly. There's a man named Cushman who's very bad to cross. He's over there, two tables across and down several seats. The big one with the bald head."

The Kid could tell which convict Schofield meant. Cushman looked like a bruiser, all right. Big, broad-shouldered, slab-muscled. Prematurely bald, because he appeared to be a relatively young man. The Kid didn't like the looks of him, or of the other men who sat around Cushman, who seemed to be the same brutal sort.

"He's bad about starting fights," Schofield went on. "You'll want to stay away from him as much as possible, Waco."

"Thanks," The Kid said with a nod. "I'll remember that."

He knew the other name Schofield had mentioned. Boozer was the prisoner who had tangled with Quint Lupo and sent him to the infirmary. Later, Boozer wound up dead, supposedly killed along with a couple other prisoners during Lupo's breakout.

It was pure speculation on The Kid's part, but if Boozer had been working with the gang all along, they might have decided it was time to get rid of him. The corrupt guards wouldn't want to take a chance on a disgruntled accomplice exposing what they were doing.

If that was true, they might approach somebody else to help them get "Waco Keene" out, and if the pattern held true, that someone might well be Cushman. It was a good thing to know.

Schofield might be loco, but he was being helpful so far.

After supper, the prisoners had an hour in their cells before lights-out. Schofield slid a Bible out from under the mattress on his bunk and spent the time reading. After what the former minister had done and the disbelief he'd expressed, The Kid thought he probably wouldn't have wanted to read the Good Book, but obviously that wasn't the case.

Maybe Schofield was looking for some loophole, The Kid mused, some way of believing again and escaping damnation. The Kid didn't think he'd find it.

When the lights went out and stifling darkness closed in, awareness of all that stone and metal between him and the outside world sunk in and made The Kid's nerves stretch taut. Somewhere along the cell block, a man laughed, and it had the sound of insanity to it.

The Kid thought Schofield was actually sort of right about one thing. The whole world might not be hell, but being locked up in prison sure was.

Chapter 14

The worst part, at least starting out, was the sheer monotony of existence inside the prison walls. The same things happened at the same times every day, from breakfast to supper to lights-out.

The Kid's job in the laundry was to stir the big vats of hot water where uniforms and bedding were washed. The work was mind-numbing and miserable. The heat and humidity made it hard to breathe and ensured that he spent his days covered in sweat. The stink of the harsh lye soap stung his nostrils.

A week passed with nothing unusual happening. He made the acquaintance of a few men he worked with, but no one approached him about an escape attempt.

That wasn't really a surprise, since Hughes and Culhane were of the opinion the gang didn't tell their targets beforehand what was going on. It was more likely Lupo hadn't had any idea he was about to "escape" until the breakout was already in progress. Secrecy was the only way to make sure no one went to the prison authorities and spilled the truth.

All The Kid could do was tend to the job he'd been given and wait. He didn't like it—he was used to action—but he had no choice.

A week later, things changed abruptly. He was assigned to work in the fields.

Each morning prisoners were loaded into enclosed wagons after their ankles were shackled together. The wagons took them to the fields, where they clambered out awkwardly and were given canvas sacks. Their job was to pick cotton, something The Kid had never done in his life.

He quickly discovered it was miserable, back-breaking work, spending long hours bent over in the sun, fingers growing raw from handling the plants.

Schofield was part of the same detail, and The Kid finally understood why the man was so tanned and weathered. He had been doing this for nearly his entire sentence, Schofield explained to him as they labored side by side.

In East Texas, not that far inland from the Gulf Coast, the growing season was long, and a lot of fields were planted in cotton. The prison even had its own gin to process the crop.

A dozen mounted guards armed with shotguns and rifles watched each group of fifty prisoners. Schofield told The Kid a number of convicts had been shot while trying to get away. Everybody knew the futility of it, but sometimes the temptation to make a stumbling run for freedom was just too much to resist.

As hard as the work was, The Kid preferred being outside to being stuck in the prison laundry. He wondered if Warden Jennings was responsible for getting him transferred to the work detail, or if it was something that would have happened on the same schedule anyway.

It didn't really matter, of course. He was there, and there he would probably stay until the gang made its move.

If the gang made its move.

If the gang really existed.

Doubts about that assailed The Kid from time to time. If Culhane and Hughes were wrong, all he was going through was for nothing.

One morning he was surprised to see Hank Cushman being loaded into one of the wagons bound for the cotton fields. Cushman hadn't been one of the pickers, and with his big, brawny frame he wasn't built for the job. But the convicts went where they were told to go and did what they were told to do, so The Kid supposed somebody in authority had decided Cushman needed to be picking cotton for a while.

That thought started suspicion percolating in The Kid's brain.

Without being obvious about it, he kept an eye on Cushman for the next few days. The big man rode in a different wagon and didn't approach him while they were in the fields. The Kid was starting to wonder if he ought to make an attempt to talk to Cushman.

Every day a trusty drove out to the fields in an open wagon with a couple water barrels loaded in the back. Several times during the day the guards allowed the convicts to gather around those barrels and get a drink, passing around a wooden dipper among them. After laboring in the hot sun, the men were always parched with thirst, so there was usually considerable crowding going on.

The men moved back quickly, though, when Cushman came up and reached for the dipper. The man who had just filled it with water handed it to Cushman without complaint.

Cushman drank, the muscles in his corded throat working as he swallowed. Then he callously tossed the dipper on the ground as he turned away. Behind him, one of the convicts picked it up and wiped away the dirt sticking to its wet surface.

Cushman saw The Kid looking at him, grinned, and walked over to him. "What's the matter with you? You don't like what I just did?"

"I don't give a damn," The Kid replied with a shrug. "I already got my drink."

"You're that train robber, aren't you? Keene?"

"That's right."

"I'm Hank Cushman."

The Kid nodded. "I know."

"Then you know you'd be smart to steer clear of me."

"I don't go looking for trouble, Cushman. But I don't step around it when it's in my way, either."

"You don't?"

"No. I go over it."

Cushman took that just the way The Kid meant it, as a challenge. His huge hands knotted into fists. For a second The Kid thought Cushman was going to take a swing at him.

The guards thought so, too. One of them suddenly moved his horse closer and called, "Hey there, you two. Back off from each other. Now!"

Cushman looked like he wanted to defy the order, but the guard had a Winchester pointed in his general direction. After a couple heartbeats he grinned at The Kid again. "Another time."

"Sure," The Kid answered easily.

"I said move," the guard snapped.

"Don't get a burr under your saddle, Hagen," Cushman told the man. "I'm goin'."

"I won't put up with anything from you," the guard growled. "You remember that."

So that was Bert Hagen, The Kid thought. Until that moment he hadn't known which of the guards was the one involved in Lupo's escape . . . if you could call it that.

Hagen was a big man—not as big as Cushman, but nobody else around there was—with a long, mean, horse-like face and a few wisps of pale hair sticking out from under the broad-brimmed hat the guards wore when they were out in the fields.

The Kid felt an instinctive dislike for Hagen, but to be honest, he felt that way about most of the men inside the prison walls, guards and convicts alike.

Still, he was glad to know which one was Hagen. He could keep a closer eye on the man.

Several more days passed. Cushman continued to work in the cotton fields, but kept his distance from The Kid.

Schofield was usually somewhere close by. Knowing what the man had done to land himself in prison, The Kid couldn't bring himself to actually like Schofield, but he felt sorry for him in a way. The guilt Schofield must feel over his actions would be enough to drive a man crazy, if he wasn't already.

Ike Calvert wasn't the usual trusty who brought the water wagon out to the fields. The Kid's eyes narrowed with suspicion when he saw the weaselly little trusty hauling back on the wagon's reins. Calvert being assigned to the job might be entirely innocent . . . or it could be the opening move in the game The Kid had been sent to crash.

When the guards called for a water break, the convicts left their sacks stuffed with cotton bolls on the ground and headed for the wagons. Even though the leg irons limited their movement, they moved along pretty quickly. A great thirst gripped them.

The Kid had been picking fairly close to where the wagon had stopped and was almost there when somebody rammed hard against his left shoulder from behind. His feet tangled in the chains and he went down, sprawling on the dirt between rows of cotton plants.

He rolled over and looked up in time to see Hank Cushman dropping toward him, obviously intending to pin him to the ground with his knees and bring those giant fists crashing down into his face.

Chapter 15

The Kid rolled hard to the side, barely avoiding Cushman's attack. Still vulnerable, he rolled back the other way. He didn't want those clubbed fists smashing into the back of his head.

Bringing his hands up, he grabbed Cushman. The big man was a little off balance, having landed on his knees in the dirt, and The Kid was able to heave him to the ground.

The other convicts began to shout excitedly. Nothing like a nice bloody fight to break up the boredom of the day's work.

Cushman was an experienced brawler and recovered almost instantly. He swung his legs toward The Kid, lifting them high so the chain hanging between them dropped neatly over The Kid's head.

Just before the chain snapped tight against The Kid's neck, he managed to get his hands up and block the metal links. He hung on to them desperately, knowing it would take Cushman only a second to crush his throat if the big convict got the leverage he needed.

The Kid threw himself backward so he landed on top of Cushman. His hands were all that was protecting his throat, so he twisted and jabbed a knee at Cushman's groin.

Cushman writhed out of the way of the blow, forcing him to let up on the pressure on the chain. Muscles in The Kid's arms and shoulders bunched as he shoved it up and away from him. He ducked his head, free of the deadly chain, and rolled again to put some distance between him and his attacker.

But is wasn't far enough, Cushman leaped after him, and they crashed together, landing in a row of cotton plants and crushing them. Cushman hammered punches at The Kid's head and body.

The Kid blocked most of the blows, but some got through and landed with stunning force. Cushman's mallet-like fist clipped the side of his head, and the impact made the whole world spin in the wrong direction for a second.

The Kid knew he had to do something or Cushman might beat him to death.

It couldn't be part of the gang's plan, he thought wildly. Cushman wasn't trying to just put him in the infirmary. He was trying to kill him.

The Kid hooked a left and a right into Cushman's midsection. It was like hitting a wall. He sent a jab against Cushman's jaw but might as well have punched a rock. The big man didn't seem to have any vulnerabilities.

One of Cushman's fists dug into The Kid's belly and took his breath away. Gasping for air, The Kid cupped his hands and slapped them as hard as he could against Cushman's ears.

That tactic finally brought a howl of pain from the man and made him heave upright. He pawed at his ears as he moved back a couple feet.

The Kid snapped out a kick and drove the heel of his boot against Cushman's left knee. The convict staggered as his left leg folded up underneath him.

The Kid came up off the ground and sent an uppercut whistling into Cushman's jaw. Finally, a punch had an effect. Cushman's head snapped back and he stumbled away another step. The Kid lowered his head and shoulders and drove forward, plowing into the man.

Cushman went over backward and toppled to the ground like a giant redwood. Instantly, The Kid landed on top of him and drove a knee toward his opponent's groin. Cushman wasn't able to get out of the way in time, and screamed as the savage blow landed.

The Kid pushed himself to his feet. Cushman, curled up around the agony gripping him, was still huge, but all the fight had gone out of him.

During the battle, The Kid hadn't paid any attention to what was going on around him. If he had allowed himself to be distracted, Cushman would have beaten his brains out.

When he glanced around as he stood with his

chest heaving for breath, he saw the other convicts herded together about twenty yards away, well covered with rifles and shotguns. Hagen and another guard were standing near the scene of the fight.

"Why didn't you . . . put a stop to this ruckus?" The Kid asked.

"What, and ruin the show?" Hagen asked with an ugly grin. "When two of you idiots start whalin' away on each other, we generally let it run its course unless it looks like somebody's fixin' to get killed. You and Cushman didn't look to be in any danger of that." Hagen laughed. "Although I'll bet Cushman's hurtin' so bad right now he wishes he was dead!"

The Kid turned away and walked over to the water wagon. None of the guards told him to stop. He leaned on the lowered tailgate and tried to catch his breath.

"You all right, Keene?" Ike Calvert asked from the seat. The little trusty looked worried.

"Yeah, I'll be . . . fine. Just . . . bruised and sore in the morning."

"You're lucky. Cushman's an animal."

"Yeah, I . . . got that idea."

One of the guards said, "A couple of you men grab Cushman and drag him into the shade of the wagon. I don't know if he'll be able to work any more today."

"If he can't, you'll have to take up the slack for him, Keene," Hagen told The Kid.

"He started the fight," The Kid pointed out. He was breathing better, but starting to hurt from the pounding he'd taken.

"I don't give a damn about that," Hagen snapped. "All I know is that at the end of the day there'd better be as many full sacks of cotton as I'm expectin'. Understand?"

"Yeah, yeah," The Kid muttered. He reached for the wooden dipper, filled it, and dumped the water over his head before refilling it and drinking.

Two of the convicts dragged Cushman under the wagon as they'd been ordered. His screams had turned into groans of abject misery.

The other men were allowed to crowd around the wagon for their turn at the water barrels. The Kid handed over the dipper and moved out of the way.

Schofield came up to him and said quietly, "You made yourself a bad enemy today, Waco."

The Kid shrugged. "Cushman's the one who came after me. I reckon he already had his mind made up the two of us were enemies."

"Maybe so, but he'll feel like he has to kill you now. The only way anybody in here will ever respect him again is if you're dead."

"People have wanted me dead before." The Kid shrugged.

"I'm sure they have. But trouble can come at you from any direction in prison, without much warning. I'll try to help you keep an eye out for it."

The Kid nodded. "I'm obliged to you for that, John."

With the excitement over, the convicts got back to work. The guards allowed Cushman to stay under the water wagon the rest of the day.

When they were loading up to head back to the prison late that afternoon, Hagen ordered him placed in the back of the wagon with the barrels. "Take him to the infirmary. I'll send a man along with you to keep an eye on him."

"Sure, boss," Calvert agreed.

The Kid didn't think that *boss* meant anything. Some of the prisoners addressed all the guards that way.

Bruises stood out on The Kid's face, and he knew his body was black and blue from Cushman's pounding fists. The fight had convinced him Cushman wasn't working with the gang. Cushman had been trying too hard to kill him.

But having the big man as an enemy was liable to complicate things. The Kid hoped it wouldn't scare the gang off and decide they didn't want to break him out of the penitentiary after all.

During the hour the lights were still lit after supper, The Kid was surprised when footsteps came along the cell block, drawing curses and catcalls from the prisoners they passed. Several men stopped in front of the cell he shared with Schofield. He was even more surprised when he recognized one of them as Warden Preston Jennings.

"Step up here, Mr. Keene," Jennings ordered. He was flanked by four guards.

"What is it?" The Kid asked as he stood up from his bunk and approached the bars. He kept his tone deliberately surly, the way Waco Keene would talk to the warden.

"It's been reported to me that you were involved in a fight in the cotton fields today," Jennings said.

"Cushman jumped me."

Lawrence, one of the guards with Jennings, snapped, "Keep a civil tongue in your head when you're talking to the warden, Keene."

Jennings lifted a hand to signal it was all right, then went on. "I've spoken to all the guards who were there, and they agree Cushman provoked the fight and you were only defending yourself. For that reason, I'm going to recommend no additional charges be filed against you."

The Kid frowned. "Charges?" he repeated. "Charges for what?"

"Murder," Jennings said. "Hank Cushman died a short time ago."

That came as a shock to The Kid. He had landed a few decent punches, and had planted his knee in Cushman's groin with quite a bit of power, but none of that should have proven fatal.

"What the hell!" he exclaimed. "I didn't do anything that would have killed him."

Lawrence stepped toward the bars. "I'm warning you, Keene."

Again Jennings gestured for Lawrence to move back. "Dr. Kendrick informed me that Cushman died from internal bleeding. If he hadn't been left lying out there in the field for the rest of the day after he was injured, it might not have happened. So all the blame doesn't lie on you, Keene, and as I said, it's been established that you fought back in self-defense. However, the final decision isn't up to me. I'll recommend to the local prosecutor that you not be brought to trial, but that's all I can do."

The Kid took a deep breath. "All right. Thanks, Warden. I really didn't mean to kill him."

Jennings gave him a curt nod. "You'll carry on with your usual activities until I receive a final determination in this matter."

With that, he turned and walked back up the cell block with Lawrence and the other guards accompanying him. The Kid shook his head slowly and went over to sit down again on his bunk.

"I heard all that," Schofield said from the other bunk. "Looks like you won't have to be watching over your shoulder for Cushman after all."

"I guess not." The wheels of The Kid's brain turned over rapidly. He had speculated from the first that Dr. Simon Kendrick might be involved with the gang, and what had happened to Cushman made him even more suspicious. He supposed it was possible Cushman had died just the way Kendrick had said, but The Kid had his doubts. If he was being targeted by the gang, they wouldn't want him killed by a vengeful Cushman before a breakout could be arranged.

It would be much easier to get rid of Cushman . . . while they had the chance. Kendrick could have killed him somehow, and since the doctor was the person responsible for determining the cause of death . . .

The theory fit together, The Kid thought as he stretched out on his bunk and rolled to face the wall. And if it was right, it was more proof—as if anybody needed it—just how ruthless the gang was.

Tired and sore though he was, The Kid had a little trouble falling asleep that night.

Chapter 16

The Kid's muscles were stiff the next morning. He bit back a groan as he climbed out of his bunk.

But he was better off than Hank Cushman. At least he was still alive.

The Kid was aware that more prisoners than usual were looking at him as he and Schofield filed into the mess hall with the rest of the men from their cell block. He tried to ignore the added scrutiny, but Schofield said quietly, "Looks like you're famous today, Waco."

"I reckon," The Kid agreed. Infamous was more like it, he thought.

He was the man who killed Hank Cushman.

Hunger got the better of curiosity as the men settled down to eat, but every now and then The Kid caught somebody staring at him. He heard whispers behind his back, too, and wondered if any of Cushman's cronies were going to try to settle the score for their friend.

Crawling into the wagon taking him to the cotton fields, The Kid noticed Cushman's friends were no longer part of that job. He was grateful. He didn't need the extra worry. The day passed in the usual manner.

Within a week the Kid's bruises faded and the aches went away. He had gotten used to picking cotton, although he knew it was something he would never enjoy, no matter how long he did it.

He was also getting restless. He didn't like being locked up. He had volunteered for the task and was ready for it to be over. . . . even though it would likely mean more danger.

Ike Calvert hadn't driven the water wagon since the day of the fight with Cushman, but he showed up again, bringing the vehicle with its pair of water barrels to a halt on the dirt lane running through the fields.

Calvert climbed down from the seat and stood to the side, rolling a cigarette while the convicts gathered around the wagon to get their drinks.

The Kid wasn't really surprised when Calvert sauntered over to him.

The trusty spoke in a voice so quiet it couldn't be heard more than a few feet away. "There's a rumor goin' around that Cushman's partners are gonna jump you durin' chow tonight. They've got knives, and they plan to cut you to pieces for what you done to Hank."

"That was an accident," The Kid said. "And Cushman started the fight, anyway."

"That don't matter none to them. They're gonna kill you, Keene . . . unless you get out of here today."

Sensing this might be what he'd been waiting for, The Kid was careful not to let anticipation show and he let out a disdainful snort. "Yeah? How in the hell am I gonna do that?" He nodded toward the guards, who were watching the prisoners closely, as usual.

"You might be surprised," Calvert said. "There are people on the outside who are interested in you, Keene. All you got to do is play along, and you'll be looked out for."

It was a little different from the approach they had taken with Quint Lupo, The Kid thought, no longer doubting such a gang really existed and Calvert was connected to it. Bert Hagen was one of the guards assigned to the cotton fields, too. The Kid had noticed. He figured that wasn't an accident.

Still sounding dubious, he said, "What in blazes are you talkin' about, Calvert?"

"There's a gun in the bottom of the water barrel closest to the tailgate."

The Kid's eyes widened slightly. He didn't have to do much acting to look surprised by what Calvert told him. "Are you tryin' to get me killed?"

"I'm tryin' to save your life, you damn fool!" Calvert dropped the stub of his quirly and ground it out savagely under his foot.

"Listen to me," he went on in an urgent half whisper. "Somethin's gonna happen in a few minutes. When it does, jump in the wagon, grab that gun, and shoot one of the guards off his horse. Then you'll be able to jump in the saddle and light a shuck out of here before anybody knows what's goin' on."

"That'll be a neat trick with my ankles shackled together," The Kid looked down at his feet and his lips drew back from his teeth in a grimace.

"Here." Without appearing to do anything, Calvert's hand moved slightly at his side.

The Kid felt something metal pressed into his palm. "Is that a key to the irons?"

"Yeah. Don't ask me how I got it."

For the first time, The Kid allowed himself to sound interested. "I wasn't planning to. Is this for real?"

"Damn right it is. I got contacts on the outside, men who can use an hombre like you. They'll be around when you make your break. Join up with them and they'll see to it you get out of here, free and clear."

"Yeah, free and clear with every lawman in the state on my trail."

"If you'd rather sit in a cell with that loco sky pilot for the next twenty years, wonderin' when he's gonna snap and murder you in your sleep, that's up to you, kid."

For a second The Kid stiffened, thinking Calvert had somehow figured out who he really was.

Then he realized Calvert had called him "kid"

because he was so much younger than the trusty. That was all.

"The gun's fully loaded?"

"Six in the wheel," Calvert confirmed.

"Sounds good. What's this distraction you were talkin' about?"

"You'll know it when it happens. Just be ready to move. The ball won't take long to get started as soon as I give the high sign. Are you in?"

The Kid hesitated, but only long enough to make the reaction look real. Then he nodded. "I'm in."

"Good. There's just a couple more things . . . When you jump up in the wagon, give me a clout on the head. Don't bust my skull open or nothin' like that, but make it look real. I don't want any of the guards thinkin' I had any part in this."

"What's the other thing?" The Kid asked.

"Don't shoot Hagen."

The Kid gave Calvert a shrewd look. "It's like that, is it?"

"Don't ask questions. Just do what I told you."

"Sure, sure," The Kid said. "Now I've got just one more thing."

"What's that?"

"This better not be some kind of double cross. If you're setting me up, Calvert, I'll make sure you're dead before I go down."

Calvert chuckled. "Don't worry about that. You'll see, Keene. Just be ready."

The Kid nodded and moved away from Calvert, but didn't stray far from the water wagon.

He watched Calvert climb back onto the wagon seat and lift his right arm to scratch vigorously underneath it. That was probably the signal. Somebody had to be watching them through field glasses or a telescope.

A few more minutes went by, and The Kid started thinking the guards would order the prisoners back to work. If the gang was going to make a move, it needed to be soon.

So why hasn't anything happened yet?

Even as that thought went through his mind, an explosion suddenly roared in the distance, strong enough to shake the ground.

The Kid's head snapped around. A column of smoke and dust rose into the air about two hundred yards away. He knew a fence of some sort surrounded the fields, although he hadn't been close enough to get a good look at it. From the sound of the blast, somebody had just made themselves a gate where there wasn't one.

"Everybody down!" one of the guards bellowed as he swung his rifle toward the startled prisoners. "Get down on the ground, damn it!"

Most of the convicts dropped to the dirt between the rows of cotton plants, wanting to be well out of the line of fire if any shooting started. A few began trying to shuffle away, futile though it might be.

The Kid threw himself to the ground, but didn't just lie there. He reached down to his ankles, thrust the key Calvert had given him into the lock on one of the leg irons, and twisted it.

If the key didn't work, he might not live through it, he thought.

But the key turned and the shackle sprang open. Moving swiftly, The Kid unlocked the other one and kicked free. He rolled over, and surged to his feet.

A guard yelled, "Hey! Keene, stop!"

The Kid ignored the warning. A quick leap carried him to the back of the water wagon.

He plunged his right hand into the barrel, reaching for the bottom. His fingers touched the hard round metal of a revolver's cylinder. Sliding his hand along it, he found the gun butt and grabbed it.

A rifle cracked. The bullet punched through the water barrel, missing The Kid's arm by a few inches as he pulled out the gun. Water began to spout out through the pair of holes the bullet left behind.

The Kid straightened and twisted. He didn't want to kill the guard racing toward him on horseback, who was just doing his job. He aimed for the man's arm, thinking it was better to risk crippling him than killing him.

He didn't have to do either. As the guard galloped past John Schofield, the former minister leaped up and grabbed him, jerking him out of the saddle. The guard let out a startled yell and tumbled to the ground.

Hoofbeats pounded. From the corner of his eye The Kid saw half a dozen riders galloping across the field from the site of the explosion. The gang was coming to break him out, he realized. Flame lanced from the guns in their hands as they traded shots with the guards.

Innocent men were going to die, The Kid thought bitterly. But their blood would be on the hands of Hughes and Culhane. The Rangers were the ones who had come up with the plan. They probably hadn't expected the gang to strike so brazenly.

The Kid lunged toward the front of the wagon. Calvert was cowering on the seat. As the trusty had told him to do, The Kid swung a punch with his left fist, smashing it against the side of Calvert's head hard enough to make the man slump to the floorboard.

Schofield stumbled up to the back of the wagon and called, "Take me with you, Waco! Take me with you!" His willingness to stay in prison the rest of his life had evaporated as soon as he saw a chance to get away. He clambered onto the tailgate and struggled to his feet, thinking The Kid was going to steal the wagon.

Just as Schofield rose, one of the guards lined his rifle sights on The Kid and pulled the trigger. The slug caught Schofield in the back instead, ripping all the way through him to whine past The Kid's head.

Schofield's eyes widened in shock and pain. He slumped forward but caught himself on one of the water barrels. "Waco . . ." he gasped. Blood bubbled from the exit wound in his chest.

"Sorry, John." There was nothing The Kid could do.

The light went out of Schofield's eyes and he pitched lifelessly to the side.

The Kid threw himself from the wagon and landed in the saddle of the horse belonging to the guard Schofield had pulled from the saddle.

Most of the convicts were on their feet again, running and hopping around as best they could with the leg irons on. The guards had been forced to retreat from the gang's attack, though they outnumbered the outlaws, and the prisoners saw it as a possible chance to get away.

The gang probably counted on that confusion to help delay any pursuit, The Kid thought. He jerked his mount around and thundered toward the charging gunmen. He saw that they were all masked.

Just like the bank robbers who had been with Quint Lupo, he thought. There was a good chance at least some of them were the same men, maybe all of them.

One of the guards spurred out, evidently attempting to cut him off.

The Kid was surprised to recognize the guard as Bert Hagen.

He had suspected all along that Hagen was part of the gang, and what Calvert had told him about not shooting Hagen pretty much confirmed that.

Then The Kid realized the outlaws were aiming high, making it look good so none of the other guards would suspect Hagen was in on the escape attempt.

The Kid played his part in that, throwing a couple slugs in Hagen's general direction but aiming well wide of him.

Hagen could always be arrested later, The Kid told himself, after the gang had been broken up.

Several prisoners lurched toward him, waving their arms and begging him to help them escape just like Schofield had done. The Kid weaved among them, jerking the horse from side to side to avoid trampling them.

Suddenly two of the masked men closed in on either side of him. One of them shouted, "Keene?"

"Yeah!" The Kid replied.

"Stick with us!"

That was exactly what The Kid intended to do.

Hughes had said the Rangers would have a man somewhere close by the prison all the time, to follow the gang when they broke The Kid out. The Kid hoped that whoever had the assignment hadn't fallen down on the job.

The explosion should have alerted anybody that something was going on. It would have been heard inside the prison, that was for sure. A large force of guards was probably on the way to find out what had happened and round up any prisoners who were trying to get away.

The other masked men fell in behind The Kid and his two escorts. They twisted in their saddles and fired behind them to keep the guards back. The fence appeared in front of them, with the gaping hole blasted by dynamite. The Kid and the masked men raced through the opening.

He was free, The Kid thought as his heart slugged hard inside his chest.

Free of the penitentiary, anyway.

In a very real sense, he was still a prisoner. He had just traded one set of dangers for another.

Chapter 17

The men didn't slow down until several miles were between themselves and the prison. They seemed to know the roads very well and didn't hesitate as their mounts lunged forward.

The Kid had a good sense of direction, but once their route plunged into the thick East Texas forests covering the landscape, he wasn't sure which way they were going. Tall pines and tangled underbrush crowded in on either side of the trail, blocking off most of the sky.

The growth stifled even the slightest breath of air, too. The Kid found himself sweating through his prison uniform, and it wasn't just from nerves.

Finally a big, bulky man crowded into the lead and raised his hand to signal a halt. As the other riders reined in, the leader turned his horse toward The Kid and reached up to pull the bandanna mask from his face.

He had craggy features dominated by a powerful

jaw and a ragged gray mustache. Despite his brutal appearance, intelligence gleamed in his eyes as he studied The Kid. "You'd be Waco Keene."

The Kid kept a tight rein on his nerves. "I'd better be, hadn't I? If you went to all that trouble and broke the wrong man out of prison, you'd probably shoot me right here and now."

"I just might, at that." The man rested a hand on the butt of his gun. "So answer the question, pronto."

"I'm Waco Keene. Satisfied?"

"Yeah, I reckon. I wanted to hear it for myself, but you wouldn't have that gun if Calvert hadn't told you where it was. I don't think that little rat would've made that bad a mistake."

That's where you're wrong, The Kid thought, musing that nobody seemed to like or respect Ike Calvert, even the men who worked with him.

"What did Calvert tell you before all hell broke loose?" the man went on.

"There wasn't time for him to tell me much. He told me the gun was in the water barrel and somebody was coming to help me get out of prison. He said he knew people who had a use for me."

"And you went along with it, just like that?"

The Kid snorted. "Who the hell wouldn't? The only thing I cared about was that it was a chance to get out of there. I don't like bein' locked up."

"Not many folks do."

The Kid looked around at the trees. "Speaking of gettin' out of there, don't you reckon we ought to get moving again? There's bound to be a whole passel of guards on our trail."

"You'd be surprised. We know these woods pretty well and can give just about anybody the slip in them. But we'll be on our way again as soon as the horses have rested a little more. It won't do us any good to ride them into the ground, now will it?"

The man had a point there.

While they were stopped, The Kid said, "You fellas know who I am, but I don't know a blasted thing about any of you, not even your names."

"That's the way it's got to be for now," the leader said. "You'll find out everything you need to know later on, when we get to where we're goin'."

The words had a rehearsed quality to them, The Kid thought, as if the man had said the same thing on a number of occasions in the past.

At least three times, if the Rangers were right, and it was sure starting to look like they were. It was possible the gang had pulled off this trick on other occasions the Rangers weren't even aware of.

The other men had lowered their bandannas. Without being too obvious about it, The Kid took a good look at them. They were all hard-faced gunmen, the sort of outlaws he had clashed with frequently in the past.

After avenging his wife's death—for all the good that had done—The Kid had wanted only to be left alone to drift with his sorrow.

But despite that resolve, he had been drawn into trouble again and again, sometimes at random and sometimes because of enemies from his past seeking vengeance. It had happened often enough he had become resigned to the fact that he naturally attracted violence.

He knew from talking to his father the same problem plagued most men who were fast with a gun. It was as if the universe compensated for the deadly abilities it had given such men by forcing them to continually test those skills.

There was no point in worrying about it, The Kid had decided. He accepted the idea that he would be forced into dangerous situations on a fairly regular basis, situations in which he would have to kill or be killed.

After a few more minutes the leader waved the group of riders into motion again. Eventually they left the trail they had been following and started along a narrower one.

The men were forced to ride single file, three men in front of The Kid, three men behind. The gloom was so thick inside the forest it was almost like night, deep and dark and forboding. The thickets on either side of the trail were impenetrable. He couldn't have gone anywhere, even if he wanted to.

The trip through the forest seemed endless. The Kid asked, "Are you sure you boys aren't lost?"

"Keep your shirt on," the leader called back. "We know where we're going."

"It's going to be dark soon."

"Doesn't matter. We'll get there."

The Kid understood how the gang had been able

to throw off pursuit in the past. They had twisted and turned so much in that wilderness, splashing across little streams every so often, not even blood-hounds were able to follow them.

That meant whoever the Rangers had watching the prison probably hadn't been able to pick up their trail, either.

And *that* meant he was really on his own now. He wasn't going to be able to get in touch with the contact man. It was one of the many things that could have gone wrong with the Rangers' plan. The Kid had to stay alive until he could figure out his next move.

Darkness settled down, and as The Kid expected, it was nearly complete inside the forest. If his horse hadn't been able to plod along behind the animal ahead of it, The Kid would have had no idea which way to go.

The men rode for at least an hour after night had fallen before they suddenly broke out of the trees and emerged into a clearing.

After the stygian blackness of the forest, the sil-very glow of the moon and stars seemed almost as bright as daylight. Blinking, The Kid looked around and saw they were on a wide, hard-packed road. The leader turned his horse to the right and the others surrounded The Kid and followed.

They were taking no chances on him deciding to cut and run now that he was free of the prison. It was like they considered him an investment and didn't want to lose him.

That was just about right, he thought. They planned to make money on him, especially in the long run.

A tree-lined lane appeared ahead of them, on the left—the first sign of human habitation The Kid had seen in a while—and he wasn't surprised when the leader turned his horse into the lane and rode toward a large house at the end of it.

As they came closer The Kid could tell it was an old plantation manor in poor repair. With a ghostly flutter of wings, pigeons flew out from under the portico, apparently spooked by the approach of the horses.

The leader reined in and motioned for the others to do likewise. As The Kid brought his mount to a halt, several of the men swung down from their saddles and surrounded him, guns drawn.

"There's no need to worry," The Kid told them. "I told you, I'm grateful to you boys. I'm not going to cause any trouble for you."

"There are certain ways we do things, and it won't do you any good to argue about them," the leader said. "Get down from that horse, Keene. Hand over your gun."

"I don't much like bein' unarmed."

The leader hefted his own revolver and snapped, "You don't have any choice in the matter. Shuck the iron or this ends right here and now."

"Take it easy, take it easy," The Kid muttered. "I said I didn't like it, didn't say I wouldn't do it."

Moving carefully so none of the men would be

tempted to get trigger-happy, he took the gun from his waistband and passed it over to the nearest of the outlaws. Then he dismounted as the men moved back to give him room.

"All right," the leader said, lowering his gun but not pouching the iron. "Come with me."

The Kid followed the man into the house, which was dimly lit by oil lamps. The place's disrepair was more apparent inside with its frayed rugs and stained wallpaper.

The leader took him along a hallway, and as they approached a pair of double doors at the end of the corridor, they passed an alcove.

The Kid glanced in there, but the alcove was too shadowy for him to see anything except a painting that hung on the wall. It seemed to be a family portrait, with a man standing behind a chair where a woman sat with a child on her lap.

The Kid couldn't make out any more details before he was past the alcove and moving through the door the big man held open for him.

The smell of mold was strong in the air, and as The Kid entered the room, he saw why. The roof of the library had leaked and the books had gotten wet.

The Kid figured most of those leather-bound volumes were ruined, sitting there on the shelves rotting. He didn't have the same love of reading his father did—Frank Morgan always had a book or two tucked away in his saddlebags—but he still thought what had happened to these books was a shame.

He didn't have long to think about that. His gaze turned instantly toward the desk dominating the room. The man sitting behind it rose to his feet to greet the newcomers.

He was tall, slender almost to the point of gauntness, and well dressed in a brown tweed suit. The pale skin of his face seemed a pallid contrast to the shock of dark hair that topped it. Deep-set eyes peered across the desk at The Kid as the man smiled. "Waco Keene! Welcome to my home. My name is Alexander Grey."

Chapter 18

A while back, The Kid had spent some time in West Texas, in a place called Rattlesnake Valley. While there he'd seen more of those venomous reptiles than he had ever wanted to.

He got the same feeling looking at Alexander Grey that he had when he'd confronted those rattlers. Even though the man was smiling and congenial, lurking under the surface was a cold, inhuman menace. When Grey held out a long-fingered hand, The Kid was reminded of a rattlesnake's wedge-shaped head poised to strike.

He stepped forward and shook Grey's hand anyway, keeping his instinctive revulsion well concealed. "You must be the boss of this outfit," he said with plenty of false enthusiasm in his voice.

"That's right," Grey replied as he released The Kid's hand. He motioned toward a leather chair in front of the desk. "Have a seat. Brattle, bring us some drinks."

"Sure thing, boss." The man who had brought The Kid to the room turned to the bar on one side of the room.

As The Kid settled in the chair, he felt like he had wandered into a stage play. The other men were familiar with their roles and had performed them numerous times before. He was the newcomer, the understudy forced by circumstances into a role of his own.

"You weren't injured when my men liberated you from your imprisonment, I hope?" Grey said.

The Kid shook his head. "I'm fine. Just mighty glad to be out of there."

"Of course you are. No man likes to be locked up."

John Schofield hadn't seemed to mind, The Kid thought . . . but then as soon as the chance to get away cropped up, Schofield had tried to seize it.

Bad luck had seen to it he took another way out of prison.

"In case you're wondering what this is all about," Grey went on, "our organization specializes in helping men with unique talents such as yourself, men who can put those talents to much better use outside prison. You have quite a reputation, Mr. Keene, and it would truly be a shame not to let you do the thing you do best."

"What are you thinkin' that is?" The Kid asked.

"Why, robbing trains, of course," Grey answered with another smile.

The big outlaw called Brattle came over with a

couple brandy snifters, setting them on the desk in front of The Kid.

"Help yourself." Grey gave another languid wave of his hand.

Letting him pick which drink he wanted was a show of trustworthiness, The Kid supposed. He reached for one of the snifters, and Grey took the other.

"To our new partnership," Grey toasted as he raised the glass.

"Let's not get ahead of ourselves. I'm grateful for your help, no doubt about that, but I don't know that I'm looking for a new partner."

Grey sipped his brandy.

The Kid couldn't see any reason they would break him out of prison only to turn around and poison him, so odds were the drink was safe. He took a sip and found it to be quite good, better than he expected to get in the run-down plantation house.

He probably shouldn't make any comment about the quality of the liquor, he reminded himself. It was unlikely the real Waco Keene had known much about brandy. He settled for saying, "That's nice smooth drinkin'."

"Thank you," Grey said. "As for our business arrangement, I'm afraid you don't have much choice where that's concerned, Mr. Keene. You see, I've invested a considerable amount of money in setting up your escape, and I intend to be paid back for that investment."

The Kid bristled. "I didn't ask you or anybody else to bust me out of prison."

"True enough, but now that we have, you owe us, to put it bluntly."

The Kid sat there with a frown on his face and didn't say anything for a moment. Finally, he shrugged and admitted, "I suppose you could look at it that way."

"Indeed I do." Grey took another sip of brandy and smiled. "But there's no need for us to argue. What I have in mind is an arrangement that will prove quite beneficial and lucrative to us both."

"Go on," The Kid said as he leaned back in his chair.

"I have Brattle and a number of other men working for me, but I need someone with more experience in your particular specialty—train robbing."

"I've held up quite a few of them," The Kid said with a note of pride in his voice.

Grey nodded. "I'm aware of that. I did a bit of looking into your history, Mr. Keene . . . or should I call you Waco?"

"Waco's fine."

"Because you were born there."

"Yep."

"You've made some nice hauls from the jobs you've pulled. But you can do even better with my gang backing you up. They're top professionals, and I have contacts among the railroads who will help us spot the best trains to hit. There's no point in risking your life for an express car that's almost empty, is there?"

The Kid shook his head. "No point at all. What would my share be?"

"Well, starting out, nothing, I'm afraid."

When The Kid frowned again and sat up straighter, Grey went on. "Your share will go toward paying off what you owe me. But later, once you've proven yourself and become a full member of the gang, you'll have a full share, of course. Maybe even a bonus, since I'll be relying heavily on you to help plan the jobs."

The Kid wondered if it was the same pitch Grey had given Quint Lupo. That was possible, although it was just as likely Grey varied the approach for each of the men he targeted, depending on who it was.

Not wanting to appear too eager to agree, The Kid shook his head. "I don't know . . ."

"Again, I'm not really giving you a choice." Grey hardened his voice. "I expect you to cooperate at least until your debt is paid. After that . . . well, if you truly don't want to be part of our organization, you'll be free to leave, although I think you'd be foolish to do so."

It was an easy enough promise for Grey to make, The Kid thought. There was no chance any of the men Grey broke out of prison would leave the gang. They were all doomed from the moment they rode away with Grey's men, although none of them had known that.

Until now. The Kid knew what Grey's plan was, and it was up to him to stop it if he wanted to live.

With a slight show of reluctance, he said, "Since you put it that way, I reckon I'd be a fool not to stick around and see how things play out."

Grey smiled again, but the reptilian coldness in his eyes didn't disappear. "I knew you'd see it our way." He turned to his second. "Brattle, show our new partner to his room."

"Sure, boss."

The Kid tossed back the rest of the brandy. Hitting on a nearly empty stomach the way it did, the liquor made him feel a little light-headed.

As he stood up, he said, "I could use something to eat. It's been a long time since that prison breakfast this morning, and it wasn't very good to start with."

"Of course," Grey said. "I'll see to it."

"How soon do you figure on pulling one of those train robberies you were talking about?"

Grey waved away the question. "Don't worry about that right now. I think we should let any uproar over your escape from prison die down first. That's one of the most important keys to running an operation such as ours—never rush anything."

"You're the boss," The Kid said.

"That's right, I am."

From the doorway, Brattle jerked a thumb. "Come on, Waco."

As they went up a curving set of stairs, The Kid said, "I guess you must be Grey's segundo."

"That's better than some things I've been called," Brattle replied with a trace of wry humor. "Sometimes the boss gets it in his head that I'm his butler. I reckon he misses the way things used to be around here. But I ask you, do I look like a damn butler to you?"

The Kid chuckled and shook his head. "Not hardly. So, is this the boss's old family home or something?"

Brattle got a look on his face like he realized he had said too much. He snapped, "Never you mind about that. Just do as you're told and you'll get along fine around here."

"All right. That's what I intend to do." The Kid paused as they reached the second floor landing. "Do you reckon I could have that gun back now?"

Brattle laughed. "You don't need a gun as long as you're here. When you need one, I'll see that you get it."

He motioned for The Kid to follow him down a hallway with a worn carpet runner on the floor. Brattle paused in front of a door, pulled a key from his pocket, and unlocked it.

"I'm startin' to feel like I'm back in Huntsville," The Kid said. "No gun, guards everywhere, locked doors . . ."

"This place is a lot better than prison," Brattle assured him. "You'll see."

The Kid went into the room. It was simply furnished with a narrow bed, an old wardrobe, a chair, and a small table with a washbasin and a lamp on it. Brattle scratched a match into life and lit the lamp.

Ragged curtains hung over the single window. The Kid wondered why Grey didn't have the place fixed up. The gang had made quite a bit of money from its string of robberies. Grey should have been able to afford to restore the place to at least a semblance of its former glory. Unless he didn't want to for some reason.

Maybe The Kid would learn more about that as the days went on.

"There are some clothes in the wardrobe that ought to fit you," Brattle said. "Somebody will be up with supper in a little while."

"Much obliged," The Kid said with a nod of thanks.

"You'll do all right," Brattle told him. "Just don't get impatient, and don't get too curious about things that don't concern you. Remember those two things, and you won't have any trouble."

"Sounds good."

Brattle nodded and went out. With a rattle, the key turned in the lock behind him.

The Kid ignored the fact that he was locked in. He'd expected it. Opening the wardrobe, he found several shirts and a couple pairs of trousers hanging inside. A pair of boots sat on the floor of the wardrobe with a neatly folded pair of socks draped over the top of them.

The Kid stripped off the scratchy woolen prison uniform, glad to be out of it. As many times as the garments had been soaked in sweat, he would have liked to take a bath and scrub himself clean before he put on fresh clothes, but nobody had offered him a bath and it seemed pretty unlikely they would. He pulled on the new clothes and felt a little better for wearing them.

He had just finished changing clothes when the key sounded in the lock again. The Kid turned toward the door, expecting to see Brattle or one of the other outlaws bringing him the promised meal.

The person standing there when the door swung open had a tray with food on it, all right, but she wasn't one of the outlaws.

She was a beautiful young woman.

Chapter 19

The Kid's mind flashed back to the Menger Hotel in San Antonio and the day he had found Katherine Lupo standing in the hallway instead of a waiter with his supper. The situation had some parallels, all right, but where Katherine was fair, the young woman in front of him was darker, with ebony hair and skin the color of coffee with a lot of cream in it. She wore a tan blouse and a long brown skirt instead of a traveling outfit. And she had indeed brought food with her, whereas Katherine had shown up with only a plea for The Kid's help.

"You are Waco Keene, yes?" The young woman's voice had a hint of an accent to it, an intriguing accent The Kid identified as Cajun.

"Yeah, I'm Waco." He put a cocky grin on his face. He figured a convict, even one who hadn't been locked up for all that long, would react that way to a visit from a beautiful young woman. He took a step toward her.

She balanced the tray holding his supper with her left hand while her right dipped into the pocket of her skirt and came up with a small pistol. "Mr. Grey said a gun of this caliber wouldn't kill you unless I shot you in the head or the heart," she informed him, "so I have permission to aim elsewhere. And I will if you try anything funny, Mr. Keene."

The Kid stopped and held up both hands in surrender, still grinning. "Take it easy, mam'selle. There's no need for gunplay."

"Not only am I armed," she went on as if she hadn't heard him, "but there are men within earshot who will be here in a matter of moments if I cry out for help."

"You won't need to," he told her. "I'm not lookin' for any trouble."

"Back up," she ordered. "Stand over there by the window, please."

He did as she told him, keeping his hands in plain sight as he backed toward the window.

Still pointing the gun at him, she carried the tray over to the table and set it down. As she straightened, she said, "You can just leave the dishes there when you're finished. Someone will get them later."

"I'm obliged to you," The Kid said with a nod. "There's just one more thing."

"What's that?" she asked with a trace of impatience in her voice.

"You know my name, but I don't know yours."

Her brown eyes flashed for a second as if she

were angry, but his charming grin had an effect on her. "I'm Beatrice."

"Mighty pleased to make your acquaintance, Miss Beatrice. I'm sure we'll be seein' more of each other."

"I'm sure," she said dryly. She left the room, locking the door behind her.

The Kid went over to the table and sat down. The plate on the tray held several slices of roast beef, a mound of potatoes, a piece of bread, and some greens. A cup of coffee with wisps of steam curling up from it was next to the plate. Simple fare, to be sure, but it was better than what he'd been getting in prison. He ate eagerly, washing the food down with gulps of the hot coffee.

He wondered if Beatrice had prepared the meal or just delivered it. He wondered who she was. Given her coloring and the fact that part of Texas was more like the Old South than the West, it was likely at least one of her ancestors had been a slave.

Having been raised in Boston as Conrad Browning, he had known a number of older people who had been fervent abolitionists during the days before the Civil War. The war had been over before he was born, though, so he didn't have any direct knowledge of those days and slavery had never really been an issue of personal importance to him.

However, that probably wasn't true of most of the people in East Texas so he considered it unlikely Beatrice was Alexander Grey's wife. Also, on a practical level, she hadn't been wearing a ring of any sort.

It was entirely possible she was Grey's mistress. She was beautiful enough that most men would want her.

It was just idle speculation on The Kid's part. It didn't have anything to do with the job he was expected to do. But he was chivalrous enough to hope if he was successful in breaking up Grey's gang, Beatrice wouldn't be hurt in the process.

Since he was locked in, there wasn't much left for The Kid to do after eating supper other than turn in and get some sleep. The strain of the day's events had left his nerves drawn taut, and he was tired from the long hours of riding. After staring up at the darkened ceiling for a short time, he dozed off and slept surprisingly well.

The rattle of the key in the lock woke him the next morning. As he sat up and opened his eyes, he wondered if Beatrice was bringing him breakfast. That would be a good way to start the day, he thought.

It was Brattle's ugly face, wearing a leering grin, that looked in at him. "Better get up, Keene. We're pullin' out."

That brusque announcement took The Kid completely by surprise. "Pulling out?" he repeated. "But I just got here last night."

"That's right. We've been waitin' for things to work out so we could have you with us when we left. We would've made our move to bust you out before we did if that big galoot Cushman hadn't jumped you the very day things were all set up."

The Kid had wondered about that since Ike Calvert had brought the water wagon to the fields that day but hadn't shown up in that job again until the day of the breakout. Based on what Brattle had just told him, there had probably been a gun in the water barrel and the gang waiting to blow up the fence that first day, too. They would have carried out the plan if not for Cushman's interference.

The Kid was convinced Dr. Kendrick had killed Cushman.

None of that, however, cleared up The Kid's confusion over Brattle's comment about them leaving the plantation.

All he had done to prepare for bed the night before was to take off his boots. He swung his legs out of bed and reached for them, saying, "Where are we going? Or am I not allowed to know that?"

"I reckon the boss will tell you when he's good and ready. That ain't for me to say. Now rattle your hocks."

"What about the other clothes in the wardrobe?" Those were the only things The Kid had to his name, other than the clothes on his back.

"Don't worry about them," Brattle said. "Somebody'll get 'em."

"Beatrice?" The Kid asked with a grin on his face as they left the room.

Brattle stopped and frowned. "Don't you be worryin' or even thinkin' much about Miss Beatrice."

"She belongs to the boss, eh?"

"You better not say anything like that around him. He won't cotton to it."

The Kid shrugged. "Fine. I've never been one for poachin' on another man's territory. Sounds sort of funny comin' from a train robber, don't it?"

Brattle didn't say anything. He just glowered darkly and motioned for The Kid to follow him.

Even before they reached the bottom of the staircase, The Kid could tell something was going on. Men hurried here and there, carrying boxes and bags, packing up the house to leave. From the looks of the activity, it wasn't a temporary trip. It struck The Kid as someone getting ready to move permanently.

If the plantation really was Alexander Grey's ancestral home, as The Kid had speculated, he was about to abandon it.

The front door was open, and the pallid light of dawn came through the opening. Grey appeared in the doorway, wearing a white suit and a planter's hat. "Ah, good morning, Waco. Sorry to drag you out of bed so early, but we have a long way to go. There's coffee and food in the dining room, but I'm afraid you won't have much time to eat. I want to get the wagons rolling."

"Just about all I have is what's on me"—The Kid spread his hands—"so it won't take me any time to pack."

That brought a laugh from Grey. "Simplicity, eh? That's a good attitude to take."

"Where are we going?"

"You'll see when we get there. I assume I can count on your discretion?"

"We're partners, aren't we?" The Kid said.

"Indeed we are." Grey slapped a hand on The Kid's back. "Come on. I could use a cup of coffee myself."

Grey's jovial false camaraderie didn't fool The Kid for a second. He knew what the man's murderous intentions were. But he put a smile on his face anyway and went with the ringleader of the gang into the dining room.

Beatrice was there waiting. "Good morning, Mr. Keene."

She looked just as lovely as the night before, The Kid thought. "Please, ma'am, call me Waco."

"Coffee . . . Mr. Keene?"

"Sure," he said with a shrug of his shoulders indicating he accepted the momentary defeat.

"For you, too, Alexander?" she asked.

"I think I have time for that. He looked over at The Kid. "You met our lovely Beatrice last night, I suppose?"

"She brought me my supper," The Kid said.

"Every home needs the feminine touch. This one was missing that for a long time. But now that Beatrice is here . . ."

So Beatrice was a newcomer, too. That was interesting, The Kid thought, although he didn't see how it would impact his mission.

"Of course, we're leaving," Grey went on, "but

when we settle in at the new place, I'm sure she'll
make a home out of it as well. Won't you, dear?"

She smiled indulgently at him. "I'll do my best,
Alexander."

The Kid ate some hotcakes and bacon and
gulped down the coffee. With that done, he said
to Grey, "If you need me to help with anything, I'd
be glad to."

"Thanks, but I believe we're about ready to go.
You'll leave with Beatrice, Brattle, and the others. I
have one more chore to finish up before I go."

They went outside, where The Kid saw all the
horses had been saddled. In addition, a buggy and
two covered wagons were parked in front of the
house. Drivers were already waiting on the wagon
seats.

Beatrice came out of the house wearing a brown
jacket over her blouse that matched her skirt. Brattle offered her his arm. "Let me help you, Miss
Beatrice."

"Thank you." She allowed him to assist her in
climbing into the buggy.

Brattle turned to look at The Kid and jerked a
thumb at the horse he'd ridden the day before.
"Mount up, Keene," he ordered.

The Kid turned his head to glance at Grey, but
the ringleader had already gone back into the
house.

With nothing to do except mount up as he'd been
told, The Kid swung into the saddle and brought
his horse alongside the buggy, where Brattle had

settled onto the seat next to Beatrice and had hold of the reins.

"You're leading the way?" The Kid asked.

"That's right. Don't go wanderin' off." Brattle gave The Kid a hard-eyed look of warning. "The boys wouldn't like it."

That would be a good way for The Kid to get shot, Brattle seemed to be saying.

"I'm not goin' anywhere except where you go," The Kid assured him.

Brattle nodded curtly. He slapped the reins against the backs of the two horses hitched to the buggy, and the vehicle began rolling along the lane away from the plantation house. The two wagons lurched into motion behind it. Half a dozen riders, including The Kid, flanked the wagons.

Brattle led the way to the road and turned in the opposite direction they had come from the night before. In the daylight, The Kid could tell it was north. The road ran fairly straight, but had some long curves that soon had the plantation out of sight behind them.

For some reason, The Kid looked back. Glancing over his shoulder, he stiffened in the saddle as he saw billows of smoke rising over the trees. The smoke was starkly black against the pale, early morning sky. He could tell from its location that the plantation house was ablaze, and knew what the last chore was Alexander Grey had lingered behind to complete.

Chapter 20

The buggy driven by Brattle finally came to a halt in front of a large house reminding The Kid of a heap of big rocks.

Grey was riding alongside the Kid as they approached the place. "It's actually an old stone ranch house where no one has lived for several years," Grey explained. "A drought wiped out the herd of the man who owned it. The county took it for taxes, and no one has bought it since then. Conditions are just now starting to improve in this area."

The Kid looked around and commented, "It still looks pretty dry to me."

The brown grass, dead flowers, and wilted look of the trees offered stark testimony to the effects of months with little or no rain.

For the past week, the wagons and riders had been traveling north and west, swinging wide around Dallas and Fort Worth into an area Grey had said was known as the Cross Timbers, a mixture of rolling, wooded hills, broad, grassy plains, rocky ridges, and brush-choked draws.

Earlier in the day, the group had traveled through a valley where a small, almost-dried-up creek ran, fording it without difficulty. From there, they had climbed gradually to the wide plateau where Battle has stopped the buggy. Distant vistas opened up in places along the edge of the plateau, but for the most part, the terrain was flat and dotted with clumps of low-growing cactus. Stretches of hard white rock created the hard surface. Horseshoes rang on those areas as the riders crossed them.

The Kid rested his hands on his saddlehorn and leaned forward to ease tired muscles as he asked Grey, "We're not going to be stayin' here permanent-like, then?"

"We'll have to wait and see," the ringleader replied. He had replaced his planter's hat with a black Stetson picked up at a general store in a small town when the group had stopped for supplies. "It all depends on how our operation proceeds."

Grey had gotten The Kid a hat, too, a flat-crowned brown Stetson. The Kid thumbed it back. "Sooner or later you're gonna have to tell me exactly what we're doin'."

"It'll be sooner than you think, now that we're here," Grey assured him. He turned to the buggy. "How do you like the place, Beatrice?"

"It's almost as large as the plantation house. Are you sure no one lives here?"

"Positive. I had the situation checked out thoroughly before I decided on this as our destination." Grey lifted his reins. "Come on. I want to get settled in before nightfall."

They rode past a small stone storage building next to a windmill and a stock tank with a low stone wall around it. Obviously there was a lot of rock in the area. Even the house had thick stone pillars flanking its entrance. The place reminded The Kid of the old castles he had visited in Europe when he was traveling as a youngster with his mother and stepfather.

"There's a settlement about three miles in that direction." Grey pointed northwest. "We'll avoid it as much as possible. We don't want to draw any more attention to ourselves than necessary."

"So this is our hideout," The Kid said. "We won't be pulling any jobs right around here. Best to stay respectable where you live."

"You're starting to understand, Waco," Grey said. "I knew you were an intelligent man."

The wagon drivers followed a path around the place toward a barn and other outbuildings sitting to the right of the main house. Brattle hopped down from the buggy and turned to help Beatrice, but Grey had already dismounted and beaten him to it.

He smiled at her as he took her hand and helped

her down from the vehicle. "Welcome to your new home, my dear." He gave a gracious wave with his other hand and led her to the thick wooden door. Grey hadn't told The Kid to go around back with the other men, so he stuck close to the ringleader.

Hot, musty air drifted out when Gray opened the door. It didn't smell too bad, The Kid thought. Despite the air of abandonment about the place, the old ranch house appeared to be in better shape than the one on the plantation.

The one Alexander Grey had torched as they left.

Grey hadn't said anything about the blaze, and neither had Brattle or any of the other men. The Kid followed their lead. He figured Grey had his reasons for what he'd done, but they probably didn't have any connection with The Kid's mission.

Grey and Beatrice went into the house and The Kid and Brattle followed. The interior of the big stone pile was dark and gloomy, reminding The Kid again of European castles. However, enough sunlight peeked through the gaps around the dusty curtains over the windows for them to find their way around the rooms.

Large, heavy pieces of furniture loomed here and there, obviously left behind when the cattleman who'd built the house abandoned it. The Kid listened for the chittering and scampering of vermin but didn't hear any, which surprised him. The house had to be well built if it had kept out rats and mice during the years it had been deserted.

"Excellent," Grey proclaimed as he looked around. "This will do just fine."

"I'll take a look at the kitchen." Beatrice headed in that direction.

Brattle suggested, "Maybe I'd better have a look around, too, boss, just to make sure the place is as empty as you think it is."

"That's a good idea," Grey replied. "Take Waco with you."

"How about a gun?" The Kid asked.

"You won't need one," Brattle said with a disdainful grunt. "There ain't been any Indian trouble around here for twenty years or more."

"I didn't say anything about Indians."

"Anything short of a Comanche war party I can handle by myself."

The Kid shrugged and went with Brattle on a quick tour of the house. The other rooms had furniture in them, too. Moving in wasn't going to be difficult.

Cleaning up might be, though. When they came back to the kitchen to report the house was indeed empty, Beatrice was standing in the center of the room with her hands on her hips and a determined expression on her face. "This place is going to take a lot of scrubbing, from the floors to the ceiling. All the bedding will have to be changed and washed, too. I'll build a fire in the stove. Brattle, can you fetch water from the well?"

"Yes, ma'am," the segundo replied. He looked at The Kid. "Come on, Keene, you can lend a hand."

The rest of the day was spent getting the place into better shape, or getting started on that job, anyway, since Beatrice kept insisting there was still a great deal to do.

The house was big enough that all the men could stay inside, rather than having to use the bunkhouse out back. The Kid took note Beatrice had her own room on the second floor, rather than sharing a room with Grey as he'd expected her to do. As far as he knew, nothing had gone on between the two of them during the trip from East Texas, but that didn't mean a whole lot. When camping out on the trail, privacy was at a minimum and everybody was worn out from the day's travel. It was no place for romance.

Now that they had reached their destination and were evidently going to stay for a while—possibly until the gang was ready to kill him, have Angus Murrell turn in his body for the reward, and move on—the need to contact the Rangers became more urgent. The journey had given him plenty of time to think, but he hadn't figured out any way to get in touch with the Texas Rangers and let them know where he was. Brattle or one of the other outlaws had watched him all the time.

They had the same sort of meal for supper that they'd been eating on the trail—bacon, beans, and biscuits, with canned tomatos and peaches.

"Tomorrow I need to go to that settlement you mentioned, Alexander," Beatrice said to Grey while they were eating at a long table in the dining room.

"If we're going to be here for a while, we need some proper food."

Grey frowned. "I said we were going to avoid the settlement as much as possible," he pointed out.

"Yes, well, that's not possible right now. We need supplies." She glanced across the table at The Kid. "Brattle and Mr. Keene can take me."

"Not Waco. Too much of a chance someone might see him and recognize him."

Grey didn't want anybody recognizing him until the gang pulled their first train holdup with him, The Kid thought.

"Well, then, just Brattle," Beatrice said.

"All right," Grey gave in. "I suppose you're right. We're going to be here for a good long while, so we can't live on what few supplies we have left."

She smiled. "Good. It's settled."

After supper, Brattle came up to The Kid and inclined his head toward the stairs. "Come on, Keene. Time for you to go to your room."

The Kid's eyebrows rose in feigned surprise. "You're going to keep on lockin' me in like you did back at the plantation? I've been with you people for more than a week now. Don't you trust me yet?"

"Ain't a matter of trust," Brattle said. "It's—"

"Just the way you do things," The Kid finished for him. "Right?"

"Well, at least you understand."

"That doesn't mean I like it."

"Nobody said you had to."

Arguing wasn't going to do any good. The Kid shrugged. "Fine. Let's go."

When the door of the room assigned to him closed behind him and the key rattled in the lock, he looked around. A bed and a small table next to it were the only pieces of furniture in the room. A candle burned in a holder on the table. No chair, no wardrobe as there had been at the plantation house.

That was fine with The Kid. His comfort didn't matter as long as he got the job done.

He went to the window and pulled the curtain back. Dust swirled into the air and tickled his nose. He leaned closer to the window and peered out.

He was on the second floor. It would be a simple matter to climb out through the window, hang from the sill, and drop to the ground.

But it was possible, even probable, Brattle had posted at least one guard outside to keep an eye on that window. He had made it clear that while they wanted The Kid as part of the gang, if he caused any problems they might kill him. Trying to escape might just get him a bullet.

Anyway, that would mean abandoning the mission. Getting away, finding the local law, convincing those star packers to get in touch with the Rangers, and setting up a raid on the old ranch, all before Grey realized The Kid was gone and bolted with the rest of the gang . . . well, those chances were practically nonexistent, The Kid thought. But he wasn't the sort of man to give up.

That stubbornness was something else he had inherited from Frank Morgan.

Despite that resolve, he put a hand on the window and tried to lift the pane, just to see if he could. If anybody asked him about it later, he could always say he was just trying to get a little fresh air.

The window wouldn't budge. The Kid studied it more closely and let out a humorless laugh.

Earlier in the day he had heard hammering and had assumed some of the men were carrying out repairs. Maybe that was true for part of the racket, but not all. The window was nailed shut. He couldn't go anywhere that way without breaking the glass. The racket of that would probably be heard all over the house.

With a rueful shake of his head, The Kid let the curtain fall closed. There was nothing left for him to do except what he had done the first night at the plantation house.

Go to bed and get some rest.

Since the room was warm and stuffy and the window wouldn't open, he stripped down to the bottom half of a pair of long underwear, blew out the candle, and stretched out on the bed with a sigh.

Beatrice had seen to it that some of the fresh sheets they had brought with them were placed on the beds, but the mattress smelled musty to The Kid. He tried to ignore it as he rolled onto his side.

He hadn't fallen asleep when he heard a soft, metallic scraping. It took him a moment to realize someone was unlocking the door and trying to be quiet about it.

He stiffened for a second, then swung his feet to the floor and stood up noiselessly. No one in the house had any reason to do him harm, at least not at that point, but he still didn't like the idea of somebody sneaking into his room.

He moved quickly and quietly to the door and pressed himself to the wall so he was behind the panel when it opened. Holding his breath, he waited.

The door swung back. The corridor was dark. No light spilled into the room, only a faint glow indicating a lamp was still burning downstairs.

A shadow moved against that glow. The figure it belonged to eased into the room.

"Mr. Keene?" a voice whispered. "Waco?"

The Kid couldn't have been more surprised, and yet he had a sense that the moment was inevitable.

His nocturnal visitor was Beatrice.

Chapter 21

Guided by her voice, he reached out and placed his hand on her shoulder. "Miss Beatrice." His voice was as quiet as hers had been.

She gasped and pulled away from him, but at least she didn't scream. It would have drawn Grey's attention and explaining to the outlaw leader just what his mistress was doing in The Kid's room might have proven awkward.

For that matter, The Kid wondered, what *was* Beatrice doing there?

"Waco? Is that you?"

"Who else would it be?" The Kid asked dryly. "I was locked in here, remember?"

"That wasn't my idea. I'm not sure why Alexander and Brattle don't trust you. It seems to me you're all on the same side."

"You could say that," The Kid agreed. *You could say that*, he thought, *but saying it didn't necessarily make it true.* Beatrice didn't have to know that.

His eyes had adjusted a little to the darkness, and he could vaguely make out her shape. She wore what appeared to be a light-colored robe.

He gave voice to the question uppermost in his mind. "I'm not tryin' to be rude, but what are you doing here? I don't reckon Alexander would take kindly to it if he knew you were in my room."

"Why not?"

"Well . . ." The Kid thought the answer to that question was pretty obvious, but if she wanted him to put it into words, he would. "I don't think he's the sort of hombre who'd cotton to having somebody messin' with his property."

A sharply indrawn breath hissed between her teeth. "I'm not Alexander's property. I'm not anybody's slave."

"Well, then, his ladyfriend."

For a moment she didn't say anything. Then she asked, "Is that what you think I am?"

"It's pretty obvious, isn't it?"

"Obvious to you, maybe." She laughed softly, surprising him. "I'm not Alexander's ladyfriend, Mr. Keene. I'm his sister."

It was The Kid's turn to stand in silence, unable to find the words to respond.

"Half sister, actually," Beatrice went on. "He and I have the same father."

"I didn't have any idea," The Kid murmured.

"There was no reason you should. You didn't know any of us until a week or so ago. My mother was a servant who worked on the plantation after the war. She was an octaroon from Louisiana who'd been a slave when she was a little girl. Her mother brought her to Texas after they were freed. They both worked for Alexander's father, and he . . . took a fancy to my mother when she was fifteen. After I was born, she and my grandmother took me and ran away, back to Louisiana."

"All right," The Kid said. "That's a pretty ugly story. How'd you wind up back in Texas?"

"My mother and my grandmother are both dead now. I didn't have anyone else. So I came back to Texas to claim my birthright."

"Things don't work that way."

"Why? Because I'm a bastard? Because some of my ancestors were slaves?"

"Take your pick," The Kid said. "I'm not sayin' it's right, just tellin' you how the law would look at it."

"That's probably true. Fortunately for me, when I showed up at the plantation and told Alexander my story, he welcomed me. He remembered me from when he was a boy and knew I was telling the truth. He said I was a member of the family. You see . . . he hates our father as much as I do."

"Is that why he set the place on fire when we left?"

"I suspect that's right. He hasn't said anything to me about it, and I haven't asked him."

They were standing in almost complete darkness. The Kid wanted to be able to see Beatrice's face. If he could see her, he would be able to judge better if she was telling him the truth.

The Kid recalled matches laying on the table. "I'm going to light the candle, if that's all right with you."

"Go ahead."

He found one and snapped it to life with his thumbnail. Squinting slightly against the glare, he held the flame to the candle wick. It caught and the flame strengthened, casting a circle of light into the room.

Hearing the floorboards creak a little, The Kid turned to see Beatrice easing the door closed. He had been right about the robe she was wearing. What he hadn't been able to tell was that it was silk and clung enticingly to her body.

Her midnight hair was pulled back from her high forehead and tied behind her head. She was strikingly beautiful and The Kid knew he didn't have to worry about her being Grey's mistress.

But she was Grey's half sister, which might also make him protective of her. Besides, The Kid had no interest in cluttering up his mission with unnecessary complications.

He was interested, though, in finding out what had brought her to his room. "What's Alexander got against your father?" he asked, partly out of curiosity and partly to keep her talking.

"My father never recovered from losing his wealth and power because of the war. He let the plantation go downhill and became a lecher and a drunkard. He . . . he raped my mother, and she wasn't the only one. Eventually his wife—Alexander's mother—confronted him about his behavior, and in a drunken rage, he choked her to death."

"Good Lord," The Kid muttered.

"When he saw what he'd done, he ran away. Alexander found his mother's body. He was only ten years old. When the authorities discovered what had happened, they took him away. It was a horrible time for him."

"I can imagine. This was after you'd already gone back to Louisiana with your mother and grandmother?"

Beatrice nodded. "Yes, thank goodness. Otherwise we would have been in the middle of that terrible mess, too. I didn't even know anything about it until I came back to Texas and went to the plantation to see Alexander. He told me what had happened and then asked me to stay."

"Wait a minute," The Kid said. "How did he wind up with the plantation? What happened to his father? Your father, too, I reckon."

"The law caught up to him eventually," Beatrice said. "He had changed his name and become an outlaw. He was tried, convicted, and sent to prison for his crimes. The plantation was lost, of course. It went through several owners, but they were never able to get it back on its feet. By the time Alexander was grown and had made some money of his own, the place was empty when he came back."

"Just like this one," The Kid mused. "So he was just squatting there, like he is here."

"The difference is he had grown up in that house and considered it his by rights, to do with whatever he wanted."

Including burning it down when he was done with it, to wipe out the place where his mother had been murdered by his own father, The Kid thought. It made sense . . . of a twisted sort, but still . . .

"That's quite a story. The sort of thing they make melodramas out of. But it doesn't explain what you're doing here in my room tonight."

A flush spread across her lovely features. She lifted a hand to the robe's neckline and toyed with the silk. "Do I really have to explain that, Waco?"

"Yeah, you do," The Kid said bluntly. "You've barely looked at me since the night Brattle brought me to the plantation. What changed your mind all of a sudden?"

"Nothing, I . . ." She looked more uncomfortable. "Darn it, Waco, why are you making this so difficult?"

"Because I figure on making some money workin' with your brother, and I'd just as soon not have him shoot me for beddin' his little sister before I can cash in on the deal."

"Listen, when I came to the plantation, I didn't know Alexander was an outlaw! It didn't take me long to figure it out, though. This isn't really the life I bargained for. I haven't said anything to him about it, but I . . . I'm afraid of what might happen."

"So you want me to rescue you, and the two of us will run away together. Is that it?" The Kid put a tone of scorn in his voice as he asked the question. The thought had occurred to him it might be a test. Grey might have sent Beatrice to find out just how easily he could be persuaded to betray the gang. Maybe she was telling the absolute truth about everything, but he couldn't afford to assume that.

"You don't have to make it sound so crass," she snapped as she glared at him.

"Why me?" he shot back at her. "Why not Brattle or one of the other men?"

"Do you really think Brattle would ever double-cross Alexander?" A humorless laugh came from her. "Besides, you've seen what he's like. The same thing goes for the others. I've had enough of brutal men in my life. Besides, you're new here, like I am. You don't have the same ties to Alexander the rest of the men do."

"You're the one who's related to him by blood," The Kid pointed out.

Beatrice shook her head. "That doesn't really mean anything," she insisted. "I don't even remember him from when I was a little girl. I was too young when my mother ran away from the plantation. For all practical purposes, I never laid eyes on Alexander Grey until about three weeks ago." She paused and leaned her head to the side. "It's true that he's been very kind to me, and I'm grateful to him for taking me in. I don't really want to betray him . . . but I don't want to spend the rest of my life cooking and cleaning for a gang of outlaws, either."

She certainly sounded sincere, The Kid thought, but he still didn't trust her. "Look, I owe your brother. I'd still be rotting in prison if it wasn't for him. I don't think I can help you."

"Are you sure?" Beatrice's fingers went to the belt knotted around her waist. "I was on my own for a while after my mother passed away. I had to do some things I'm not proud of to survive. I learned a lot. I know I could make it worth your while to help me, Waco."

The Kid's jaw tightened. Before his marriage, when he was still the spoiled, rich young man known as Conrad Browning, he wouldn't have hesitated to take a beautiful woman like Beatrice to bed. The same was true of Katherine Lupo.

But he wasn't that spoiled young man anymore, and he had a job to do.

On the other hand, if Beatrice was telling the truth, she might prove to a valuable ally somewhere down the line, so he didn't want to anger her so much that she wouldn't have anything else to do with him.

He reached out to touch her arm and stop her from untying the belt. "Let me think about it. We're already here, so we might as well stay for a while."

"Until you're such a part of the gang you won't want to turn on Alexander?"

"I can't help you right now. That doesn't mean

things will always be this way. I've got to see how it plays out."

She sighed and stopped fiddling with the belt. "All right. We'll give it some time. But can I trust you not to say anything to Alexander about this?"

"Hell, he doesn't trust me completely yet. He's made that clear. So I'd be a fool to tell him his sister was in my room in the middle of the night, wouldn't I?"

She smiled. "I suppose so. Just don't take too long to make up your mind, Waco. I could change *my* mind, you know. It's a woman's prerogative, they say."

"Let me take a look out in the hall before you leave. We don't want anybody spotting you sneakin' out of here."

"Especially since we didn't actually do anything. That would be a real shame, wouldn't it, to get in trouble over nothing?"

"I wouldn't say it was nothing," The Kid told her. "It's just not something yet."

He opened the door enough to look out into the hall and see that it was empty. Then he went back to the table and blew out the candle before opening the door wide enough for Beatrice to slip through.

In the darkness, she somehow found his face and brushed her lips across his cheek. Then she was gone and The Kid closed the door quietly behind her.

The night certainly hadn't gone the way he expected, he thought as he went back to the bed and stretched out on it.

He wondered if Beatrice was reporting to Alexander Grey that "Waco Keene" hadn't fallen for the scheme, no matter how much she had tempted him. He wondered if she was really Grey's sister or if Grey had concocted that melodramatic story as part of the plan to test the new recruit's loyalty.

Everywhere The Kid looked there were unanswered questions, including the one of how he was going to get in touch with the Texas Rangers. And it didn't seem the answers were forthcoming any time soon.

He rolled over and went to sleep.

Chapter 22

The night passed quietly, and the next morning Beatrice and Brattle went to the nearby settlement in one of the wagons. They came back that afternoon with supplies.

"Any problems?" Grey asked as he helped Beatrice down from the wagon seat.

"No," she told him. "No one seemed to pay any attention to us. We didn't stop anywhere except at the general store."

Grey nodded, obviously pleased. "Excellent. We're going to do our best to be good citizens around here."

The Kid helped unload. He noticed they had bought enough provisions to last for several weeks.

For several days, everyone concerned themselves with putting the ranch house back in good shape and cleaning up around the place in general. The Kid did his share of the work without complaining, but he began to think he ought to speak up soon and ask Grey when they were going to pull their first job. He didn't think Waco Keene was the sort of hombre to do such menial work without getting tired of it.

He still didn't have a gun, and Brattle or one of the other men continued keeping an eye on him all the time except at night, when he was locked into his room.

He said something about it to Grey, pointing out that if the house ever caught fire, he would be doomed if no one came to let him out.

"That won't happen," Grey assured him. "You're worth too much to us, Waco."

"How do you mean?" The Kid asked. Surely Grey wasn't alluding to the reward they hoped to collect on him. Not so early in the game.

"For your experience as a train robber, of course," Grey answered easily. "We're counting on you."

The Kid grunted. "Haven't seen any signs of it so far."

"Soon, my friend, soon," Grey told him.

The next day, The Kid had just carried a couple buckets of water into the kitchen for Beatrice when she said, "Have you thought any more about what we talked about, the first night we were here?"

The Kid glanced around to make sure none of the other men were close enough to overhear. He didn't want anybody carrying the news to Grey that he and Beatrice were keeping secrets with each other.

"Don't worry, we're alone," she told him. "Alexander is upstairs, and unless one of them followed you in, the rest of the men are outside. I wouldn't have said anything otherwise." She came closer to him and put a hand on his arm. "So have you thought about it?"

"Reckon I have," The Kid admitted, and that much was true. He had pondered the question of whether Beatrice had been telling him the truth that night, or if the whole thing was just part of some convoluted plot by Alexander Grey.

If she'd been telling him the truth, he wanted to find some way to help her. But it was going to have to wait until he had broken up the gang, he had decided, assuming he could even pull that off. He would certainly do what he could to see to it the law didn't treat her as if she were just another member of the gang.

"Well?" she prodded him. "What do you think? Can you do it?"

The Kid was saved from having to answer the question by a sudden commotion outside. Men shouted angrily, and as he turned toward the front door with a puzzled frown on his face, a gun went off, the report muffled somewhat by the house's thick stone walls.

"What in blazes?" he exclaimed. Grateful for the distraction, he hurried out of the kitchen.

Grey appeared at the top of the stairs as The Kid started across the big front room. The ringleader had a pistol in his hand and wore a surprised expression on his face. "Was that a shot I heard, Waco?" he called as he clattered down the staircase.

"I reckon so, boss."

The Kid reached the front door first and had just grasped the latch when Grey said sharply, "Wait a minute!"

When The Kid paused, Grey went on. "You're not armed."

The Kid thought Grey was going to go first, but the man surprised him by pressing the pistol into his hand. If there was any more gunplay, Grey obviously wanted The Kid to handle it.

Even with the small caliber pistol, it felt really good to wrap his fingers around a gun butt. The thought flashed across his mind that he could take Grey prisoner and use him as a hostage to get away. Then he could turn Grey over to the law and send the Rangers back there.

By which time the rest of the outlaws would have scattered, he reminded himself. And what would happen to Beatrice in the meantime? Could he manage to rescue her, too?

Doubts intruded instantly. He didn't know for sure the gun Grey had just given him was even loaded. It could be a trick or a test of some sort, too.

The pause to consider all of that lasted only a fraction of a second.

Then The Kid did what Waco Keene would have done. He jerked the door open and charged out to see what all the ruckus was about.

A couple men were rolling around on the ground, fighting. Fists flew and thudded against flesh and bone. The Kid recognized one of the combatants as a man called Dodge, a member of Alexander Grey's gang.

The other man was a stranger. A saddled horse The Kid hadn't seen before stood nearby, moving around nervously as if spooked by the fight and the gunshot. He quickly put everything together in his mind. The stranger had ridden up to the house, Dodge had challenged him, and somehow heated words had been exchanged, leading to the battle.

The Kid spotted a revolver lying on the ground, and the stranger's holster was empty. Clearly, the stranger had fired that shot, but it must have missed because Dodge didn't seem to be wounded.

It was only a matter of time before the other men converged, drawn by that gunshot, but at the moment The Kid and Grey were the only witnesses to the battle.

Suddenly, the stranger landed a solid punch to Dodge's jaw that sent him rolling away. He snatched up the fallen Colt and wheeled around, lining his sights on Dodge.

The Kid acted instinctively, firing before the stranger could pull the trigger. The small caliber pistol made a sharp, wicked crack as it went off.

The stranger yelled in shock and pain and dropped the Colt. He jerked his right arm back and cradled it against his body. Blood welled from the furrow The Kid's bullet had plowed in his forearm.

"Don't try it again," The Kid warned, though he didn't think it was likely the wounded man would.

"You shot me!" the stranger said.

"You were about to shoot one of my pards. You're lucky I just winged you instead of killing you."

In truth, that fancy shot had been more luck than anything else. The Kid was fast and accurate, but shooting the gun out of a man's hand was the stuff of dime novels. He'd been trying to fire a warning shot in front of the stranger, but the bullet had nicked the man's arm and produced an even more dramatic effect than intended.

"I wasn't gonna shoot him!" the stranger protested. "I just didn't want him jumpin' me again!"

The Kid shrugged, obviously not moved by the complaint. "Looked to me like you planned to ventilate him."

Dodge slapped dust off his shirt and pants. "That's the way it looked to me, too, Waco. I'm much obliged to you for stoppin' him."

"Dadblast it!" the stranger howled. Blood dripped from his fingers as he held his wounded arm. "What loco kind of place is this?"

He was short, no more than five and a half feet tall, but his arms and shoulders were heavily slabbed with muscle. His high-crowned brown hat had fallen off during the fight, revealing close-cropped sandy hair. He was probably between twenty-five and thirty, The Kid judged, and his range clothes showed plenty of signs of wear and tear.

"All I did was ride up to see about askin' for a

job," the stranger went on, "but after gettin' shot I ain't so sure I want to work here anymore!"

"You're a ranch hand?" Grey asked.

Brattle and several other members of the gang came pounding around the corner of the house then, guns drawn, but Grey lifted a hand and motioned for them to take it easy, letting them know the situation was under control.

"That's right," the stranger said. "I've ridden for three or four outfits around here. You can ask the owners about me if you want. Name's Tyler."

"Well, Mr. Tyler, what makes you think we'd be hiring here?"

Those massive shoulders went up and down in a shrug. "Rode by the other day and saw somebody was fixin' the place up. Old Jonah Rankin had a pretty good spread here at one time. I figured somebody finally bought the place from the county and was gonna try to make a go of it again. Seein' as how I'm sorta between ridin' jobs . . ."

"Say no more," Grey told him. "An understandable mistake, I suppose."

Brattle asked, "You want us to run this peckerwood off, boss?"

"Not at all," Grey said. "What sort of hospitality would that be, to shoot a man and then force him to leave?"

"It'd be more hospitable not to shoot him at all," Tyler said through teeth gritted against the pain of his wound.

"Yes, I suppose." Grey turned to Beatrice, who

had followed him and The Kid to the front door. "My dear, do you think you could patch up this young man's arm?"

"Of course," she said, although The Kid thought she didn't look too enthusiastic about the prospect of cleaning and bandaging that bloody bullet gash. She put a smile on her face and told Tyler, "Come in."

Brattle said, "I ain't sure you should trust this short-growed runt, boss."

Tyler's jaw thrust out pugnaciously. "Short-growed runt, am I? Mister, I'm so tough if I was any taller it wouldn't be fair to all the other fellas in this part of the country."

Grey laughed. "It's all right, Brattle. I'm not going to offer Mr. Tyler a job, mind you, but there's no reason we can't be neighborly."

"No job, huh?" Tyler said. "You sure about that? I'm a top hand, mister."

"I'm sure you are, but I have all the riders I need right now."

Tyler sighed. "Oh, well. Can't blame a fella for tryin'." He smiled at Beatrice. "I'm comin', ma'am. I'm mighty obliged to you for fixin' me up."

The two of them went into the house. Grey told the other men to get back to their work, then said quietly to The Kid, "Would you mind keeping an eye on our visitor, Waco? He seems to be exactly what he claims, a drifting cowboy, but I don't want to leave Beatrice alone with him."

"That's probably a good idea, boss." The Kid

looked down at the pistol on his hand. "You want your gun back?"

Grey frowned in thought for a second and then shook his head. "No, I believe I'll let you keep it for now."

"Oh? In that case, I'd rather have something bigger, like a Colt .45, maybe."

Grey grinned and clapped a hand on The Kid's shoulder. "Don't push your luck, my young friend. I said you can keep it for now. And as soon as Tyler rides away, I expect you to give that gun to Beatrice. Understand?"

"Sure. You don't trust me yet."

"We're getting there."

The Kid nodded and followed Grey into the house. Grey went upstairs, and hearing voices in the kitchen, The Kid walked out there and found Tyler sitting at the table with his bloody sleeve rolled up while Beatrice swabbed at the bullet crease with a wet cloth.

Tyler winced a little at the pain, but kept a smile on his face. "I sure appreciate you takin' care of me like this, ma'am."

"It's the least I can do," Beatrice told him. "Now hold still. I'm going to get some whiskey."

Tyler's smile widened into a grin. "That's mighty kind of you. I could use a drink right about now."

"It's to clean the wound, not to drink."

The grin on the young cowboy's face disappeared and was replaced by a crestfallen expression. "Oh."

Beatrice laughed at his disappointment. "I'll be right back." She looked at The Kid, who had reversed one of the chairs at the table and straddled it. The pistol was tucked into the waistband of his jeans. "Don't let him run off."

"I won't," The Kid promised.

The Kid supposed Beatrice was going to get the whiskey from the parlor where he'd seen bottles of liquor. When she had left the room, he nodded toward the wounded arm Tyler had stretched out on the table. "For what it's worth, I was just trying to make you drop the gun. I really didn't mean to wing you like that. It was sort of an accident."

Tyler smiled as he looked down at the raw furrow on his forearm. "I know."

Then he lifted his eyes to meet The Kid's. "Not even Kid Morgan is that good a shot."

Chapter 23

The Kid stiffened. His hand moved instinctively toward the gun at his waist.

Tyler shook his head as if warning him not to try anything. His left hand moved over the thin layer of flour on the table, left over from Beatrice mixing the dough for biscuits that morning. His index finger swiftly traced a symbol in the white powder.

He drew a circle first, then a five-pointed star in the middle of the circle.

The same shape as the badge of the Texas Rangers.

The Kid's eyes widened slightly in surprise. He recognized the symbol.

Tyler's hand moved again, casually sweeping across the table and wiping out the design as if it had never been there. He smiled faintly as he met The Kid's intent gaze.

Everything was clear. Someone had actually followed the gang through the wilderness between the prison and the Grey plantation. And someone, maybe the young man who called himself Tyler, had followed them from the plantation to the ranch in the Cross Timbers.

The Kid knew the young cowboy was his contact man from the Rangers.

There was no time for them to say anything else. Beatrice came back into the kitchen carrying a bottle half filled with whiskey.

"This is going to sting," she warned as she took a clean cloth and soaked it with the liquor.

"I'm tough," Tyler told her. "I can stand it, ma'am. Especially if you'll smile at me while you're doin' it."

She did smile as she began swabbing at the wound with the cloth.

The bite of the whiskey on raw flesh made Tyler grimace, but he put a grin back on his rugged face. "Not bad at all."

"You should probably have a doctor take a look at this," Beatrice said. "It might need a few stitches, and I can't do that."

"Yes'm. I'll go see Doc Steward over in the settlement as soon as I get a chance. I hear tell he's a pretty good sawbones."

"Don't wait too long," she warned. "You don't want it to fester."

"No, ma'am."

Brattle came into the kitchen while Beatrice was wrapping a bandage around Tyler's forearm and tying it into place. He was carrying Tyler's Colt. He set the gun on the table and dropped five bullets beside it. "I unloaded this hogleg. Just so you don't get tempted to use it again."

"You don't have to worry about that, mister," Tyler said. "This trouble was all just a big misunderstandin'."

Brattle grunted. "Don't misunderstand again. As soon as the lady's done patchin' you up, you need to haul your freight off this range."

Tyler nodded. "Yes, sir, that's just what I intend to do. I never meant to stir up a ruckus."

"That should do it," Beatrice said as she finished tying the bandage into place. "You take care of that wound, Mr. Tyler. Be sure and check the dressing."

"Yes'm, I will." Tyler looked at Brattle. "What about my hat?"

"It's still out there on the ground where it fell. You can get it as you're leavin'."

"Thanks." Tyler got to his feet and smiled again at Beatrice. "And I'm obliged to you as well, ma'am, like I told you." He glanced at The Kid. "Though I don't believe I'll thank you for shootin' me, mister."

"You wouldn't be welcome anyway," The Kid replied with a sneer.

Tyler looked back at Beatrice. "Ma'm, I don't know if you're partial to scenic views or not, but there's a hill about half a mile west of here where you can see for a long way. Mighty pretty from up there. Since you're new around here, I thought you might like to have a look at it sometime."

"Thank you, Mr. Tyler, I'll do that," Beatrice said

politely, but The Kid could tell she wasn't really interested in some scenic view.

He, on the other hand, was very interested in what Tyler had just said, even though he couldn't show it. He knew the Ranger's words had been meant for him. Tyler was conveying a message. That hill would be his vantage point for keeping an eye on the ranch . . . and on The Kid.

That didn't help much, since the gang still had him on a tight rein, but maybe in the future it would.

Brattle and Tyler left the kitchen.

Remembering what Grey had told him, The Kid took the pistol from his waistband and set it on the table. "Alexander told me to give this to you when you were finished working on Tyler."

"He still doesn't trust you?"

"Evidently not. But he claims that's going to change soon."

Beatrice hesitated, then said quietly, "Is anything else going to change soon, Waco?"

"We'll have to wait and see," The Kid told her.

She wasn't aware that something had already changed, something very important.

The Texas Rangers were on the job.

That evening after supper, Grey told The Kid and Brattle, "Come into my office."

Grey had taken over one of the rooms downstairs and turned it into his office and library, unpacking the books he'd been able to salvage from the water-damaged volumes in the plantation house. A big rolltop desk left behind by the previous owner of the ranch took up the center of the room.

The Kid and Brattle followed him into the room. Grey put his finger on the map spread out on a table. "This is our first job, gentlemen."

As The Kid leaned over to study the map, Grey traced his fingertip along a straight line marking the course of the railroad. "Fort Worth to the east, Weatherford to the west. And halfway between, a flag stop at a little settlement. That's where you'll be waiting for the train."

The name Weatherford rang a bell in The Kid's mind. He thought back to when he was still Conrad Browning and the conversations he'd had with his father, before the tragedy that had given birth to Kid Morgan.

Frank Morgan, The Drifter, had been born and raised in that part of Texas, he recalled. Frank had spent quite a bit of time in and around the town of Weatherford, including a visit a few years earlier when he'd met up with an old flame who was married to a judge.

The Kid didn't recall the woman's name, and Frank had been sort of close-mouthed about the whole business, but at the time Conrad Browning had gotten the feeling Frank suspected the woman's daughter might be his child.

It was odd to think he might have a blood relative—a half sister—so close by.

Another memory worked its way into The Kid's

head. Frank had come back to the area to attend the young woman's wedding. She had gotten married to a Texas Ranger, The Kid suddenly recalled.

That Ranger's name abruptly sprang into his mind. *Tyler Beaumont.*

"Waco? Something wrong?"

Grey's voice broke into The Kid's stunned thoughts. Trying not to show what he was thinking and feeling, he shook his head. "No, go ahead with what you were sayin', boss. I'm listenin'."

"This is no time for wool-gathering," Grey said with a frown. "This is important."

"I know that. Sorry. You were sayin' that we'd stop the train there at that little place called . . ." —the Kid leaned closer to the map—"Aledo?"

"That's right. It's ranching country all around there, so no one will think twice about a bunch of cowboys riding into the settlement. There's a little depot, which you'll take over so you can raise the flag and stop the train. Once you have it stopped, two men will deal with the engineer and fireman while the rest of you empty out the express car."

"What'll it be carrying, boss?" Brattle asked.

"A shipment of cash bound for banks in Midland, Odessa, and El Paso. There'll be a couple deputy U.S. marshals guarding it, but that's all. The railroad doesn't want to draw attention to the shipment. It totals sixty thousand dollars."

Brattle let out an awed whistle. "That's a damn fortune! We won't have to pull another job for a year."

Grey shook his head. "Maybe we won't have to,

but that won't stop us," he insisted. "This is just the beginning. We'll all be very rich men by the time we're finished, thanks to Waco here."

"Looks to me like you've already got this planned out," The Kid commented. "I'm glad you busted me out of prison, mind you, but I don't see why you even need me."

"Because of your expertise in robbing trains, of course. We're going to go over every detail of the plan so you can tell us whether you think it will work. If there's anything you want to change, you can let us know and we'll figure out some other way of going about it."

The Kid frowned, encountering another tricky aspect of the role he was playing. He'd never robbed a train in his life. He had been a passenger on a couple that had been held up, but that was completely different.

Still, as a businessman he had developed a pretty good head for strategy and tactics, and since adopting the life of a fighting man he had refined that ability. Mostly knowing what to do was just a matter of common sense.

"First thing is, what's the law situation down there? Is there a local star packer we're gonna have to deal with?"

Grey smiled. "See, you're already proving valuable. I don't know for sure. I expect there'll be a town constable or maybe a deputy sheriff who has an office there, but we'll have to find out, won't we?" He looked at Brattle. "You'll need to send a couple boys over there to do some scouting. We have five days before that money shipment goes through."

Brattle nodded. "I'll take care of it, boss. What else?"

"That's a good question," Grey said. "What about it, Waco? What else will we need to know?"

The Kid leaned over and rested his hands on the table as he studied the map again. "We'll need to figure out the best getaway. And for that you're going to need a better map. I want one with as much detail as you can find on the surrounding countryside. Better yet, I want to take a look at the country myself."

A dubious expression came over Grey's lean face, as if he didn't like the idea of The Kid leaving the ranch. He didn't want anybody spotting Waco Keene and identifying him.

Of course, The Kid looked nothing like the real Waco Keene, so nobody was going to mistake him for the bank robber. But Grey and the others didn't know that, and The Kid's life was riding on the gang's ignorance of that fact.

"I suppose it can be arranged," Grey finally said, "but you'll have to be very careful."

The Kid nodded. "Sure. I don't want to do anything to mess this up." At least not until he had enough evidence to put Alexander Grey and the rest of the outlaws behind bars for a long time. For that, he would have to cooperate until after they had pulled at least one robbery.

But after that, maybe he could signal the Rangers to move in . . . and maybe find out if the stocky young lawman called Tyler was really his brother-in-law!

Chapter 24

The Kid spent the next few days riding through the countryside between the ranch and the settlement where the train robbery would take place, which was about fifteen miles south of the gang's current headquarters.

Brattle and at least one other man were with him at all times.

The Kid didn't see any point in arguing about being guarded. He wanted the robbery to go off without any hitches. It was the last piece in the puzzle. He also wanted no one getting hurt. He figured the loot could be recovered later.

He wasn't going to lead a posse straight toward the ranch, so his getaway plan was to start off in the opposite direction, south, before swinging west and then cutting north again. The terrain in all directions was hilly but not particularly rugged, so some hard riding would be needed to put distance between themselves and any pursuit.

The hope was, of course, that the gang would have an insurmountable lead before any posse could be formed to give chase.

In the evenings, Grey, Brattle and The Kid discussed the plan. If the train was on schedule, it would pass through the settlement at five minutes after three in the afternoon. The depot was just a little one-room affair, set off to the side of a block of businesses facing the track.

"Only one freight clerk works there, so he shouldn't present much of a challenge," The Kid pointed out. "Two men could take him, while the others wait nearby for the train to pull in."

He didn't want the townspeople noticing anything unusual was going on, so it was his suggestion the gang not move on the depot until about a quarter to three.

Somewhere Grey had gotten his hands on a topographical map, and in the evenings The Kid went over it with him and Brattle, marking the course he thought they should take and pointing out things that might slow them down.

Grey was impressed by the way The Kid anticipated problems. "I knew it was a good idea to get you to join us, Waco. You're going to be worth your weight in gold."

Or in bounty money, The Kid thought wryly.

The day of the holdup dawned bright, hot, and still. When it was time to go, Brattle squinted at the brassy sky. "I don't like it, boss. Feels to me like there's a storm comin'."

"Nonsense," Grey claimed. "It's a beautiful day. There's not a cloud in the sky."

"Right now there ain't. Thunderstorms can blow up mighty quick-like this time of year."

"Well, it shouldn't have any effect on what you're doing, " Grey insisted. "If anything, a little rain will just make it harder for anyone to follow you."

He was right about that, The Kid thought. A hard rain would wash away the prints their horses left.

As they mounted up, Beatrice came to the door of the house and watched them. She had a worried look on her face. It was the first time since the gang broke The Kid out of prison—and the first time since Beatrice had been reunited with her brother—that they were riding off to commit a crime . . . if she had been telling The Kid the truth. Her gaze lingered especially long on him.

He hoped Grey wouldn't notice that.

When the men were all in their saddles, Grey addressed them. "Good luck to all of you, although I'm sure you won't need it with Brattle and Waco leading the way. And speaking of Waco . . ." He held up a gunbelt and holstered Colt and handed it to The Kid.

"I was wonderin' if I was going to have to do this unarmed," The Kid said as he buckled on the weapon. He drew the revolver from its holster and opened the cylinder, only to look up in surprise. "It's unloaded."

"That's right," Grey said. "Here's the way things

work in this organization, Waco. You don't carry a loaded gun yet, and you don't wear a mask. The other men do. You're already a wanted man, so you don't have to worry about concealing your features, but none of them have posters out on them and I'd like to keep it that way. I'm sure they would, too."

The Kid frowned. "Nobody told me anything about this," he snapped. In reality, those developments came as no surprise, knowing what he did about the holdups in which Quint Lupo had participated.

"You've known all along that we have our own way of doing things," Grey said, his voice hardening. "You also know I'm in charge here."

"Sure. It just seems like if there's any shooting, I'm liable to be in a mighty bad spot with an unloaded gun."

"Consider that an incentive to make certain there aren't any problems involving gunplay. We're in this to make money, not to shoot up the place."

"Yeah, I guess," The Kid said with obvious reluctance. "I don't much like the idea of paradin' my face around, either. I may be wanted for breakin' out of prison, but if I get tagged with new train robbery charges, every bounty hunter in the state will be looking for me."

"That's something you'll just have to get used to. You *are* a fugitive, after all. None of us are."

Still playing the part of Waco Keene, The Kid glanced around at the other men. He tried to look worried, angry, and desperate. They gave him flat, hard stares in return.

He let resignation take over with a sigh. "Fine. As long as I get my share."

"Don't worry, you will," Grey assured him.

The Kid lifted his reins. "Let's ride, then." He didn't look back, but could feel Beatrice watching him as he and the other men rode south. Without being too obvious about it, he glanced toward the hill to the west Tyler had mentioned.

If the stocky Ranger was up there, keeping an eye on the ranch through high-powered field glasses, he was bound to see them riding away and could probably guess they were headed out to pull a robbery.

The Kid wondered if he should make some sort of unobtrusive sign, then decided against it. They were probably too far away for the Ranger to even see anything like that.

He was on his own.

A line of ominous, dark blue clouds had moved up on the southwestern horizon by the time the gang neared their destination. Brattle eyed those clouds suspiciously. "Told you it was gonna storm."

"It'll be all right," The Kid said. "That won't stop us from doing what we need to do."

A range of low hills overlooked the settlement. As the riders headed down the slopes toward the block-long row of buildings making up practically the entire town, The Kid's eyes followed the railroad tracks running straight as a string east toward Fort Worth and west toward Weatherford.

Everything was quiet and peaceful at the moment . . . but it wouldn't stay that way, The Kid knew.

There were only a few residences in the settlement, just enough to provide homes for the people who ran the half-dozen businesses, which included a couple mercantiles, a drugstore, a restaurant, a saddle shop, and a ladies' dress shop.

Those establishments depended on the cattle spreads surrounding the settlement for their existence. The families who owned the ranches and the cowboys who worked for those outfits furnished customers for the businesses. In the middle of the week, Aledo was a pretty sleepy place. A couple horses were tied up at the hitch rack in front of the restaurant, and a wagon was parked in front of one of the general stores.

That was encouraging. The fewer people around when the gang stopped and boarded the train, the less likely anybody would try to interfere.

One of the gunmen licked his lips and asked, "Is there a saloon in this backwater?"

"No, there's no saloon," Brattle replied. "We're in a dry county here."

"No booze in the whole blasted county?" The

outlaw sounded horrified, as if he couldn't believe such a thing.

"You don't need to get drunk anyway," Brattle told him. "We're here to rob a damned train, not to fill our guts with whiskey."

They appeared to be nothing more threatening than half a dozen cowhands as they rode around the block of buildings to the front.

The Kid looked at the depot, which was a small, redbrick building about fifty yards from the eastern end of the block. The road they had been following crossed the railroad tracks next to the depot and continued on south.

Alexander Grey had given The Kid a turnip watch and assured him it kept perfect time. The Kid took the watch out of his pocket, flipped it open, and saw that the hour was 2:35. A half hour until the train was due. Ten minutes or so before he and Brattle would enter the depot and take the freight clerk prisoner.

In the meantime, the other four outlaws would split up, two men going to each of the mercantiles. They wouldn't do anything to draw attention to themselves.

When they heard the train's whistle as it approached the settlement, they would converge on the depot. Along the way they would pull their bandannas up to mask the lower halves of their faces.

As the men dismounted, a low rumble of thunder

sounded, far to the southwest where the roiling, blue-black clouds continued to gather.

"Told you," Brattle said again. "We'll be lucky if it don't come a cyclone. You've always got to worry about that this time of year."

"I think I'm going to worry more about other things," The Kid said.

For one, he was curious whether or not Tyler had followed them to the settlement. If he had, he might be tempted to interfere with the train robbery. That would be a lawman's instinct, after all, to step in whenever he saw a crime being committed.

The Kid was sure Tyler had strict orders to stay out of whatever happened and hoped the young Ranger would follow those orders. The arrival of a lawman might set off a shooting scrape and ruin everything.

The scouting carried out by the men had determined that the settlement had no constable, only a deputy sheriff who covered that whole part of the county and wasn't there very often.

The Kid hoped the man was far away.

Brattle sat down on the steps leading up to the high boardwalk running in front of the businesses, took out the makin's, and started rolling a quirly. The Kid lounged against a post beside him. The other four men went into the general stores, as planned.

No one else was on the street.

"Looks good," Brattle said quietly. "With some

good luck we'll light a shuck out of here before anybody even knows what's happenin'."

"That's the plan." In apparently idle curiosity, The Kid thumbed back his hat and went on, "How long have you been workin' for the boss?"

"Long enough to know he don't like folks askin' a bunch of damn fool questions about him," Brattle replied without hesitation. "And long enough to know if I do what he says, I'll wind up a lot better off."

The Kid shrugged. "Didn't mean to pry. Just passin' the time of day, that's all."

"It'll pass just fine without you sayin' anything."

The Kid realized Brattle was nervous. Maybe it was because of the weather, or maybe he always got that way before a job. It didn't really matter. As long as The Kid could count on Brattle to hold up his end of the chore, that was all he cared about.

Glancing toward the west, The Kid saw a lone man about four hundred yards out, riding toward the settlement. His eyes were sharp, but he couldn't make out any details at that distance except the rider didn't seem to be getting in any hurry.

"Somebody coming," he said under his breath to Brattle.

The big, ugly segundo had set fire to his cigarette. He dropped the match to the dirt and ground it out under his boot toe.

"I see him. Probably just a cowhand, like we're supposed to be. His boss sent him into town to pick up somethin' at the mercantile, or else he sneaked off to get himself a phosphate or some licorice at the drugstore."

The Kid hoped that was the case. But it might be a complication they didn't need. The man could be armed, and tempted to use his gun if he realized the train was being held up.

The Kid didn't want anybody to die. Not him, not a member of the gang, and certainly not any innocent citizens.

"Should we go on over to the depot before that hombre gets here?" Brattle asked.

"Let's wait a few more minutes," The Kid replied in a hushed voice. "It won't hurt to see where he's goin' before we make our move."

Still taking his time, the man rode into the settlement, but instead of heading for the block of businesses, he angled his horse toward the depot.

The Kid muttered a curse. Having someone else at the depot when he and Brattle went in to take it over was definitely a complication they didn't need.

It was even worse than that, he realized a moment later. The newcomer swung down from his saddle and tied his mount's reins to an iron hitching post next to the redbrick building. As he turned toward the door, he glanced in the direction of The Kid and Brattle, as if wondering who the two strangers lingering in front of the general store were.

The threatening clouds in the southwest continued to move closer, but the sun was still shining brightly over the town. That sunlight reflected from something fastened beside the breast pocket of the man's shirt.

That object glinting in the sun had to be a law badge, The Kid thought.

The deputy sheriff had shown up at the wrong place and the wrong time, and all hell would likely break loose with The Kid powerless to stop it.

Chapter 25

The Kid wasn't the only one who had spotted the lawman's badge shining in the sun. Brattle angrily tossed his quirly to the ground and muttered an explosive curse under his breath. "It's that damned deputy! Why'd he have to show up here today, of all times?"

"This is bad luck, all right," The Kid said. "But it doesn't mean we're going to abandon the plan."

As they watched the deputy step into the depot, Brattle's hand dropped to the butt of his gun for a moment. His fingertips caressed the smooth walnut grips as if drawing strength from them. "We'll have to kill the stupid SOB, that's all there is to it."

The Kid shook his head. "There won't be any killing unless it's absolutely necessary," he insisted. He didn't have much confidence Brattle would pay attention to what he said. In reality The Kid wasn't running the show. Brattle was actually in charge of the train robbery.

At least that's what Brattle and the other members of the gang believed.

As long as he was alive, though, Kid Morgan didn't consider himself powerless. He just had to figure out how to handle the situation . . . and quickly.

The Kid tugged his hat brim lower and told Brattle, "Let's go. Follow my lead."

Brattle grunted as he stood up from the boardwalk steps.

The Kid couldn't tell if he was going to cooperate or not.

As they strolled toward the redbrick building, thunder rumbled again in the southwest. A gust of wind hit suddenly, swirling dust around the two tall figures crossing the open ground. Bright fingers of lightning clawed across the blue-black wall of clouds. The sun still shone where they were, making the clouds look even darker and more threatening.

No more threatening than the immediate future, The Kid thought. He had heard the eagerness in Brattle's voice when the outlaw spoke of killing the deputy. In the long run, such a murder would actually play right into the hands of Alexander Grey's master scheme.

If a lawman died in the course of the robbery, and "Waco Keene" was the only member of the gang who was identified, the reward on Keene was bound to go up considerably. Grey would be quite pleased.

The Kid was determined not to let that happen.

Brattle paused right outside the door of the red-brick building. He pulled up his bandanna and settled it across his nose. With his hat brim pulled low, most of his face was concealed. He put his right hand on the butt of his gun and reached for the doorknob with his left.

The Kid beat him to it, grasping the knob and twisting it. He wasn't going to give Brattle the chance to go in shooting. He threw the door open and swiftly stepped inside. Brattle crowded in behind him.

The Kid's gaze took in the scene instantly. The deputy sheriff stood in the depot's one room, an elbow propped on one end of the counter. At the other end were scales for weighing freight.

A stocky, middle-aged man who wore his gun with the butt tilted forward, the deputy was shooting the breeze with the freight clerk perched on an empty, overturned crate. The clerk was younger, skinnier, and wore spectacles. He was dressed in black trousers and a white shirt with sleeve garters.

Both men turned their heads to look at the new-comers, and both jaws dropped in surprise as they saw the bandanna mask covering Brattle's face.

The Kid knew the deputy's instinct was to grab for his gun. Brattle, using that as an excuse to shoot the man down, was already drawing his revolver.

The Kid leaped forward, knowing he had only a split second to act. In a blur of speed, his empty revolver leaped from his holster to his hand. He struck with the quickness of a snake, bringing the gun barrel down on the deputy's head.

The blow crushed the lawman's hat and thudded solidly against his skull. The Kid hoped the hat had cushioned the impact enough that the deputy's skull wasn't cracked.

The deputy's eyes rolled up in their sockets. With a groan, he collapsed into a heap on the floor.

The Kid kept moving, driving his left shoulder into the freight clerk's chest and ramming him against the wall. As The Kid held the man pinned there, he jammed the Colt's barrel against the soft flesh under the clerk's chin.

"Give us any trouble and I'll blow your brains out," he growled.

The clerk's eyes were so wide they looked like they were about to pop right out of his head. He couldn't speak or even nod with The Kid's gun pressed against his chin, but he was so frightened The Kid was confident he wasn't going to put up a fight.

"I'm gonna let you go," The Kid went on as he eased off a little on the pressure with the gun barrel. "But if you so much as squawk you'll be dead a half second later. You understand what I'm tellin' you?"

With the gun barrel moved back slightly from his throat, the clerk was able to nod. "I g-g-got it, mister."

"You better not be lyin', you little peckerwood." Brattle's voice was slightly muffled by the bandanna.

"That's Waco Keene holdin' a gun on you, and he'd just as soon shoot you as look at you."

The Kid gave Brattle a quick, hooded glance, the same way the real Waco Keene would have reacted to having his name tossed around in the middle of a robbery.

Grey wasn't taking any chances on The Kid not being identified as Waco Keene. Brattle had orders to throw the name out while there were witnesses present.

There was no time to worry about that. The Kid moved back a step. He kept his left hand against the clerk's chest, holding the man against the wall.

The deputy hadn't budged since he sprawled on the floor. The Kid glanced down at him, saw to his relief the man was breathing. He also saw the deputy's gun had fallen out of its holster when he collapsed.

Moving quickly, The Kid pouched his empty iron, bent down, and scooped the deputy's Colt from the floor. Its grips rested comfortably against the palm of his hand. The weight of the weapon felt good, too.

Brattle stiffened. The Kid knew what the outlaw was thinking. He should have grabbed the lawman's gun while he had the chance. The Kid was armed, and that might change everything.

The Kid knew it might not change a thing. He still wanted the robbery to take place successfully. Giving Brattle a curt nod, he tried to make him understand the plan would continue just as it was supposed to. There wasn't going to be any double cross.

Thunder rumbled, closer. At the same time The Kid heard the far-off wail of a train's whistle.

"Train's early," he snapped. He gave the clerk a hard look. "You're gonna step out there and raise the signal for the train to stop, amigo. Got that?"

"I-I'm not supposed to . . ."

The Kid ignored the stammered protest. "Don't even think about tryin' to run away. We'll both have our guns pointed right at you, and if you do anything but raise that signal, we'll kill you. At this range we can't miss."

"So don't try anything funny," Brattle added. "You'll be dead mighty quick if you do."

"Just don't . . ." The clerk had to stop and gulp before he could go on. "Please just don't hurt the engineer. He's m-my father-in-law."

The Kid could tell that Brattle was grinning under the bandanna.

"Well, ain't that cozy?" the outlaw said. "Both of you workin' for the same railroad."

The Kid said, "Don't worry, nobody's gonna get hurt as long as they do what they're told. We're just after the money in the express car."

"Wh-what money?" the terrified clerk asked.

The Kid thought he was telling the truth. The clerk didn't know about the shipment of cash bound for the banks in West Texas. Well, that made sense, The Kid supposed. There was no reason for the clerk to know.

Grinning, he used his left hand to lightly pat the man's pale cheek. "You let us worry about that. It's our job. Your job is to make sure that train stops. Now get out there and raise the flag."

The flag was actually a red metal signal attached to a pole, raised and lowered by means of a lever.

Brattle opened the depot's rear door, the one closest to the tracks, and The Kid motioned with the deputy's gun for the freight clerk to follow orders.

Still pale and gulping, the clerk stepped out of the building, walked the ten feet or so to the signal, and reached up to grasp the lever and pulled it down.

The signal rose, letting the engineer know he needed to stop at the settlement.

"Good job," The Kid called softly to the clerk. "Now get back in here."

The clerk turned, and for a second The Kid saw something he didn't like in the man's eyes behind the spectacles. It was the wild hope he could leap away and escape being shot if he was fast enough.

"Don't try it," The Kid warned.

The defiance went out of the clerk's body with a visible slumping of his shoulders. He said miserably, "Don't kill me, mister. Please. I did what you told me."

"Get on in here," The Kid said again.

The clerk entered the depot. Brattle closed the door behind the young man.

Then with startling suddenness, Brattle's gun

rose and fell. It came down in a vicious, chopping blow on the back of the clerk's head.

The Kid heard the crunch of bone shattering. "What the hell!" he exclaimed as the clerk fell to his knees and then pitched forward onto his face. He lay on the depot floor, unmoving except for a tendril of bright red blood worming its way out of his ear.

"Didn't want to have to be keepin' an eye on him while we were busy," Brattle explained. "So I thought I'd knock him out for a while."

The Kid dropped to one knee beside the clerk and reached out to roll the man onto his back. The clerk's eyes were turning glassy, and his chest was still.

"You killed him!"

Brattle shrugged. "Reckon I hit him a little harder than I meant to." His casual tone made it clear the clerk's death didn't bother him the least little bit.

Rage welled up inside The Kid. Brattle had committed cold-blooded murder right in front of him, and for a second The Kid was tempted to use the deputy's gun and ventilate the outlaw.

Brattle was watching him closely. The Kid knew if he made a move to fire, Brattle would return his shots. In the close confines of the little train station, chances were good both of them would die.

The Kid controlled his emotions and straightened. In a cold voice, he said, "Well, I guess he won't be tellin' anybody Waco Keene ramrodded this holdup, anyway."

Brattle chuckled. "See how well things work out?"

Outside, thunder pealed again as the storm continued its approach.

And thunder of another kind rumbled as the train rolled in with smoke billowing from the locomotive's diamond-shaped stack. Brakes squealed as they gripped the drivers, and rods clattered as the train came to stop.

It was time for the gang to get to work.

Chapter 26

The Kid went to the front door of the depot and looked out. The other four outlaws had heard the train approaching and converged as they were supposed to. All four men were near the depot and had their masks pulled up. Two of them split off and headed for the locomotive to take care of the engineer and fireman.

The Kid turned to Brattle and nodded.

They went out the rear door onto the small platform. Out of habit, the engineer had brought the train to a stop with a freight car next to the platform, since passengers rarely boarded there. Most of the time when the signal was up, it meant somebody had something they wanted to ship.

The express car was right behind the freight car. As The Kid and Brattle hurried toward its door, The Kid glanced toward the engine.

One of the outlaws leaned out from the cab and gave him a thumbs-up to let him know the engineer and fireman had been taken prisoner and were under control. That was one less thing to worry about.

The Kid reached up and hammered a fist on the express car door. "Big wreck up the line! Emergency trains coming! You fellas are gonna have to move over onto the siding to let them through!" It was a lie, but he figured it was one worth trying.

A man's voice demanded through the door, "Who the hell are you?"

Before The Kid could answer, Brattle turned sharply toward him. "Here comes the conductor."

The Kid looked over Brattle's shoulder. The conductor was hurrying forward from the caboose. Brattle was standing with his back to the blue-uniformed man, so the conductor couldn't see the mask over the outlaw's face.

"Here now, what's going on?" the conductor asked as he came up to them. "Did I hear you say something about an emergency—"

He stopped with a gasp as Brattle whirled and jabbed a gun barrel into his chest.

"Yeah, it's an emergency, all right," Brattle growled from under the bandanna. "You're gonna get a hole blowed right through you if you don't convince those fellas in the express car to open up!"

"Oh, my God! Don't shoot!" The conductor's hand dipped toward the pocket of his coat, and The Kid knew he was going for a small pistol. It was a foolhardy move, but conductors were known for their scrappy nature.

The Kid stepped in and grabbed the man's arm, wrenching it behind him before he could reach the gun. Dipping into the man's pocket, he pulled out the pistol. "Don't try anything else," he warned. "We don't want to kill you."

"Maybe Keene don't," Brattle said, "but I don't mind blowin' you to hell, mister."

There was that name again, The Kid thought. Brattle was being sure to provide another witness by saying it to the conductor.

The Kid felt the irrational impulse to throw Brattle's name out there, too, but he suppressed it. "Just get them to open the door."

"There are two deputy marshals in there, and the express messenger is armed, too," the conductor said.

Two of the other outlaws ducked around the near end of the express car, stepping over the coupling. After checking out the other cars, they had run along the far side of the train so their movements wouldn't be visible from the row of businesses.

"No passengers," one of them reported. "Just freight cars and the express car."

Brattle prodded his gun barrel harder against the conductor's chest. "Looks like we've got those guards outnumbered now," he said in a tone of gloating satisfaction.

"Blast it, what's going on out there?" one of the men in the express car demanded. "Redmond, are you there?"

The conductor swallowed hard. "Open up, Ketchum. There's a, uh, problem up the line. I need to talk to you about it."

The Kid heard a thump as the bar on the inside of the door was drawn back. He nodded to the conductor. "You just might live through this, mister."

The Kid motioned for Brattle to step back against the side of the car. He did the same, positioning himself on the other side of the express car door as it began to slide open. They kept their guns pointed at the conductor.

Despite that threat, the man was unable to conceal the fear on his face. As one of the deputy marshals guarding the money shipment stepped into the doorway, he got a good look at the conductor and realized instantly that something was wrong. With an angry curse, he started to swing up the double-barreled shotgun he held.

The Kid acted faster, reaching up, grabbing the man's belt, and heaving him out of the car. The shotgun went flying, and the lawman had time only to let out a startled yell before he plowed face-first into the cinders of the roadbed.

Brattle bulled the conductor aside and shouted, "Drop 'em!" as he pointed his gun into the car. The other two outlaws crowded up behind him.

The men in the car weren't going to surrender without a fight. A gun cracked, and Brattle returned the fire, flame gouting from the muzzle of his Colt. The other two outlaws joined in. Shots rolled from their guns.

With a dull boom, a shotgun went off inside the car. It didn't sound that much different from the thunder of the approaching storm.

The Kid didn't know where the buckshot went, but none of the outlaws appeared to be wounded. It must have been a wild blast, triggered as a wounded man was falling.

Brattle and the other two men scrambled into the express car.

The deputy marshal The Kid had yanked out of the car stumbled to his feet. The Kid rapped him on the head with the Colt, stretching him out senseless on the ground.

A little sick because he knew Brattle and the others had been shooting to kill, he looked into the express car and saw its two defenders lying on the floor in bloody heaps. He couldn't let on how he was feeling, so he grabbed the conductor by the collar and roughly shoved the man toward the door. "Get in there and open the safe," he ordered.

"I—"

"Don't waste your breath tellin' me you can't," The Kid snapped. "I know good and well you can. And unless you want to wind up like those two, you will." Alexander Grey would pay for this, he vowed. Either by death or imprisonment, the outlaw mastermind would pay.

It was the only thing that would lessen the stain of blood on The Kid's own hands.

And even that wouldn't wipe it out, he knew. By helping the gang he'd been doing what the Texas

Rangers wanted him to do . . . but the freight clerk and the two men in the express car were just as dead as if he'd really been Waco Keene.

The clerk had been married, too. The fact that the train's engineer was his father-in-law was proof of that. So he'd left behind a widow and quite possibly some children. The Kid had no way of knowing if the same was true of the dead guards, but he didn't have time to think about it.

At gunpoint, he forced the conductor into the car. The man fumbled a key from the pocket of the dead messenger and took another key from his own pocket. It took both to open the safe.

When the thick steel door swung back, it revealed half a dozen heavy canvas bags on shelves inside the safe. Brattle backhanded the conductor, knocking him off his feet and stunning him.

Then Brattle dragged one of the bags out of the safe, jerked it open, and reached inside to pull out a banded sheaf of twenty dollar bills. "This is it!" He waved the money triumphantly. He stuffed the bills back in the bag and started handing the sacks to the other men.

"Got the horses ready to go, out here!" a man called from outside. He was one of the two outlaws who had taken over the locomotive. If any shooting started, their orders were to knock out the engineer and fireman and grab the gang's horses from the hitch rack. Obviously they had followed through on that plan.

The robbers leaped out of the car, taking the

sacks of money with them. The Kid had one of the sacks in his left hand. It was heavy, but not as heavy as his heart. Anger burned fiercely inside him at the thought of those three dead men.

The outlaws swung up into their saddles almost as one. They galloped toward the rear of the train and swung around the caboose, leaping their mounts over the rails.

Somewhere behind them, a man yelled in alarm. Either the conductor or the surviving deputy marshal had come to, or someone else had discovered the train had just been robbed.

At that moment, thunder crashed again and lightning shot across a sky gone dark above the settlement. The storm had moved in while the men were looting the express car.

Rain sheeted down, falling in thick curtains blown around by hard gusts of wind. The Kid lowered his head against the downpour. Like the other men, he was soaked to the skin in a matter of moments.

No one would be able to come after them in the deluge, he told himself. The rain and the gloom hid them from sight as they fled. And any hoofprints their horses left would be swiftly washed away.

But not the blood, The Kid thought.

That was going to take time.

A lot of time.

Chapter 27

As they had planned beforehand, the gang made their getaway to the south, riding hard for several miles before The Kid and Brattle brought their horses to a stop and signaled for the other outlaws to do likewise.

Brattle raised his voice over the sound of the rain pouring down. "Nobody can follow us in this weather. There's no point in us keepin' on this way!"

The Kid nodded, agreeing with him. If anybody had seen them riding away from the railroad tracks, those witnesses would know they had started south. The inevitable search for them would focus on that direction. "We might as well swing west for a ways, then head for the ranch."

"Sounds good to me. I ain't no duck! The sooner we're out of this weather, the better."

The summer thunderstorm was a powerful one, but it hadn't spawned any cyclones, as far as The

Kid knew. Just hard rain, frequent lightning, and gusty winds.

All of those things started to taper off as the outlaws rode west, traveling at a fast pace but not an all-out gallop as they had been earlier. The farther west they went, the lighter the rain fell, until it stopped completely.

"That's one good thing about these Texas gully-washers," Brattle said as the horses splashed through mud puddles. "They don't usually last very long. Wouldn't surprise me if we saw the sun shinin' in a little while."

His prediction proved to be correct. A short time later, breaks appeared in the clouds, even while thunder still grumbled and growled to the east where the storm had moved on.

Sunlight slanted through those gaps and quickly warmed a day that had turned chilly while the storm was passing through. The air soon felt sticky and steamy. The Kid's soaked clothes were uncomfortable.

"We made a good haul," Brattle said with a grin on his ugly face. "The boss said there was supposed to be sixty grand in that money shipment, and from the looks of it, he was right."

"Yeah, but what's his share from that? What's yours?"

"You don't need to be concerned with that right now. Your share's goin' to pay back the boss, remember?"

The Kid shrugged. "I was just wondering how

much he's gonna collect for sitting in that ranch house while the rest of us do the real work and run all the risks."

Brattle surprised The Kid by throwing his head back and laughing. "You think you're the first hombre who's tried to stir up trouble that way? You're wastin' your time, Keene. All of us are collectin' more loot than we ever did workin' on our own. We don't care how much the boss makes for bein' smart enough to put this deal together." He turned in the saddle to look at the other outlaws. "Do we, boys?"

The question brought more laughter from the men. Dodge said, "Far as we're concerned, Waco, Mr. Grey earns every penny he takes."

"Fine," The Kid said, his voice curt. "I was just thinkin' out loud, that's all."

"Best to do as you're told and not think too much," Brattle said.

They rode on in silence, gradually curving back to the north, crossing the railroad tracks, riding through a wide basin, and then climbing a ridge commanding a view of fifteen or twenty miles to the east.

The Kid spoke up again. "I didn't care for the way you kept tossin' my name around, Brattle."

"What's it matter? The law's already lookin' for you."

"Yeah, but once word gets around that I was mixed up in this robbery, the reward being offered for me will go up . . . especially since we left three dead men behind us."

"They shouldn't have put up a fight. Anyway, you don't have to worry about that, Keene. All you have to do is stick with us and you won't get caught."

No, not until they were *ready* for him to get caught, The Kid thought. And by then it would be too late.

Somehow he had to get a signal to Tyler and let him know it was time for the Rangers to move in. The Kid could testify about the robbery and the killings, as well as Alexander Grey's part in them.

He didn't know where that would leave Beatrice, who would be on her own again, but there was nothing he could do about that. Maybe he could use some of Conrad Browning's money to help her get started in a new life, if her pride would allow that.

The Kid started seeing familiar landmarks, and knew they were getting close to the old ranch. Brattle knew it too, because he reined in. "I'm gonna need that gun back now, Keene."

"Gun?" The Kid said.

"Don't be stupid," Brattle snapped. "You know what I'm talkin' about. That gun you scooped up after the deputy sheriff dropped it."

The Kid smiled and reached for the butt of the Colt tucked in his waistband. Brattle moved quickly, gripping the handle of his own revolver, and The Kid sensed the other outlaws behind him were ready for trouble, too.

"Take it easy," he drawled. Moving slowly and

deliberately, he took hold of the weapon and drew it. Then he reversed the gun and held it out butt first toward Brattle.

"You try anything fancy like a road agent spin, and the other fellas will blast you full of holes," Brattle warned.

"If you haven't figured out by now that we're on the same side, Brattle, I don't know what I can do about it. I carried my weight in that holdup, didn't I?"

"Yeah, but the boss's orders say you don't carry a loaded gun around the place unless he okays it." Brattle took the Colt from The Kid. "I don't make the rules."

The Kid didn't say anything as they hitched their horses into motion again. For a second, he had considered blasting Brattle off his horse and then turning to shoot it out with the other men. Four against one odds were pretty bad, but he had won against some long odds in the past.

Not today, he told himself. Too much depended on him staying alive for a while longer.

They followed the ridge for a couple miles before it sloped down into another valley with a creek running through it. The plateau where the ranch was located was on the far side of that valley. The Kid could see the hill serving as Tyler's lookout point looming to the west. It seemed likely the young Ranger was watching them.

As they started across the valley, The Kid reached into the canvas sack hanging from his saddlehorn by a short length of cord and pulled out a bundle of money.

"What are you doin'?" Brattle asked as The Kid riffled his thumb along the edge of the greenbacks.

"Just thought I'd take another look at this loot, since pretty soon I'll be turning it over to the boss and won't ever see it again."

"I told you, stick with us and you'll have more money than you know what to do with. Now put that away. You're makin' me nervous."

"Why should it bother you? You think we'll run into somebody who'll see it and figure out we stole it from that train?"

"Maybe it sounds far-fetched, but it could happen. Now put that money back in the sack, damn it."

"All right, don't get a burr under your saddle." The Kid replaced the money.

"I'll get whatever I want under my saddle!" Brattle exclaimed, annoyed.

The Kid grinned. "I'm not sure that even makes sense."

"It makes sense enough to me," Brattle snapped. "Come on. We're almost back to the ranch."

He heeled his horse into a trot, and the others matched his pace. The slope leading up to the plateau was a fairly easy one, so the horses didn't struggle.

Twenty minutes later, the six men rode up to the old stone ranch house. As they reined in, the front door swung open and Grey stepped out, an eager expression making his pale face look a bit less cadaverous than usual. His eyes lit up at the sight of the canvas money bags hanging from the saddles. "Success!" he exclaimed.

"That's right, boss," Brattle said as he swung down from his horse. "Everything went off without a hitch, except we got mighty wet when a thunderstorm blew through."

The Kid's mouth tightened. Without a hitch, Brattle had said. That was true enough for the members of the gang, The Kid supposed, but not for the three dead men they had left behind.

"Dodge, Hendry, you take care of the horses," Brattle went on. "The rest of you, let's take this money inside."

Grey came up to The Kid. "Any problems for you, Waco?"

The Kid shook his head. "Not really." He paused. "Brattle was a little free about using my name."

"Is that so?" Grey frowned, as if he hadn't given Brattle the order to do just that. "Well, I don't suppose it'll make much difference in the long run, will it? You're already a fugitive from justice, after all."

"That's what I told him, boss," Brattle put in.

The Kid had expected Beatrice to come out and greet them, too, but he hadn't seen any sign of her. He told himself there was no reason to worry about her, but even so he realized he would be glad when he saw for himself that she was all right.

The two men Brattle had picked out led the horses around to the barn while everyone else went into the house. They entered the cavernous front room, and Grey motioned to a large table. "Dump the money there," he ordered. "I'll count it and find out just how well we did today."

Grey used that *we* as if he had been right there with them, The Kid thought, shooting it out with the hombres inside the express car. He might as well have been. Without his evil brain behind all of it, those men would still be alive.

The Kid saw the greed on the man's face as he looked at the greenbacks spilling from those canvas sacks, and was glad Brattle had taken the loaded gun away from him. At that moment, he was mighty tempted to put a .45 caliber bullet right between Alexander Grey's reptilian eyes.

Beatrice came into the room then, and a surge of relief went through The Kid. He thought she looked happy to see him, too, but she glanced away quickly so Grey wouldn't notice her reaction.

"Look at that, Beatrice," Grey said as he waved a hand at the pile of bills on the table. "Another installment on a fortune that will dwarf anything our father ever had, eh?"

"I don't care about that, Alexander," she said. "I don't care about anything that has to do with him."

"I can't say that I blame you for feeling that way. He's a despicable man." Grey smiled. "But enough about that. Would you like to help me count this?"

Before Beatrice could answer, a flurry of gunshots suddenly erupted somewhere outside. Everyone stiffened in alarm. The Kid thought the shots came from the barn.

Brattle jerked his gun from its holster and yelled, "Somebody must've jumped Dodge and Hendry!" He took off at a run for the back door. So did the other outlaws.

Grey told Beatrice, "Stay here!" and started to follow.

The Kid hesitated. It was a chance to grab Beatrice and get out of there. If he could get his hands on a couple horses . . .

"Come on, Waco!" Grey threw the order over his shoulder, putting an end to that idea.

It would have been a long shot anyway, The Kid told himself.

He ran out of the house behind Grey. The shooting had already stopped as they emerged from the big stone pile. They were in time to see Brattle and another man half dragging, half carrying a limp, bloody figure out of the barn.

The Kid's breath froze in his throat as he recognized the wounded man. Brattle and the other man dumped the intruder at Grey's feet. "Look who Dodge and Hendry caught skulkin' around the place, boss."

It was the young Texas Ranger called Tyler.

Quite possibly Tyler Beaumont.

Kid Morgan's brother-in-law.

Chapter 28

Blood stained Tyler's shirt in a couple places, but his eyelids fluttered and his chest rose and fell. The Kid was glad to see the man wasn't dead.

But that situation might not last long. At any second, Grey could order his men to finish filling the young Texas Ranger with lead.

"What's that young rapscallion doing here?" Grey demanded.

"Don't know for sure, boss, but he wasn't up to anything good." Brattle held out his hand. "I found this in a hidden pocket on the back of his gunbelt."

Brattle was holding Tyler's Ranger badge.

Grey snatched it out of his segundo's fingers. "A Ranger! Then when he showed up here before, he wasn't just looking for work, like he claimed."

"I reckon not," Brattle agreed. "You want us to go ahead and kill him?"

Grey looked like he was going to issue the order, in which case The Kid knew he would have to make a grab for a gun and try to shoot it out with the gang. He had already had to swallow too much. He wasn't going to stand there and do nothing while they murdered Tyler.

Before Grey could say anything, Beatrice exclaimed from behind him, "Alexander! You can't—"

"I told you"—Grey swung to face her, his voice sharp—"when you showed up on the plantation, Beatrice, that I was very pleased to see you and that you were welcome to stay, but you weren't to interfere in my business. Do you remember that?"

Her chin came up defiantly as anger sparked in her eyes. "Of course I do. At the time, I didn't know what your business was."

"Well, now you know," he snapped. His narrow shoulders rose and fell in a shrug. "But that doesn't change the fact there's a good reason to keep this man alive . . . for now. Brattle, tend to his wounds and see to it he's well guarded at all times."

"But, boss—"

"I want to question him and find out exactly what brought him here," Grey cut in. "I want to know if he's aware of who we really are and what we're doing, or if he was just snooping because someone new moved in on this ranch."

"We can't let him go," Brattle argued. "Not after shootin' him."

Grey smiled coldly. "I didn't say anything about letting him go. We'll deal with that problem. But I intend to find out as much as I can from him first."

He jerked his head toward the barn, indicating Tyler was to be held prisoner out there.

"This is an unpleasant development in what had been a very promising day," Grey went on to nobody in particular as Brattle and the other outlaw picked up Tyler's senseless form and toted it toward the barn. "But I suppose I'll feel better about things again once I've counted that money. Let's get back to that." He turned toward the house and asked over his shoulder, "Are you coming, Waco?"

The Kid watched the other outlaws disappear into the barn with Tyler and wondered if he would ever see the young Ranger alive again.

"Waco?"

"Yeah, sure, boss." The Kid forced himself to sound nonchalant. He figured it was all right to let some of his nerves show. "I just don't like the idea of a Ranger snoopin' around here."

"Neither do I, but it may not mean anything."

"What'll we do if we find out they're on to us?"

"We'll have to clear out, I suppose, and find somewhere else to serve as our headquarters. That would be a shame, because I like this place. Let's not borrow trouble." Grey smiled. "I'll find out the truth later on, assuming, of course, the lawman doesn't succumb right away from his wounds. I can make him talk."

The chuckle that came from Grey made chills go down The Kid's spine.

"Yes, that Ranger will tell me everything I want to know before he dies."

* * *

The haul from the train robbery wasn't an exact sixty thousand dollars.

When Grey counted the money in the canvas sacks, the total came to $59,380. That was still a large sum of money, more than most folks saw in their entire lives. Not much compared to the sums Conrad Browning used to deal with all the time, of course, The Kid reflected, but a fortune for most people.

"We'll work out the division of the spoils later," Grey told Beatrice, who was sitting in one of the room's armchairs with a frown on her lovely face, "There'll be a share for you as well, my dear."

"I don't want any of it, Alexander."

"Nonsense. You contribute to our efforts by cooking and taking care of us. You deserve some money of your own in return for that."

She shook her head. "I really don't want to argue about it."

"All right. But you can't stop me from setting some aside for you." Grey looked over at The Kid. "And of course I'll take what would have been your share into account against the expenses I incurred in securing your freedom from prison."

"That's fine," The Kid said with a nod. "But with a job of this size, my share ought to cover a big chunk of those expenses."

"I'll let you know how the figures work out," Grey said noncommittally.

The Kid knew good and well that would never happen.

Brattle came into the room. "We patched up that Ranger, boss. He's awake now if you want to talk to him. A couple shots of whiskey braced him up some."

"Excellent, Brattle." Grey said. He left the room with his big, ugly second-in-command.

The Kid started after them, but Beatrice stood up quickly and moved to intercept him. "Waco, I don't care about the money," she said in a low voice. "I just want to get out of here."

The Kid didn't doubt her sincerity. He wished he could give her what she wanted, but with the gang holding Tyler prisoner, he couldn't cut and run yet.

"I'll do what I can." It was a promise as vague as the one Grey had just made to him about the money. He knew that, but there was nothing else he could do.

Trying to ignore Beatrice's plaintive look, he went after Grey and Brattle, catching up to them before they reached the barn.

Tyler was sitting on the ground with his bloody shirt off and bandages wrapped around his midsection and upper left arm. His arms were pulled behind him and tied around one of the posts supporting a stall gate.

His haggard face showed the strain he was under, but not even a flicker of recognition filled his eyes as he looked up and saw The Kid, Grey, and Brattle coming into the barn. Tyler was thinking clearly enough not to give away The Kid's identity.

The other outlaws stood around the Ranger in a half circle. The ominous threat they represented hung in the air like the stink of gunsmoke.

"Well, Mr. Tyler," Grey greeted him with false joviality. "I see you decided to pay us a return visit."

"There was no need for your hands to start blazin' away at me like that," Tyler said sullenly. "I just thought maybe things had changed since I was here—"

"Don't waste your time and mine by lying about looking for a job," Grey said. "We both know that's a lie. You already have a job." He took the Texas Ranger badge from his pocket and held it up so Tyler could see it.

Grim lines settled over Tyler's face at the sight of the silver star in a silver circle. "You found that, did you?"

"My men did, yes. So you see there's no point in lying. What I want to know is what brought you here the first time and then today."

Tyler didn't even glance at The Kid. He kept his attention focused on Grey. "I came here startin' out because this ranch has been abandoned for quite a while and when I spotted somebody livin' here, I was curious. That's all. Most folks get pretty close-mouthed when they're talkin' to a lawman, even when they haven't done anything wrong, so that's why I spun that yarn about lookin' for a ridin' job."

"What made you come back?"

"Well, hell, that gunnie of yours shot me!" Tyler jerked a nod in The Kid's direction.

"Only to keep you from shooting one of my men," Grey pointed out.

Tyler started to shrug his shoulder, but stopped with a wince as the movement caused his wounds to hurt. He couldn't really shrug anyway, because of how his hands were tied.

"That wasn't the only thing. I just had a hunch somethin' wrong was goin' on here. The whole place just didn't feel right. I still don't know what it is, but I'm mighty certain now that you fellas are up to no good."

With a slight frown on his face, Grey appeared to think about what Tyler had told him. After a moment he said, "I believe you're telling the truth."

"Hell, with the fix I'm in, I'd be pretty dumb to make it worse by lyin' to you, wouldn't I?"

"I don't know. That's hard to say." Grey drew a pistol from his pocket and pulled back the hammer as he pointed it at Tyler. "Perhaps you should try again to convince me before I pull this trigger. So tell me, Mr. Tyler, what exactly do you know about us?"

Tyler's eyes widened. No matter what sort of control he had over his emotions, he knew he was staring death in the face. He wouldn't have been human if it didn't affect him.

The Kid knew it, too, and tensed as he watched Grey's finger on the trigger. If it started to tighten, he planned to leap forward and knock the gun toward the barn's ceiling before Grey could fire.

Even if he succeeded, that would probably postpone Tyler's death, and his own, by no more than a few minutes, but he didn't think he had a choice.

Tyler swallowed and licked his lips. "Damn it, I'm tellin' you the truth! Yeah, sure, I'm a Ranger, and I was suspicious of you fellas, evidently for good reason. But I don't know who you are or what you're doin' here."

He was trying to convince his captors of that so Grey wouldn't order the gang to make a run for it, The Kid thought. Tyler was trying to trade his own life for more time. If he didn't report in on a certain schedule, maybe Rangers would come looking for him.

And he was trying to protect The Kid's secret, too. The Kid wasn't sure his own life was worth that sacrifice.

The moment stretched out until he thought his nerves were going to snap. Then Grey tilted the pistol's barrel up, lowered the hammer, and slipped the gun back into his pocket. "Now I'm convinced you're telling the truth."

"It's about time," Tyler muttered.

"Unfortunately, that won't save your life."

Grey nodded curtly to Brattle, who grinned and reached for the gun on his hip.

"No, I think I'd prefer not to have any more gunshots right now," Grey went on. "It would be best to dispose of him in a more discreet manner."

"Whatever you say, boss," Brattle replied, shrugging. "Hendry, hand me that knife you carry. Mr. Grey, you might want to move back. Blood tends to squirt out sometimes when you cut a man's throat."

"Yes, of course," Grey murmured. "I wouldn't want to ruin this suit."

Tyler fought to keep his face expressionless, but The Kid could see the horror in the young lawman's eyes as Brattle and Grey calmly discussed cutting his throat.

The Kid was horrified, too, but didn't have time to give in to the feeling. He thought furiously to come up with a way to save Tyler's life. "Wait a minute," he said as Hendry handed a heavy-bladed Bowie knife to Brattle. "Wouldn't it be better to keep him alive for a while?"

"Why would we want to do that?" Grey asked with what sounded like genuine curiosity.

"I agree he's probably telling the truth," The Kid said. "But if he's not . . . if any more Rangers come around here . . . it might come in handy to have a hostage."

"Do you really think the Rangers would bargain for his life?"

"I don't know, but they might."

Grey considered the suggestion, taking so long about it Brattle finally said, "Well, boss, do you want me to cut his throat or not?"

"For now, no," Grey decided. "We'll hang on to him, as Waco suggested. He's proven to be pretty cunning so far."

The Kid tried not to let the relief he felt show on his face. "That's the smart thing to do, Mr. Grey. I don't think you'll be sorry."

"You had better hope that I'm not," Grey said, "because I can promise you, Waco, if I'm sorry, you will be, too."

The threat was clear in his voice.

Just as clear as the hum of an angry diamond-back's rattles.

Chapter 29

They left Tyler tied up in the barn with a couple outlaws standing guard over him. Brattle would set up a schedule so the Ranger would be guarded around the clock.

The Kid saw a thin sliver of hope. "I can take a turn, too, if you want." That might give him the chance to knock out whoever was paired with him, so he could free Tyler and both of them could get out of there.

However, Grey shook his head at the suggestion. "You're much too valuable to spend your time on menial work like that, Waco. We'll enjoy the success of this one for a day or two, then you and I need to sit down and start planning our next job."

"Whatever you say, boss," The Kid agreed.

For now, Tyler was alive, and The Kid considered that a victory.

When they were back inside the house, Beatrice

asked, "What happened out there? Is . . . is that young man dead?"

"Of course not," Grey said heartily. "I had a talk with him, and he admitted he came over here because he was suspicious of us. I'm sure he regrets that idea now."

"Are you going to kill him?"

"Not unless it becomes absolutely necessary. As you can imagine, I'd prefer not to give the authorities any more reasons to pursue us than we have to."

From Beatrice's expression, The Kid could tell she wasn't happy with her brother's answer.

She asked, "What about his wounds? Shouldn't a doctor take a look at them?"

"That's not going to happen," Grey replied with a shake of his head. "Brattle's quite competent when it comes to patching up bullet wounds."

"I can take a look at him—"

"Not necessary," Grey cut in. "It's all taken care of, dear sister. Don't give it another thought."

"Well . . . all right. If you say so, Alexander."

He laughed, bent, and gave her a kiss on the forehead. "I say so. Now, there's a big empty valise upstairs in my room. Would you mind bringing it down? I think we can pack all this money in it."

"That valise is pretty heavy, even empty. I'm not sure I can handle it."

"I can get it," The Kid volunteered. He might be able to find a gun or some other weapon in Grey's room, too.

Grey shook his head. "No, that's all right. I'll

fetch it down myself." He started to leave the room, but stopped and looked back at The Kid and Beatrice. "I can trust the two of you together here with all that cash, can't I?"

He was smiling, but The Kid sensed an undertone of warning in his voice.

Beatrice laughed. "Of course you can. I'm your sister, and if Waco wanted to betray you, he's had plenty of chances before now, hasn't he?"

"Not really, but I take your point. I'll be back in a few minutes."

They listened to his footsteps going up the stairs. When they heard the door of his room open, Beatrice moved quickly over to The Kid and whispered, "Waco, did they kill that Ranger?"

The Kid shook his head. "He's still alive. Your brother was telling the truth about that."

"But they're going to kill him sooner or later. You know they are. We have to get out of here. We can't be mixed up in the murder of a Texas Ranger."

"I'm already wanted by the law, remember?" The Kid asked dryly. "And after today there are going to be murder charges hanging over my head. Three men died during that robbery, including a couple deputy U.S. marshals."

"Oh, my Lord . . ." Beatrice covered her mouth with her hand for a moment, visibly shocked by what The Kid told her. "I still say we should go. If we're ever going to have a chance to get away—"

"I can't," he told her as he shook his head again. "I'm sorry. It's just not the right time." And wouldn't be until he could free Tyler. The Kid had to continue playing the dangerous game that could end up being the death of them all.

Before Beatrice could argue any more, they heard the sound of Grey coming back down the stairs with the valise and moved apart. The Kid was sitting in one of the armchairs and Beatrice was standing idly by the table when Grey came into the room carrying the large valise.

He set it on the table. "Give me a hand with this, would you, Beatrice?"

"Of course."

Together they packed the money into the big canvas suitcase. It all fit, nearly three thousand twenty-dollar bills.

Grey smiled as he lifted the valise and felt the weight of it. "That's what I call doing a good job of packing," he said with smug satisfaction.

Before The Kid or Beatrice could respond, Brattle hurried into the room. The segundo's air of urgency told The Kid that something was wrong. He let himself hope Tyler had gotten away somehow.

"There are a couple riders comin', boss. You're gonna want to see this, but you may not like it."

"What the hell?" Grey said with a frown. "Murrell's not here already, is he? I didn't send for him—"

"It ain't Murrell," Brattle risked interrupting.

Grey looked worried . . . and angry as he took the pistol from his pocket. "The Rangers?"

"Nope, not the Rangers."

"Damn you, Brattle, spit it out!"

"Looks like Bert Hagen and Ike Calvert."

The Kid was surprised, but Alexander Grey looked absolutely thunderstruck. "Hagen and . . . and Calvert? But how . . . They're supposed to be in Huntsville."

Grey's back stiffened as resolve came over his pale, gaunt face. "I'm going to get to the bottom of this," he snapped. "Come on." He stalked out of the room.

As he followed Grey, Brattle gestured for The Kid to come, too.

"Better stay here," The Kid told Beatrice.

"No, I want to see what's going on," she insisted.

"I reckon it'll be all right, Keene," Brattle said. "Those two hombres work for the boss, after all. Although it don't make any sense, them bein' here right now."

They joined Grey in front of the house and watched the two riders approach. Although Bert Hagen was no longer wearing his prison guard's uniform and Ike Calvert was dressed in civilian clothes, The Kid recognized both men. Calvert had a derby hat perched jauntily on his head.

As they reined their mounts to a halt, Hagen said, "Sorry to show up like this without any warning, Mr. Grey. There's big trouble brewin', and we figured you needed to know about it as soon as possible."

Grey ignored him and looked at Calvert. "I never expected to see you again. I never wanted to see you again."

The rat-like little convict grinned. "No need to take that tone, son. I've done everything you asked me to, haven't I? Anyway, a boy shouldn't talk that way to his own father."

Beside The Kid, Beatrice gasped. "It *is* him. I . . . I remember seeing pictures of him."

So did The Kid. As he struggled to comprehend what was going on, he recalled the family portrait he'd seen in the old plantation house . . . that Alexander Grey had burned to the ground. If he'd had a chance to take a closer look at that painting, he might have recognized Ike Calvert. Or Isaac Grey, to give the man what was probably his real name.

He remembered Beatrice telling him that after murdering his wife, the elder Grey had changed his name and become an outlaw.

The Kid knew where the man had ended up. How Alexander Grey had come to set up the operation with his estranged father was unknown to The Kid, but he supposed that didn't really matter. Hagen dismounted without being asked. So did Calvert, which was the only way The Kid could think of him.

Grey demanded, "What are you doing here? What do you want?"

"To help you, of course," Calvert said. "It was time to cut and run, Alex. The law's on to what we've been doin'."

"What are you talking about?"

"I was workin' in the assistant warden's office,

sweepin' out the place, you know, and I always like to look around when nobody's there. You never know what you might find." Calvert grinned. "Like part of a letter the assistant wrote to a ladyfriend of his. Seems he was tryin' to impress her by tellin' her all about how him and the warden were helpin' the Texas Rangers by getting a fake prisoner on the inside of an outlaw gang." Calvert leveled a finger at The Kid. "Him! He ain't Waco Keene at all! He's a damned Ranger!"

The accusation didn't take The Kid by surprise. He had figured out where things were going several moments earlier, although he hadn't known exactly how Calvert had discovered his identity. Warden Jennings might be trustworthy, as Captain Hughes claimed, but obviously he had placed *his* trust in the wrong man.

Unarmed, The Kid's only chance lay in trying to brazen it out. "That's crazy! I don't know what some blasted warden wrote, but I'm sure not a Texas Ranger!"

That was true enough, as far as it went.

"Yes, he is," Calvert insisted. "They figured out somehow what we've been doin'. They tricked us into bustin' Keene, or whatever his real name is, out of prison and takin' him into the gang, and the Rangers'll probably be comin' down on our heads any minute now!"

Grey turned his cold, serpent-like gaze on the newest member of his gang.

The Kid knew nothing he could say was going to convince Grey that Calvert was wrong.

"I smuggled Ike out of the prison and we got here as quick as we could to warn you, boss," Hagen began.

"It's all right," Grey said. "It all makes sense now, why that Ranger has been sneaking around here. He's your partner, isn't he, Waco?"

"I don't know anything about this—"

"Like I told him, don't waste your time lying. You've just been waiting until after we'd pulled a job so you'd have more evidence against us. You were going to signal him so he could tell the Rangers to go ahead and raid the place. But he ruined everything by sneaking in and getting captured before you could give him the high sign." Grey laughed and shook his head, then turned back to Hagen and his father. "So you see, there's nothing to worry about. All we have to do is get rid of these two lawmen, and we can carry on as before. It's a shame we won't be able to have Murrell turn in the body for a nice, fat reward like we did with Lupo and the others, but I suppose we can accept that loss."

Brattle said, "A couple Rangers turn up missin', boss, and the rest of those badge-totin' buzzards will start wondering what happened to 'em. And that fella Tyler might've told his bosses we were holed up here. I think it'd be better if we moved out, and mighty quick-like, too. Maybe tonight."

Grey rubbed his jaw and frowned in thought.

"That's good thinking, Brattle. You may well be right. We can't take the chance. Take Waco—we'll still call him Waco for the sake of simplicity—take Waco out to the barn and put him with the other one."

Brattle grinned and reached for his gun. "Sure, boss. I'd be glad to."

The Kid knew he had run out of time. Putting up a fight might be futile, but he wasn't going to give up and let them kill him.

He launched himself at Brattle in a diving tackle. As he crashed into the segundo, he made a grab for Brattle's gun.

The impact of the collision knocked Brattle off his feet. He grabbed The Kid's shirt and dragged him down, too. His fist slammed into The Kid's jaw. The Kid drove his knee into Brattle's belly as men shouted around him. Grey's voice went up in pitch as he yelled, "Get him! Get him!"

The Kid closed his hand over the cylinder of Brattle's gun and twisted the weapon free. He got his elbow under Brattle's jaw and levered the man's head back, breaking loose of his grip.

As The Kid rolled over, he flipped the gun around and wrapped his hand around the butt. But he didn't have a chance to use it. Hagen loomed over him and swung a vicious kick, catching him in the head. Skyrockets exploded behind The Kid's eyes. A wave of darkness welled up and threatened to overwhelm him.

Another kick smashed into him, digging painfully into his ribs. He curled up and gasped for breath.

Consciousness was slipping away from him, no matter how desperately he fought to hang on to it.

He heard Grey order, "Take him out to the barn, but don't kill him yet! I want that pleasure myself."

It was the last thing The Kid knew as blackness washed over him, taking away the pain and everything else.

Chapter 30

An unknown time later, The Kid swam up out of the black pool that had sucked him under. His head throbbed with pain, but he ignored it. He couldn't afford to surrender to the agony. He had to figure out a way to escape.

Returning to consciousness, he moaned and moved around.

A voice called quietly, "Kid? Kid, can you hear me?"

The Kid pried his eyes open and looked over at Tyler. The wounded Ranger was still tied to the post in the barn.

It took only a moment for The Kid to realize he was in the same situation. His arms had been jerked awkwardly behind him, and his wrists were lashed together around a post. He was sitting on the hard-packed ground with his legs stuck out in front of him.

Squinting, The Kid looked around. A lantern hung on a nail driven into another post, casting a yellow circle of light over the two prisoners. On the other side of that circle, the outlaw called Hendry sat on a stool, a six-gun held loosely in his hand.

Hendry grinned at them. "So, both of our pigeons are awake now. I'll have to let the boss know. He wanted to kill the Ranger first, but wanted you awake to see it, Mister Waco damned Keene."

"That's not . . . my name," The Kid muttered. He took a deep breath, strengthening him some and making the pounding inside his skull lessen a little. He lifted his head. "They call me Kid Morgan."

No point in secrets any longer—not with death dangling by a thread over him and Tyler.

Hendry's eyes widened. "Kid Morgan . . . I've heard the name. Damned if I haven't. You're supposed to be some sort of gunfighter. Are you tellin' me you're really a Texas Ranger?"

"Of course I'm not a Ranger, you blasted idiot!" The Kid's mind grasped at any hope, no matter how slender. He took something that had really happened and twisted it to his purposes. "I don't know anything about some crazy plan the Rangers hatched. I was arrested and thrown into prison because I was mistaken for Waco Keene!"

Hendry gave his head a shake, as if trying to wrap his brain around what The Kid was telling him.

"When Calvert said somebody was going to bust me out, of course I went along with it," The Kid continued. "I would have been a damned fool to do anything else. And I've been pretending to be Waco Keene ever since, because that's who your boss thought I was. You've got a good operation here. I wanted to be part of it for real."

"I never heard nothin' about Kid Morgan bein' an outlaw," Hendry protested.

"I wasn't . . . until I got sent to prison for something I didn't do. Now I just want to get back at all the damned lawmen for doing that to me."

The sound of slow clapping came from the open double doors of the barn. Alexander Grey stood there, a sardonic smile on his face. "My, that was quite an inventive story. Totally ludicrous, of course, but with a tiny shred of possibility someone might take it seriously. Not me, however. I can see right through what you're trying to do, Mr. Morgan. That *is* what you said your name is, isn't it?"

The Kid didn't waste his time or breath trying to convince Grey the situation he'd described had actually happened to him in New Mexico Territory. It wasn't worth the effort. He looked up at the man. "You've got it all wrong, Grey. I'm not a Texas Ranger."

"Well, if you're not, then you're working with them, which is just as bad," Grey said as he strolled across the barn toward the prisoners. "Let's not delay here. Everything is packed up, including the loot from that robbery today, and we're ready to leave. The only thing left to do is take care of you two." He paused and frowned. "I'm really not happy about having to abandon this place. It would have made an excellent headquarters for us for a while."

"That's too damned bad, isn't it?" The Kid said.

"Yes, it is." Grey jerked his head at Hendry. "Go on and join the others. I'll be there shortly."

"Sure, boss." Hendry stood up and went out of the barn as directed.

The Kid tugged at the rope around his wrists. With only Grey to face, if he could get loose he stood a chance of overpowering the mastermind and getting his hand on a gun.

The bonds were too tight, though. No matter how hard The Kid strained, he couldn't get any play in them. Eventually he might have been able to work his way loose, with the loss of plenty of skin in the process, but Grey wasn't going to give him that much time.

Grey stood in front of the prisoners. "I thought about shooting you. I thought about letting Brattle cut your throats, too. He would have enjoyed that. But I decided both of those methods would be too quick, and relatively painless. I think you'd suffer a lot more if you burned to death."

A shiver went through The Kid at the sound of evil pleasure in Grey's voice. "What are you going to do? Burn down the barn, like you did the plantation house?"

Grey's lips drew back from his teeth. "That house didn't deserve to stand any longer! It was a monument to one man's evil, and it's only fitting that it was wiped off the face of the earth."

The Kid thought back to what the deranged preacher John Schofield had told him. "You can burn something down, but that doesn't change the past. Everything a man does is still there, whether any sign of it is left or not. Your father still murdered your mother."

"I see dear Beatrice has been spilling the family secrets. Well, no matter. Yes, my father murdered my mother. I won't deny it."

For a second The Kid thought Grey might lose control while talking about his father, and that might have led the man to make a mistake. "But you let him live."

Grey shrugged, coldly unemotional. "He serves a purpose. You two don't." It appeared he was mostly concerned with the money his scheme could make.

But concerned with cruel revenge, too, as he proved by taking a match out of his pocket and waving it around. "I'm going to set fire to the hay in the back of the barn. The flames should spread quickly, but it'll still take them several minutes to reach these stalls. You'll have that time to think about how foolish you were to try to stop me, and to ponder how it's going to feel to burn alive. I've heard that's the most painful way to die, but then how would anyone know for sure, eh?"

"You son of a—" Tyler raged at him. "You're loco, you know that?"

"On the contrary. I'm sane enough to know this world is a cesspool and the only thing it's good for is whatever we can rip away from it." Without saying anything else, Grey walked to the back of the barn.

The Kid heard the match rasp into life.

Grey returned with a smile on his face.

"Good-bye, gentlemen. I hope it hurts like hell." He turned and stalked toward the double doors.

As he did, The Kid heard the faint crackle of flames and caught a whiff of the first tendril of smoke.

Grey hadn't quite reached the door when another figure appeared in the opening. Beatrice darted past him, avoiding the startled grab he made for her. With her long skirt swirling around her legs, she ran over to The Kid.

"Waco!" she cried as she dropped to her knees beside him. She reached behind him to tug at his bonds and looked over her shoulder at her brother, pleading. "Alexander, you can't do this!"

Anger contorted Grey's face as his long-legged strides carried him to her. He took hold of her arm and hauled her roughly to her feet, drawing a cry of pain from her.

"So you've fallen for this Ranger, eh? You prefer him over your own flesh and blood?"

"No, Alexander," Beatrice whimpered. "I just don't want you to kill them, that's all. You . . . you're better than that.

"There's where you've made quite a mistake, my dear. I'm *not* better than that. Not at all. I'm no better than I have to be." He started dragging her toward the doors. "Come on. We don't have much time."

"Alexander, no, no!" She tried to pull free from his grip.

Grey used his other hand to slap her. The blow cracked viciously across her face and rocked her head to the side.

Brattle came running in. "Boss, the gal got away from—"

"I told you to watch her!" Grey yelled as he pushed the stunned Beatrice into his segundo's arms. "Put her in the buggy and get her out of here! Now!"

The flames were crackling louder in the rear of the barn.

Brattle glanced at the fire and jerked his head in a nod. He tightened his grip on Beatrice. "I got her this time, boss."

She wasn't struggling anymore as Brattle took her out of the barn.

Grey glanced back at The Kid and Tyler one last time, laughed, and hurried after the others.

Over the sound of the fire, The Kid heard hoof-beats and wagon wheels outside as the outlaws pulled out.

Tyler groaned as he strained to no avail against his ropes.

"Damn it, Kid. I'm sorry I got you into this mess!"

"You didn't." The Kid moved his hands as much as he could, feeling around on the dirt behind him. "It was my own choice to get mixed up in the plan. I wouldn't mind knowing what you were doing here, though, instead of sitting up on that hill like you were supposed to."

Tyler grimaced. "I thought it would be a good

chance to snoop around while all of you were gone. I figured we could use all the evidence against Grey we could round up. But you got back a mite sooner than I expected, and I didn't have a chance to get away before those two hombres with the horses spotted me."

The Kid supposed he couldn't fault Tyler for that. Then his heart slugged hard in his chest as his fingertips brushed against the thing he was looking for. "There's one more thing I have to know. Tyler's not your last name, is it?"

"No, that's my front handle. My full name is—"

"Tyler Beaumont," The Kid finished for him.

Tyler stared at him in surprise. "How in blazes did you know that?"

"My father is Frank Morgan."

Tyler gaped at him. "Morgan! I . . . I never put it together. But that means . . . my wife Victoria . . ."

That was the girl's name, The Kid recalled. "That's right, she may be my half sister. Frank wouldn't talk about it much, but that's the feeling I got, anyway."

His hands were busy behind his back as he talked.

"Then you and I could be brothers-in-law," Tyler said. "And we wind up stuck in the same mess like this. That's just loco!"

"Isn't it, though?" The Kid grimaced as pain lanced into his wrist. He ignored it and kept working. "Sometimes the world is . . . a lot smaller than we . . . expect it to be . . . Uh!"

With a jerk, the rope around his wrists came apart. As Tyler watched, shocked, The Kid brought his arms around in front of him. Blood dripped from a couple cuts on his wrists.

In his right hand he clutched the small folding knife Beatrice had tried to place in his hand as she was pretending to tug at his bonds. She'd been awkward about it, and the knife had slipped from her fingers to fall behind him.

The Kid had a bad moment then, thinking Grey might spot the knife and their last chance would be gone, but he'd had been too angry with his sister to notice.

There had been a few harrowing seconds when The Kid couldn't find the knife . . . but he had, and was free.

He flexed his fingers rapidly to get the blood flowing again as he hurried over to kneel behind the post where Tyler was tied. Flames had spread all the way across the barn's rear wall and were working their way up the side walls. Smoke made both men cough as The Kid started sawing at Tyler's bonds.

"I'll try not to cut you too much—"

"The hell with that!" Tyler burst out. "Just get me loose so we can get out of here!"

Less than a minute later, the ropes fell away from the Ranger's wrists. The Kid grabbed Tyler's arm and helped him to his feet. With smoke coiling thickly around them and flames casting a nightmarish glow over everything, they stumbled toward the doors.

They had just emerged from the barn when the thunder of hoofbeats welled up close by. Guns crashed in the night.

The Kid and Tyler stumbled to a halt at the sight of the outlaws who had left a short time earlier galloping hellbent for leather back to the ranch.

Chapter 31

The outlaws weren't shooting at him and Tyler, The Kid realized a second later. The men were twisted in their saddles to throw lead at someone behind them. They were being chased, not doing the chasing.

The Kid could think of only one reason for the gang to act like that.

Tyler figured it out, too, and let out an excited whoop. "The Rangers must be right on their tails!"

"Yeah, but with that fire behind us, we're good targets, too!" The Kid warned.

Sure enough, some of the outlaws had spotted them. Muzzle flashes split the night as bullets whined in the direction of The Kid and Tyler.

"Split up!" The Kid barked. "Try to get hold of a gun!"

"Now you're talkin'!" Tyler shouted as he broke into a run.

They veered apart, and luckily the outlaws had

more pressing worries than two escaped prisoners. They left their saddles and took cover wherever they could as another volley of gunfire roared out from the riders pushing them closely.

The Kid had a pretty good idea what had happened. Grey, Brattle, and the others had run right into a force of Rangers shortly after leaving, and they'd been forced to flee back to the ranch, the closest spot where they could put up a fight.

A man on horseback loomed up close beside The Kid. In the garish light spreading out from the burning barn, he recognized the outlaw called Dodge.

Recognizing The Kid, he yelled a curse and tried to swing his gun around to blast a shot at him. The Kid grabbed Dodge's arm and shoved it aside as the revolver roared. Dodge yelled again as The Kid hauled him out of the saddle and sent him crashing to the ground.

The Kid pounced, snatching the gun out of Dodge's hand and whipping it against the outlaw's head. Dodge went limp. He was knocked out cold.

For all The Kid knew the gun was empty, but he reacted instinctively as a slug sizzled past his ear from behind. Whirling and dropping to one knee he lined the sights and pulled the trigger. The Colt bucked in his hand.

The slug punched into the outlaw's guts. He doubled over, dropped his gun, and collapsed. The Kid ran over to him and scooped that weapon from the ground, filling both hands with iron.

He spotted Alexander Grey running toward the ranch house, dragging a struggling Beatrice with one hand while he carried the valise full of money with the other. Brattle, Bert Hagen, and Ike Calvert followed close behind Grey, engaged in a running battle with the Rangers as they covered Grey's retreat.

Once they were behind the thick stone walls of that house, they would be able to hold off the Rangers for a while, The Kid thought. Eventually those dedicated lawmen would root out their quarry, but would likely pay a high price in blood.

He ran toward the side of the house, then slid along it until he found an open window. He stuck the guns in his waistband and pulled himself up and into the darkened, castle-like building.

Drawing the revolvers again, he waited tensely, listening. Shots racketed from the front of the house, sounding like quite a battle. Eventually the Rangers would be able to circle, come in from behind the place, and the outlaw defenders wouldn't be able to hold it.

The Kid planned to speed that up.

He catfooted through the rooms, guided by the roar of gunshots. When he reached the door of the big front room, he paused.

No lights burned in the room, but the red glare from the burning barn lit up the place, casting black, eerie, dancing shadows around the room. Brattle, Hagen, and Calvert had torn the curtains from the windows and broken the glass so they could shoot out easier.

Beatrice was crying and trying to get away from her brother. Grey lost patience and backhanded her savagely across the face, knocking her to the floor. He set the valise on the table, drew a pistol from his pocket, and went to join the others as they tried to fight off the Rangers.

Working by feel in the dark hallway, The Kid counted the rounds he had left in the two revolvers. One still held three bullets, but the other had only one cartridge left in its cylinder. He quickly transferred a bullet from one gun into the other so he had two rounds in each.

Four shots for four men. No room for error. In the rage that gripped him, The Kid was beyond caring.

His hands tightened around the gun butts as he stepped out and raised the Colts.

"We're all gonna die here!" Calvert whimpered as he paused in his firing.

"Shut up, you old coot!" Grey told him. "You deserved to die a long time ago."

"He's not the only one," The Kid called in a loud, powerful voice.

The outlaws whirled to meet the new, unexpected threat. As Brattle came around, The Kid squeezed off a shot from his left-hand gun and saw the slug smash into the segundo's forehead and on into his brain. The impact snapped Brattle's head back as the bullet exploded out the back of his skull.

The Kid fired the right-hand gun at the same

time, sending a bullet driving into Hagen's chest. The renegade prison guard crumpled.

That left Grey and Calvert. Father and son. The Kid heard a bullet from Calvert's gun sing past his ear as he triggered both Colts again. Calvert cried out and rose up on his toes, staggering back against the window behind him. He might have tipped over the sill and fallen out of it if several shots from outside hadn't struck him in the back at that moment, flinging him forward like a bloody rag doll.

Alexander Grey was still on his feet, and The Kid's left arm stung where a slug from Grey's gun had lanced it. He was wounded and out of bullets, and he had failed to kill Grey.

The Kid dropped the empty guns and threw himself forward as Grey fired again. The bullet sang over his head as he landed on the table and slid across it, snatching up the valise full of money. Grey kept pulling the trigger, but The Kid held up the valise and felt the bullets thudding into it as the thick sheafs of greenbacks served as a shield.

He crashed into Grey and they went down. The gun flew from Grey's hand, skittering across the floor.

The Kid ignored the pain in his arm and slammed punches against Grey's face and body. Grey might have fancied himself a criminal mastermind, but physically he was no match for Kid Morgan. The Kid locked his hands around Grey's throat and rammed the man's head against the floor. He squeezed harder and harder, fully intending at that moment to choke the life out of Alexander Grey.

"Waco!" Beatrice cried. "Waco!"

Her voice penetrated the red haze in his brain and caused him to glance up. Shock went through him at what he saw.

She had picked up her brother's gun and was pointing it at him. "Don't kill him. I can't let you kill him."

"Beatrice . . ."

"He deserves to hang."

The Kid realized she wasn't threatening him.

She was covering Grey.

He pried his fingers from around the man's neck and sat back, breathing heavily.

The front door crashed open then. The Rangers had decided to risk a charge when the shooting from the house stopped. Tyler yelled, "Kid! Kid, are you in here?"

"Over here," The Kid replied wearily.

Tyler rushed over to him, and to The Kid's surprise, so did Asa Culhane.

"Kid, you all right?" Culhane asked. "Hell, you're bleedin'."

"The arm? It's fine." The Kid put a hand on the table to brace himself as he climbed to his feet. Culhane reached out to help him.

"There's the hombre behind all of it, Sergeant," Tyler said to Culhane as he pointed at Alexander Grey.

"Did you kill him, Kid?"

The Kid looked at Beatrice, who had set the pistol on the table when the Rangers came in. He shook his head. "No, I didn't kill him. He'll live . . . to hang."

The Kid sat in the lobby of the best hotel in Fort Worth and watched Asa Culhane cross the vast room toward him. The Ranger was carrying his black Stetson, and his Western-cut suit and string tie made him look more like a wealthy cattle baron than a lawman.

Culhane took a seat in a well-padded armchair beside the The Kid and balanced the hat on his knee. "How're you feelin', Kid?"

"You mean this?" The Kid looked down at his left arm, which was supported by a black silk sling. "The doctor says I ought to wear this thing for a few more days, but I don't really need it. I could throw it away and saddle and ride right now."

"I don't doubt it." Culhane sighed. "Well, I put that gal on the train like you asked me to. I think she was a mite peeved at you for not seein' her off yourself."

"I didn't think it would be a good idea."

"She don't hold no grudges against you. Shoot, without you speakin' up for her, she might've been in trouble with the law, too. Cap'n Hughes thought she ought to be charged as an accomplice to everything the gang did after she showed up at that plantation. Accordin' to the letter of the law, he's probably right."

"But being good and proper Texans, the letter of the law is less important than justice being done, am I right?"

Culhane chuckled. "You sure are. Anyway, she's on her way back to Louisiana. I don't know what she's gonna do when she gets there."

Neither did The Kid, but at least Beatrice would have the money to do whatever she wanted to. He had already wired instructions to Claudius Turnbuckle to see to that. She could start a new life without having to look back . . . if she could bring herself to do it.

Sometimes it was awfully hard to forget about the past, even when you wanted to.

"What about Tyler?" The Kid asked.

"Ranger Beaumont? He got a chewin' out for leavin' his post like that . . . and a commendation for helpin' us round up those owlhoots. He's gonna have to be on his best behavior for a while, though. He come mighty close to gettin' the both of you killed. If I hadn't come along to check on him and seen what sort of trouble you boys was in, you'd have been outta luck. Same as if there hadn't been enough Rangers on hand at the Veal Station post to go after that bunch. You heard that old sayin' about the skin o' your teeth, Kid? I'd say that you're livin' proof of it!"

The Kid thought about all he had lost over the

past few years and said wryly, "Yeah, I'm mighty lucky, all right."

But he supposed it balanced out. For every time he'd been tormented as viciously as if all the imps of Hell were after him, there were other times when a guardian angel was watching over him. That was the only way to explain the triumphs and tragedies of his life.

"You gonna come down to Huntsville to watch the hangin' when it's time for Alexander Grey to swing?" Culhane asked.

"He hasn't even gone on trial yet," The Kid pointed out.

"No, but the trial starts next week, and it won't take long. With you and Ranger Beaumont to testify against him, he'll hang, all right. No doubt about that."

"I don't have any interest in watching it. I'll stay for the trial, but then I'll be moving on. And if I never see or hear anything about Alexander Grey again, that'll be just fine with me."

Culhane fidgeted with his hat for a second and then looked up at The Kid again. "Does that, uh, mean you ain't gonna be takin' the Rangers up on that offer?"

"To pack a badge full-time?" The Kid shook his head. "I don't think I'm cut out for that, Asa. I'm too much of a drifter."

Just like my father, he thought. *We are all our father's sons.*

"Well, I can't say as I'm surprised." Culhane put

his hat on and heaved himself to his feet. "But since you're gonna have to hang around Fort Worth for a while until the trial's over, you're gonna need something to help you pass the time."

The Kid groaned as he stood up, too. "You don't have some other little chore for me to do, do you? Something that involves me getting shot at or blown up?"

Culhane chuckled. "Not hardly. I just thought you might like some company, that's all. I know somebody who's grateful to you for helpin' clear her old pa's name." Culhane nodded toward the other side of the lobby.

The Kid looked over there and saw the tall, blond, lovely figure of Katherine Lupo standing just inside the door.

The Ranger said something behind him, but The Kid didn't hear what it was. He was already crossing the room to meet Katherine as she started toward him.

Turn the page for an exciting preview of

SIDEWINDERS: TEXAS BLOODSHED

by William W. Johnstone
with J. A. Johnstone

HOME SWEET DEADLY HOME

If there's anything better than going home
to Texas, it's getting paid to do it.
For Scratch Morton and Bo Creel,
always on the hunt for funds, the job is taking
three vicious criminals from Arkansas to Tyler,
Texas, for trial. Little do they know one of the
criminals, the beautiful woman, is the most
dangerous of all. Soon the journey home turns
into a race for buried treasure, a shoot-out, and
another double cross—until Scratch and Bo
are making one last mad, bullet-sprayed dash
through the land of their birth . . .
or the land of their death.

SIDEWINDERS: TEXAS BLOODSHED

On sale now, wherever Pinnacle Books are sold!

Chapter 1

Scratch Morton peered up at the gallows and said, "I'd just as soon go somewheres else, Bo. This place surely does give me the fantods."

"You don't have anything to worry about," Bo Creel told his old friend, "if you haven't done anything to give Judge Parker cause to order you hanged."

Scratch frowned and shook his head. "I dunno. They don't call that fella the Hangin' Judge for no reason. He can come up with cause if he wants to."

Bo laughed and said, "Come on. We don't have any business with the judge, hanging or otherwise."

The gallows they'd been looking at was no ordinary affair. It stood off to one side of the big, red-brick federal courthouse in Fort Smith, Arkansas, and had eight trapdoors built into it. When huge crowds gathered on the broad courthouse lawn to watch convicted criminals put to death, it was quite a spectacle at times. It wasn't that unusual to see eight men kicking out their lives at once at the end of those hang ropes.

As Scratch had said, Judge Isaac Parker wasn't known as the Hanging Judge for no reason.

The Texans continued strolling past the courthouse. It was a crisp, cold, late winter day, and large white clouds floated in the deep blue sky above Fort Smith. Off to their right, bluffs dropped steeply to the Arkansas River where it curved past the city, forming the border between Arkansas and Indian Territory.

Bo and Scratch had been to Fort Smith before— they had been almost everywhere west of the Mississippi in their decades of wandering—but it had been a while, and after stabling their horses, they had decided to stroll around town and have a look at the place to see how much it had changed.

They probably should have started somewhere besides the courthouse and its adjacent gallows, Bo mused. His old friend Scratch was generally a law-abiding sort, as was Bo himself, but they had wound up on the wrong side of iron bars a few times in their adventurous lives, albeit briefly and usually because of some sort of mistake.

Both men were about the same height. Age had turned Scratch's hair pure silver and put streaks of gray in Bo's dark brown hair, but the years hadn't bent their rugged bodies. Bo was dressed in a sober black suit and hat that made him look a little like a hellfire-and-brimstone preacher, while Scratch was the dandy of the pair in high-topped boots, whipcord trousers, a fringed buck-skin jacket over a white shirt, and a cream-colored Stetson with a fancy band.

Scratch's fondness for the flashy extended to his guns, a pair of long-barreled, ivory-handled Remington revolvers that rode comfortably in cut-down holsters. Bo, on the other hand, as befitted the conservative nature of the rest of his attire, carried a single Colt .45 with plain walnut grips.

The similarity between them was that both Texans were fast on the draw and deadly accurate with their shots when they had to be, although they preferred to avoid trouble if that was at all possible.

Trouble usually had other ideas where they were concerned, though.

In fact, one ruckus or another had been dogging their heels ever since they had met as boys in Texas, during the infamous Runaway Scrape when the Mexican dictator Santa Anna and his army chased the rebellious Texicans almost clear to Louisiana. However, General Sam Houston had known what he was doing all along, and when the time finally came to make a stand, the Texicans lit into Santa Anna's men in the grassy, bayou-bordered fields near San Jacinto and won independence for their land and people.

Despite their youth at the time, Bo and Scratch had been smack-dab in the middle of that epic battle, and each had saved the other's life that day. That was the first time, but hardly the last.

They probably would have been fast friends for life

anyway, even if they had settled down to lives as farmers and ranchers as they had intended. But Fate, in the form of a fever, had come along and taken Bo's wife and children from him after several years of that peaceful existence, and rather than stay where those bitter memories would have haunted him, he rode away and set out on the drift.

He hadn't gone alone. Scratch had ridden with him, and the two of them had seldom been apart for very long since. They had wandered all over the frontier, taking jobs as ranch hands or shotgun guards or scouts when they needed to. Bo was a more than fair hand with a deck of cards and kept money in their pockets most of the time just by sitting in a poker game now and then. His preacher-like appearance didn't hurt. Because of it, folks tended to underestimate his poker-playing ability.

As they passed some steps leading down to the courthouse basement, Scratch shivered, but not from the chilly temperature.

"Hell on the Border," he said. "I've heard about that jail Parker's got down there in the basement. Sounds like a doggone dungeon if you ask me."

"I'd just as soon not find out firsthand," Bo said.

The creaking of wagon wheels made him look to his right. A wagon with an enclosed back was approaching along the drive that ran in front of the courthouse. One man perched on the high driver's seat, handling the reins hitched to the four-horse team. He wasn't all that big, but he had broad shoulders, a prominent nose, and a drooping black mustache. He looked plenty tough and was well armed with two pistols worn butt-forward and an old Henry rifle laying on the wagon seat next to him.

Pinned to the man's coat was a deputy U.S. marshal's badge, Bo noted.

He and Scratch walked on past the entrance to the jail as the wagon rolled up behind them. The deputy hollered at his team as he hauled back on the reins and brought the vehicle to a halt. Bo glanced curiously over his shoulder and saw the lawman climbing down from the seat.

The deputy was probably either delivering or picking up some prisoners, Bo thought. Either way, it was none of his or Scratch's business. He heard a lock rattle, then the deputy called out, "All right, climb down outta there, you—"

That was as far as he got before he let out a startled yell. A second later, a gun went off with a boom that rolled across the broad courthouse lawn.

"What in tarnation?!" Scratch exclaimed as he whirled around.

Somehow, Bo wasn't surprised that trouble had erupted right behind their backs.

Chapter 2

Bo turned quickly, too, his hand going to his gun as he did so. He saw the deputy marshal who'd been driving the wagon wrestling with a burly, unshaven man as they fought over possession of the deputy's rifle.

Another man and a woman were dashing away across the courthouse lawn.

"Those prisoners are escaping!" Bo snapped. "Come on, Scratch!"

It never occurred to him to just stand there and watch the drama unfolding, which is what most people would have done. In fact, there were already a number of bystanders gawking at the struggle behind the wagon or at the fugitives running past them.

The Texans started running, too. Luckily, the direction in which the escaping prisoners had fled sent them on a course that Bo and Scratch could intersect at an angle. If that hadn't happened, they probably wouldn't have had a chance to catch up, because the prisoners were younger and faster.

The woman was especially swift. She'd hiked up her long skirt, and her bare calves flashed in the winter sunlight as she sprinted for freedom. Long, curly blond hair bounced on her shoulders and back as she ran. Scratch, who was a little faster on his feet than Bo, went after her, while Bo targeted the tall, skinny hombre with long black hair.

Bo's pulse was pounding hard after only a few feet. He knew he couldn't hope to win a distance race with this long-legged gent, so he took a chance and launched himself off his feet in a diving tackle at the man's legs.

He almost fell short, but he was able to get a hand on one of the man's ankles. The fugitive let out a startled yell as he pitched forward out of control. The yell turned into a pained grunt as his face plowed into the grass and dirt of the lawn.

The impact of Bo's own landing on the ground knocked the breath out of him and stunned him for a second. He knew, though, that he didn't have time to lie there and recover. He scrambled onto his hands and knees and lunged toward the man he had tripped up.

The fugitive rolled over and brought a mallet-like fist swinging up at Bo's head. Bo twisted so that the blow landed on his left shoulder instead.

The punch packed enough power that it made his arm go numb all the way down. He dropped on top of the man, driving his right elbow into the fugitive's belly as he did so. Sour breath gusted from the man's mouth into Bo's face.

Years of finding himself in such rough-and-tumble brawls had given Bo plenty of experience. He considered himself an honorable man, but when you were fighting for your life, no holds were barred and no blows were too low. He aimed a knee at his opponent's groin. That was usually the quickest way of ending a fight.

It probably would have been in this case if the knee had landed. But the man blocked the blow with a thigh and slammed clubbed fists into Bo's jaw. The brutal wallop sent Bo rolling across the lawn.

The man lunged up into a stumbling run and scrambled after him. He bent, reaching for the Colt in Bo's holster.

Bo had no idea who the man was or why that deputy marshal had arrested him and brought him here to Fort Smith, but he knew it wouldn't be a good idea to let an escaping prisoner get his hands on a gun. Bo jerked his right leg up at the last minute and planted the toe of his boot in the man's belly.

The man's own momentum, along with a heave from Bo's leg, sent him flying through the air above the Texan. He crashed down hard, and this time the soft lawn didn't cushion his fall. He landed on one of the flagstone walks instead.

Bo rolled over, came up on a knee, and drew his gun. He leveled the Colt at the fugitive, who was also gasping for breath now as he lay on the ground.

"Don't move . . . mister," Bo warned as he tried to catch his own breath. "I'll blow one of your knees apart if you do, and you'll never walk right again."

The man's face contorted in a snarl. He started to push himself up and said, "I'll never walk again after they hang me, anyway!"

That made sense. He didn't have anything to lose. Bo's finger tightened on the trigger.

Meanwhile, Scratch had given chase to the blonde. She must have heard him coming after her, because she glanced over her shoulder at him with wide blue eyes. Seeing him closing in on her, she increased her speed.

Scratch didn't have enough breath left to curse, or he would have. Instead he just tried to run a little harder.

The woman had almost reached the streets that ran through Fort Smith's business district. If she made it into that maze of hills and buildings and people, she would stand a good chance of getting away. Scratch knew that. If he drew one of his Remingtons and took a shot at her, he could probably bring her down, even on the run like this.

But he had never liked the idea of shooting at a woman, even one who must have broken the law. Nor did he know what crimes this particular gal was charged with. Gunplay didn't seem called for.

And he couldn't close the gap, so it was starting to look like she was going to escape.

She likely would have, too, if a man leading a team of mules hadn't emerged from the mouth of an alley just as the woman rounded a corner and started along the street. She let out a startled cry and had to come to a sudden stop to avoid running into them.

Scratch saw that and poured on the last of the speed he had in reserve. He reached out and grabbed the collar of the blonde's dress as she tried to dart around the mules and their startled owner.

With a loud rip, the garment tore, splitting down the back and exposing a considerable expanse of smooth, creamy skin. Scratch bunched his fingers in the fabric and didn't let go. He tried to haul the woman closer so he could get hold of her.

"Help!" she screamed. "This crazy old coot's trying to rape me!"

Well, shoot! Scratch thought. That was a smart move on her part. They had gone around a corner and were out of sight of the courthouse now, and the folks who'd been walking along this street had no earthly idea what was going on. Naturally, they believed the woman's apparently terrified claim that she was the victim here.

The man with the mules let go of the reins and came toward Scratch.

"Let go of her, you varmint!" he yelled.

A woman cried, "Somebody fetch the law!"

More men shouted threatening curses as they

closed in around Scratch. He couldn't fight all of them, and he sure couldn't hang on to the blonde if they jumped him.

So he did the only thing he could. He pulled the woman closer to him with his left hand, drew his right-hand Remington, and bellowed, "Everybody back off, dadblast it!"

From the corner of his eye, he saw the woman's hand come up. Sunlight flashed on something she was holding. He jerked his head back, and it was a good thing he did, otherwise the small straight razor she had flicked open would have cut his throat neatly from ear to ear.

She grunted in fury as she twisted in his grip. The dress ripped even more. She slashed down at his arm with the razor, and he had to let go of her and yank his arm back to avoid being cut. As it was, the blade sliced through the sleeve of his buckskin jacket.

She could have run again then, but rage made her come after Scratch instead. She swiped the razor back and forth at his face, forcing him to give ground. Scratch was more tempted now to shoot her, but if he did that, some of the bystanders might open fire on him.

Somebody grabbed him from behind, wrapping strong arms around him and saying, "I got him, ma'am! He won't hurt you now!"

The same couldn't be said of the blonde. With her face twisted in lines of hate, she kept coming, obviously intent on carving Scratch's rugged face into bloody ribbons.

Back on the courthouse lawn, Bo was about to fire at the prisoner he'd been battling when somebody suddenly stepped past him and swung a leg in a well-aimed kick. The man's boot crashed into the fugitive's jaw and laid him out again. The newcomer moved in and brought the butt of his rifle crashing down on the back of the man's neck.

Bo recognized the rugged-looking deputy marshal who had driven the wagon up to the courthouse. More law officers swarmed past him and grabbed the unconscious fugitive.

The deputy swung his rifle toward Bo and snapped, "Put that gun down, mister. Better yet, holster it. You're makin' me nervous."

Bo pouched the iron as he came to his feet. Obviously, the deputy had overcome the man he'd been fighting with at the wagon, maybe with help from other deputies who'd come running out of the courthouse.

"Did you see which way that yellow-haired gal went?" the lawman went on.

"She was headed that way," Bo said as he pointed toward the downtown area. "My partner was after her."

"Come on, then. She's the most loco one in the whole bunch!"

Bo and the deputy ran toward Fort Smith's business district. They heard a lot of yelling, and as they rounded a corner they saw a group of people in the street. Through gaps in the crowd, Bo caught a glimpse of Scratch being held from behind, his arms pinned by a burly townsman.

The blonde that Scratch had pursued was coming at him, a razor in her uplifted hand.

The deputy skidded to a halt and fired three shots into the air, cranking off the rounds as fast as he could work the Henry's lever. The roar of the shots made people in the crowd gasp, curse, and fall back.

They also made the woman hesitate, and Scratch took advantage of the opportunity to lift his left leg in a kick that caught her wrist and sent the razor flying from her fingers.

Disarmed, the woman whirled around to flee again. The deputy snapped the rifle to his shoulder and fired again, this time through a narrow gap in the crowd. The bullet smacked into the paving stones at the woman's feet.

The deputy worked the Henry's lever and called, "Next one goes in your back, Cara! You know I ain't foolin'!"

The mob that had surrounded Scratch and the woman was vanishing rapidly as people scrambled for cover. There was nothing like a few gunshots for clearing a street in a hurry. The deputy had an unobstructed aim now as he settled the rifle's sights on the woman's back.

She must have known he would kill her rather than let her get away, because she stopped and raised her hands. The torn dress hung open almost indecently, revealing her smooth back down to the curve of her hips.

"Marshal, that woman needs something to wear," Bo said, his chivalrous instincts coming into play even in this situation.

"Don't worry about that murderous whore," the lawman muttered.

More deputies who had come running from the courthouse closed in around the blonde. They jerked her arms behind her back and clapped handcuffs around her wrists. Only when she was securely manacled did one of the men take off his coat and drape it around her shoulders where the mutilated dress was threatening to slip down and expose even more of her.

The lawman who stood next to Bo and Scratch finally lowered his rifle and stepped aside to let the other deputies lead the prisoner past them.

"Lock her up, boys, but don't put her in with Lowe and Elam," he ordered. He turned to the Texans and looked like he was about to say something else, but a stentorian shout interrupted him.

"Brubaker!"

"Aw, hell," the deputy muttered. "Here comes Parker."

Chapter 3

It was the famous Hanging Judge stalking along the street toward them, all right. Bo had seen photographs of Isaac Parker before, although he had never met the man and certainly never appeared before him in court.

Parker didn't cut that impressive of a figure at first glance. He was a medium-size man with dark hair and a Vandyke beard, dressed in a brown tweed suit.

You had to get close to him to see the unquenchable fire for justice that burned in his eyes.

As judge for the western district of Arkansas, which included Indian Territory, he rode herd on one of the wildest areas in the country. The tribes who had been settled on reservations in the Territory several decades earlier were peaceful for the most part, but they had their share of criminals and troublemakers just like any group will.

For the most part it was white owlhoots who made

Indian Territory such a lawless, untamed region. Smugglers, bootleggers, rustlers, bank robbers, thieves, road agents, and murderers of all stripes viewed the Territory as a refuge beyond the reach of the law.

That wasn't strictly true. The various tribes had their own police forces, such as the Cherokee Lighthorse, but those officers dealt only with Indian matters. Judge Parker employed a force of tough deputy marshals to patrol the Territory and bring in lawbreakers, but they were spread pretty thin.

Bo had heard it said that a lot of Parker's deputies were little better than outlaws themselves, and for all he knew, that might be true. The one called Brubaker certainly looked mean enough to have broken a few laws in his time.

Parker strode up to them and said in his powerful, commanding voice, "I'm told that three prisoners in your custody have escaped, Brubaker. Is this true?"

"No, sir, it's a dadblamed lie," the deputy responded without hesitation. "They gave me a mite of trouble, but they're all locked up now, Your Honor, or they will be as soon as the boys get Cara LaChance behind bars."

Parker's eyes flashed with interest. "You arrested the LaChance woman?" he asked.

"Yes, sir, along with Dayton Lowe and Jim Elam. The rest of Gentry's bunch gave me the slip, but as soon as I provision up again, I'll be headed out on their trail."

"Not so fast," Parker said. "I may have another job for you." He looked over at Bo and Scratch and frowned. "Who are these men?"

Brubaker scowled and said, "They, uh, gave me a hand corralin' them prisoners."

"Gave you a hand?" Scratched repeated incredulously. "Why, if we hadn't pitched in, two of 'em would've got away, and you durned well know it, mister."

Brubaker was about to frame an angry response when Parker stopped him with an upraised hand. The judge looked at Scratch and asked, "Is that a Texas accent I hear?"

"Texan born, bred, and forever," Scratch answered without any attempt to keep the pride out of his voice. Despite their years of wandering elsewhere, he and Bo had never lost the drawl that was part of their Lone Star heritage.

"I'm Bo Creel, Your Honor," Bo introduced himself. "My pard here is Scratch Morton."

Parker nodded and said, "I'm pleased to meet you, gentlemen, and you have my sincere thanks for your assistance in this matter." He glanced at Brubaker, whose face was flushed with anger. "Those prisoners never should have gotten loose in the first place. How did they manage that, Brubaker? Why weren't they shackled in the back of that wagon?"

"They were, Judge," Brubaker replied. "I put the irons on 'em myself. There ain't no doubt about it. But when I swung open the door on the back of the wagon, Lowe jumped me and tried to get my rifle away from me. While I was tusslin' with him, the other two jumped out and lit a shuck. They got loose somehow, but durned if I know how."

"Did you search them before you locked them up?" Bo asked. "Some people are real good at picking locks if they've got a little steel bar."

"Are you tryin' to tell me how to do my job, mister?" Brubaker shot back hotly. "Of course I searched 'em! What kind of blasted fool do you take me for?"

"Nevertheless, the prisoners were loose when you got here and unlocked the door," Parker pointed out.

Brubaker looked angry and miserable at the same time.

"The girl must'a had somethin' hidden somewhere on her," he admitted. "I ain't gonna speculate on where, because I searched her so blamed good I was embarrassed about it for fifty miles! But if any of that bunch is tricky enough to pick some locks, it'd be Cara LaChance."

"I agree," Parker said with a nod. "But at least they're still in custody. We're fortunate about that." He looked at Bo and Scratch again. "I repeat, we're obliged to you gentlemen for your help. I'd offer you a reward, but the federal government doesn't provide me with an abundance of cash to operate my court."

"That's all right, Your Honor," Bo said. "We were glad to pitch in."

"Yeah," Scratch added. "Even if that blond hellion almost did cut me up with a razor."

Parker's rather bushy eyebrows rose.

"A razor?" he said. "I hadn't heard about that. So she had a razor hidden on her person, too, eh?"

A muscle in Brubaker's jaw jumped a little as he gritted his teeth and growled.

"I'll make the whore talk," he said.

"You've delivered the prisoners," Parker said. "Your job is done."

Brubaker looked like he wanted to argue, but he didn't say anything.

Parker nodded to Bo and Scratch, said, "Good day, gentlemen," and turned to walk back to the courthouse.

"I hope you don't plan on standin' around waitin' for me to thank you," Brubaker told the Texans.

"We didn't do it for thanks or a reward," Bo said. "Just didn't want any outlaws getting loose to raise more hell."

"We ain't overfond of outlaws," Scratch put in.

Brubaker snorted and stomped after Parker.

"Well, I reckon we can go get us a drink now," Scratch went on. "That's what I had in mind to start with. I remember a certain tavern on one of these hilly streets from the last time we passed through here."

"I do, too," Bo replied. "Why don't we go see if we can find it?"

They found the tavern without much trouble and were glad it was still in business. The place was a dim, cavelike room in a stone building with very thick walls, built into the side of a hill. Warm in the winter, cool in the summer, it was run by a burly, redheaded Irishman named Michael Corrigan, who pointed a blunt finger at Bo and Scratch from behind the bar as they came in and declared in a loud voice, "I remember the two o' ye! Start any more trouble and this time I'll bust yer heads open with me trusty bungstarter!"

"We didn't start the trouble last time, dadgum it!" Scratch protested.

"And that was years ago," Bo added. "How do you even remember it?"

Corrigan scowled darkly at them.

"Some things ye don't forget, boyo," he said. "It took me nearly a week to clean up all the damage from that ruckus!"

"We're peaceable men," Bo insisted as the Texans came up to the bar. "All we want are a couple of mugs of beer."

"That I can do ye for," Corrigan said.

"And maybe some coffee later on," Scratch said.

"Aye, that, too."

Corrigan drew the beers and slid the mugs

across the hardwood. Bo paid for the drinks, and he and Scratch carried them to a table in one of the rear corners of the tavern. The place wasn't very busy at this hour, so it was no problem finding a place to sit.

"This is more like it," Scratch said after he'd leaned back in his chair and taken a long swallow of the beer. "Nobody tryin' to wallop us, stab us, or shoot us."

"Better not get used to it," Bo replied with a chuckle.

"Oh, I ain't gonna. It don't seem to matter how hard we try to steer clear of trouble, it finds us. I'm just hopin' that little fracas was our share of it for this trip."

Bo shared that hope, but like his old friend, he wasn't going to count on it.

"Did you get a look at that gal I was scufflin' with?" Scratch asked after a moment.

"I did," Bo replied. "She was pretty good looking."

Scratch snorted.

"Too good lookin' to be an outlaw gal, if you ask me," he said. "But she cussed like a bullwhacker, and she sure went after me with that razor. Reckon that just goes to show you, you can't always tell what somebody's like by lookin' at 'em."

"You should've figured that out a long time ago," Bo said.

"Oh, I did. I ain't no babe in the woods, as you

well know. But when you see a gal like that . . . Oh, shoot, you know what I mean."

Bo knew what his friend meant, all right. Scratch had an eye for a pretty girl and had always been that way. He thought they all ought to be as nice and sweet as he wanted them to be.

Unfortunately, that wasn't always the case, and sometimes Scratch had to pay a price for his idealism and romantic nature.

From time to time, Bo had been fooled by women himself, although with his practical nature that was more difficult. He had an instinctive wariness Scratch lacked.

But Scratch's more reckless personality had gotten them out of plenty of scrapes in the past, too. They made a good team, which was one reason they were still riding together after all these years.

After a while, Corrigan brought cups of coffee over to them. As he set the cups on the table, the tavern keeper said, "I've got some stew in the pot. Would ye like some?"

"That sounds mighty fine, Mike," Bo told him. "Thanks."

Corrigan nodded and started to turn back toward the bar. He paused as the door opened and a man came inside. The newcomer closed the door behind him a little harder than was necessary.

"What's got yer dander up, Forty-two?" Corrigan asked.

Deputy Marshal Brubaker ignored the question

and strode up to the table. He glared at Bo and Scratch.

"I've been lookin' for you two," he said. "Somebody told me they'd seen a couple of Texans come in here. Let's go."

"Go where?" Bo asked.

"We ain't under arrest, are we?" Scratch added.

"No, you ain't under arrest, but we're goin' to the courthouse," Brubaker said. "The judge wants to see you, and I mean right now."